The Long, Tall, Short Stories of Sue Jones

Sue Jones

Image & Design Credits:

Cover design by Richard J Fairhead.
Cover illustration Storyblocks.com
Typeset in Garamond 12/18;
book layout by Richard J Fairhead.
richard@rsdt.org

Publisher's Cataloging-in-Publication data

Jones, Sue.
The Long, Tall, Short Stories of Sue Jones / Sue Jones
p. cm.
ISBN 979-8-68752-380-6

For my beloved girls,
Natasha, Victoria, Emily,
Rebecca and Charlotte

Short Stories

A CHANGE OF HEART

The envelope was printed and the letter had been posted in Portland, Oregon. Serena had several pen pals in the States who were constantly moving around the country, so decided to open it later at her leisure. Greg would be at the gym that evening, working out for the final fitting of his wedding suit, and the letter, doubtless giving a detailed account of a conquest or escapade, would fill her time nicely. She popped it into her handbag and promptly forgot all about it.

Greg's office was just around the corner from Serena's. He was into investments, she was a solicitor's secretary. They often met in the small café in the square at lunchtime. Greg was already there when Serena arrived with umpteen bags dangling from each arm.

'Hi, Honey, been relieving the stores of their merchandise again?'

'Just a few bits and pieces, you know.'

'I'm a guy, how would I know?'

'Greg, are you sure there is nobody in your family able to fly over for the wedding?'

Greg tended to clam up when his family was mentioned. Serena sensed he'd had a rough childhood and wanted to leave it where it belonged: on the less desirable streets of Philadelphia.

'Yeah, I'm sure.' His response was not said in a snappy manner, exactly, but it was clear the matter was closed as far as he was concerned. 'So, how has your morning been?'

'As ever, busy, busy, busy. Yours?'

'I sealed a deal.' He put the tip of his index finger against the tip of his thumb to indicate an O. 'I'm talking about a seriously big deal here, sweetie.'

'Great! Things just keep getting better and better.'

'They sure do.'

Serena was late home from the office. There was a muddle of issues chasing each other around in her head and making her feel slightly giddy. The wedding was only three weeks away and there was still so much to do, even though it was to be a fairly small affair to conceal the fact that Greg's guests numbered just two. Serena wished they could leave London behind and jet off to some exotic location and get married on the beach, but she was sure her mother had been planning the event from the moment she was born. It would break her parents' hearts if she didn't have her *big day* in the little church in which they had been married.

Serena drew the letter from her handbag then put it back again. She wasn't in the mood for a load of mundane drivel. She called her best friend, Jane, and invited her to the flat to share a bottle of wine or two to help her unwind. Jane, having just broken up with her latest boyfriend, was only too happy to oblige.

Jane threw herself onto the sofa, instantly reached for the bottle of wine on the coffee table beside her, and filled a glass. She then emptied the entire contents of a large bag of cashew nuts into a small bowl and placed it on her midriff for easy access. Jane always binged when there was no man in her life. Serena threw her a warning glance.

'Don't worry, it's okay; the bridesmaid dress was a touch too big anyway. I gave up carbs completely to please Steve. Bastard!'

'I never thought he was right for you.'

'Is any man? There must be something wrong with me, Serena; every time things start to get a bit serious they bugger off. Am I that scary?'

'Only when you are drunk.'

'Right.'

'And pressing your nose against every jeweller's window on a second date might give the wrong impression.'

'Um, good point.'

'You are great, Jane. Any man who can't see that doesn't deserve you.'

The girls drank steadily until midnight, by which time Jane was well and truly loaded. Serena covered her with a quilt and went to bed. She awoke at half past two expecting to find Greg beside her, but he wasn't. He turned up just as she was getting ready for work.

'Met up with some colleagues for a drink, then went to a casino,' he told her. 'Cleaned up, made some big bucks.'

Serena was too groggy to respond beyond giving him a quick kiss before leaving. There was no point getting uppity about his failure to call and tell her he would be out all night. He always won in the war of words. They'd only had one serious argument since getting together and in its wake Serena had fallen into a fit of despair so deep it took her days to climb out. She didn't want to go through that again.

She noticed that Jane had neatly folded her quilt and straightened the cushions on the sofa before leaving for work. Quite how Jane contrived to outdrink her by a considerable margin and feel no effects the following day was a mystery. Practise, she supposed.

Celia and Edgar Brent-Charlton faced each other across the breakfast table. 'You are very quiet this morning, dear,' remarked Edgar.

'Just thinking.'

'Worrying more, I fancy.'

'A little.'

'About the wedding. You are not sure you chose the right outfit?'

'Edgar! You make me sound so shallow.'

'Sorry.'

'It's Greg. At dinner last night Frieda was talking about Patrick. She knew everything about him before he and Sally got married.'

'Well, she would, Patrick's family lived next door, the children grew up together.'

'That's true, but we know almost nothing about Greg, his past, his parents, his upbringing, and Serena seems to know little more.'

'She loves him to distraction and he seems smitten with her; perhaps that's all we need to know.'

'It makes me uneasy.'

'There is little we can we do. She's twenty-six, we must trust her judgement. Stop worrying, darling.'

Celia didn't, of course, she was Serena's mother; it was her job to worry and fret. And Edgar, despite his endless attempts to allay his wife's misgivings, as her father, had plenty of his own.

Greg phoned to say he was meeting a client at lunchtime and would see Serena in the car park at five. Serena was still feeling a little fragile, so decided to eat lunch at her desk. She popped out to the bakery next door for sandwiches and made coffee in the office. She opened her handbag for a packet of tissues and noticed the unread letter.

A photograph slipped out of the envelope and onto the desk. It was a snapshot, a happy family snapshot: mum with a tiny girl in her lap and a boy of about four standing beside her, and behind them stood dad, smiling broadly at the camera. And dad was Serena's intended, Greg Hudson.

It was some time before Serena felt sufficiently composed to read the letter.

Dear Serena,

You will have seen the photograph by now and be in a state of shock and distress, I have no doubt. Please believe me when I tell you how much it grieved me to write this letter, but I must acquaint you with certain facts about my husband, Greg Hudson. Yes, he is, alas, still my husband. He disappeared before divorce proceedings could be initiated on the grounds of adultery, citing at least four women.

He is a womaniser, a serial cheat, Serena, and marrying you would make him a bigamist, a criminal. I would have no problem seeing Greg brought to justice, but you are an innocent party and need to be protected from the fate that befell me and other women – children, too, perhaps. Until now, as far as I know, I was the only one who got the ring, the only one he committed to in the act of marriage. You might imagine how the revelation of your wedding appalled me.

I remember so vividly how I felt when I learned of Greg's infidelity, how our children cried because daddy wouldn't be living with us any more, how difficult life became with no means of financial support other than what I was able to earn and handouts. But life somehow finds a level and my children have been my salvation. All that he ever gave me of true worth. I sometimes actually pity him for not having the privilege of knowing two such wonderful little people.

I have a steady boyfriend now; he may not have Greg's looks or charm – what man does? – but he is honest and caring and he has become beautiful in my eyes because I love him so dearly. I want nothing more than to give my children the father they deserve. He wants nothing more than to make our family complete, almost certainly to increase it.

Forgive me, Serena, for upsetting your world with these dismal tidings, but better now than later, I think you will agree. We are in this together, I need to be free of Greg Hudson and so do you. I have enclosed all the details you need to contact me. Please, please contact me.

You will be wondering how I know about you, Greg and your plans. You have a pen friend in Tacoma called Ruth. She was married very recently, as you know. It is an amazing stroke of good fortune that she happened to marry my brother and they have moved into a house in my street. She is my new best friend – my brother chose well; oh, that the same could be said of me! Anyway, I happened to see the last letter you sent her spread out on the coffee table and spotted Greg's name. The photograph you included confirmed his identity.

Yours,

Naomi Hudson

PS Get tough, get even, Serena, but don't get bitter. It'll harm you, not him. Take it from one who knows. As a security measure, my cousin mailed this letter in Portland. It would not do for Greg to see a Washington postmark, he might become suspicious. You must deal with this miserable situation in your own way, but I would advise secrecy. Greg is very talented at sniffing out a conspiracy. I don't want him to escape the consequences of his behaviour this time. From what Ruth has told me about you, I know that you won't either, for how many lives may yet be ruined on his account.

Serena determined to phone Naomi the following evening: local time. She couldn't cry because her boss would question her; she couldn't talk to anybody because, as Naomi said, there had to be secrecy, total secrecy. She began to feel shaky and sick so ran to the toilet where she threw up. It was there that Marilyn, from reception, found her. 'Hey, Serena, you're not, are you?'

'What?'

'Preggers?'

No inquiry could have hit Serena harder. She scrunched herself up on the floor of the toilet, leaned over the bowl again and spewed up what little was left in her stomach. 'No,' she managed to splutter.

'Well, you must have a bug or something; I'm going to call a taxi to take you home.'

The taxi took Serena to a small hotel in Chelsea. She checked in, went to her room and, beneath the cover on the bed, howled like a creature caught in a trap. Totally drained, she slept for an hour or so. When she awoke she was filled with an emotion so acute she hardly knew how to contain it. It was a cocktail of anger, indignation, disgust and determination. Even in this moment she knew that these feelings were the key to survival, the key to making her strong enough to deal with this shattering experience and not be destroyed by it.

At ten past five her phone rang. 'Hi, Honey, I'm by the car, where are you?'

'Hi, Greg, sorry, I should have called you earlier. Listen, one of my school pals rang, she's had some dreadful news and is in an awful state; I left the office early to spend some time with her. I think I'll have to stay tonight.'

'What's up?'

'I'll tell you when I see you, okay?'

'I guess. Well, good luck. Bye sweetie, see you tomorrow.'

'Okay, love you.'

'Love you back.'

Wow! Perhaps Serena's father hadn't wasted his money on drama lessons after all. But how well would her theatrical talents stand up when she came face to face with the lying, cheating, conniving swine who had stolen the thing most dear to her, her trust?

She spotted him first. He was sitting outside their favourite coffee shop in the midday sun, his paper spread out before him. The very sight of him filled her with revulsion. She thought of all the actors who were obliged to *get intimate* with co-stars they didn't find particularly appealing, for the sake of their art – perhaps it was even harder if they did, she thought wryly.

He looked up and saw her approaching. 'Hey, sweetie,' he said, getting up and throwing out his arms to embrace her.

'Greg, darling, I've missed you so much.'

'How is your friend, what has happened, exactly?'

'Her husband was killed in a car crash.'

'Oh, God, how awful!'

'Yes. She has small children, it's hard to imagine how she'll cope on her own.'

'I am so sorry for her loss, what a tragedy.' Serena didn't know whether she was more shocked at Greg's capacity to feign concern, or her own to blatantly lie.

As Serena's hatred of Greg grew, so did her resolve to trounce him. She found she could morph into character with scary ease. She began to wonder where *she* ended and *the character* began. Perhaps she would never find her real self again, that *was* a worry.

The thing Serena dreaded most was the lovemaking – of course it was no longer lovemaking, but sex, pure, raw, flesh-gratifying sex. If she was not able to respond to Greg convincingly, it would be curtains for sure; he was an expert and couldn't be fooled. She drank enough wine to become mildly anaesthetised and focused all her thoughts on how much this was going to cost him. She had never before employed so much aggression when engaged in carnal activity, and he had never enjoyed it more. Greg might not have to pull a wad of bank notes from his wallet and leave them on the bedside cabinet, but he *was* going to pay for his sins, *BIG TIME!*

The church looked magnificent with bows and bells and flowers adorning every window ledge and pew end.

Serena entered through the west door on her father's arm. She was aware of the guests turning to admire her as she made her way down the aisle, but she did not look at any of them. If she glimpsed the expression of love and pride she knew would be on her mother's face, with a tear or two running down her cheeks, she'd be undone completely.

She put herself into a sort of trance as the service progressed, as if observing the event from outside. and then they came, the words she'd been waiting for:

Therefore, if there is any one present who can show just cause why these two persons may not be lawfully joined together in matrimony, they should now declare it or hereafter remain silent.

'I can,' said Serena.

'I beg your pardon?' inquired the Vicar.

'I have a reason,' said Serena. 'This man, Gregory George Hudson, who is about to take me as his bride, is already married. His wife is the lady in the large hat sitting at the back of the church, and the man beside her is her lawyer. There are also two policemen waiting in the vestibule.'

A DATE WITH THE MATCHMAKER

All sorts of people stepped through the door of Sally Dunstan's dating agency. Despite the numerous services offered online these days, there was still a demand for her services. For a number of reasons those seeking a soulmate or escort often needed a go-between: somebody who could judge their requirements better than themselves.

Sally had learned not to create a mental picture of her clients before they arrived in her office. The voice on the end of the telephone rarely correlated with its owner. She was, therefore, practically immune to surprise.

She had, however, received a call the previous day from a man claiming to be Ebenezer Scrooge. His voice had been gruff, his manner so curt it was rude, and he was due to arrive at any moment. She doubted he would be late. He wasn't.

He strode into the room wearing a threadbare frock coat and a tall hat, the brim of which looked as if it had been chewed away by an army of mice. He carried a walking stick topped with a shiny brass knob, this was clearly for effect; for, if slightly stooped, he was in no way reliant upon it for support.

Sally fought the urge to burst out laughing. This prankster, she didn't doubt, would expect such a response and she, being of a perverse nature, was determined to thwart him.

Sally had seen several adaptations of *A Christmas Carol* and had to admit she'd never seen a more authentic-looking incarnation of one of literature's most beloved characters. There was nothing about him that betrayed his true identity. He might be a stranger, he might not, but if he was up for a bit of fun she was happy to oblige.

'Mr Scrooge, Ebenezer, so nice to meet you, please, do sit down.'

'Scrooge, I prefer Scrooge,' snarled Scrooge, elaborately arranging himself on the small chair in front of Sally's desk.

'I apologise, Mr Scrooge. We try to be informal at *Perfect Partners*, it creates a more relaxed atmosphere. Most of our clients like it. You may call me Sally.'

'No, Miss Dunstan is more appropriate, I believe.'

'As you wish. Wretched weather we're having.'

'Haven't noticed,' snapped Scrooge.

'I'm afraid prospective partners in your age group are a little thin on the ground at present, Mr Scrooge.' Or under the ground, thought Sally.

'I have your fee in my pocket and expect satisfaction. I need a wife.'

'A wife! This is a dating agency, not a marriage bureau, Mr Scrooge.'

'Same thing. Can you find me one?'

'Mr Scrooge, relationships usually start with the meeting of two consenting parties, and that is the extent of my commitment to my clients at *Perfect Partners*. The falling-in-love part, which does sometimes lead to marriage, is quite beyond my powers.'

'I have neither the time nor the inclination for observing social niceties such as falling-in-love; I need a wife as soon as may be. If she has hair, teeth, reasonable eyesight and all her limbs are in working order, I'm sure I will deem her acceptable.'

'Mr Scrooge, when it comes to romance, if expectation is in the basement of success and realisation on the top floor, you cannot hope to get from one to the other without first climbing the stairs.'

'Never heard of lifts, Miss Dunstan?'

'I was merely trying to make a point, Mr Scrooge.'

'So, you can't oblige me?'

'Mr Scrooge, you are not being reasonable. Quite frankly, you come across as someone living in Dickensian times not the 21st century. A lot of sexual equality separates us from the Victorians.' Scrooge adopted a crestfallen expression and Sally realised that she'd so wholeheartedly thrown herself into her present role that she actually felt sorry for him, for Scrooge, not the man behind the disguise. 'Have you ever been married?'

'No.'

'Had many relationships?'

'None.'

'At the risk of sounding rude, may I ask why you feel the need of a partner now?'

'Not a partner, a wife, it must be a wife.'

'A wife, then.'

'I've been having these dreams.'

'Dreams!'

'Yes, unearthly, truly horrible night terrors. They are visitations in which certain aspects of my character, shortcomings, seemingly, materialise to mock and cajole me into deep reflection.'

'And in what way do these visitations indicate the need of a wife?'

'I see a woman, she's dressed all in white and stands in the corner of my bedchamber. All the while she points with the index finger on her right hand to the ring finger on her left hand. When the spirits, the demons, are all about me, whining and screaming and groaning, penetrating the very depths of my tormented soul, she makes to come to me, but they will not let her pass because she wears no ring. It is a sign, you see, a sign that I must find a wife if I am to know any peace.'

'That's simply dreadful!'

'Will you help me, I am desperate?'

'I wonder, have you considered therapy to rid you of these apparitions?'

'Therapy?'

'Yes, therapy, psychotherapy, hypnotherapy, sod it, I don't know, aroma-bloody-therapy.'

'Miss Dunstan, these apparitions, as you describe them, are not a figment of my imagination, they are quite real.'

'You could move to a different house.'

'I was born in that house and fully intend to die in it. The greater part of my wealth is tied into my home, I am not a man of insubstantial means, you must understand. Besides, do you suppose the demons would not pursue me?' Scrooge now let out a huge sigh that set his chest rattling and wheezing. 'I need a wife, a comely, dutiful little widow would do.'

'This is where you worry me, Mr Scrooge. You make a woman sound like a commodity. A woman is not like a bottle of cough mixture that you can keep in the cupboard until you need it – the cough mixture, that is – then put back as soon as you regain your health.'

'I would not abandon my wife once she has exorcised my home of its unwelcome guests.'

'I am exceedingly pleased to hear it.'

'No, indeed, they might return.'

A silence fell on the couple. Scrooge seemed to sink down inside himself in despair. Sally regarded him carefully with a sympathetic eye because she'd been so beguiled into believing him real. He had walked off the page and lodged himself in her psyche; fiction had become fact.

In the ten years Sally had been running her agency, she had never before encountered any man with less to recommend him than Scrooge. Physically he was utterly repulsive, his manner was objectionable, he stank of mothballs, and his character seemed fixed by such archaic notions of the way the world was supposed to operate that she wondered if he was beyond redemption. But he did have money! He might even be encouraged to part with some of it if he had a shrewd spouse.

Sally decided that a wife for Scrooge would have to be the very antithesis of the sort he had in mind. What was called for was a "she-who-must-be-obeyed" sort; a strident woman with the constitution of an ox, the body of a sumo wrestler, and a voice that could shatter glass. A female not averse to overlooking idiosyncrasies aplenty in the pursuance of financial gain, a female for whom spooks would hold not the least trepidation. She had a few ladies in mind, two *pain-in the-ass* maiden aunts for a start.

Sally's mobile started to buzz: a text message from her friend, *HI, C U at 8*. Back in the real world, she looked at Scrooge and detected the hint of a smile behind the thick stubble covering his lower jaw. 'I have a proposal for you, Mr Scrooge, you can take me out to dinner tomorrow evening, and I will waive your fee. I will teach you how to properly treat a lady. I should warn you, I'm not a cheap date.'

'A cod lot at the chippie won't do, then?'

His voice was deep and soft and *very* sexy. He removed his disguise slowly, the coat, hat, wig, stubble, and wrinkled film of skin that made him wince and draw in his breath. Scrooge now lay in a heap on the carpet and in his place sat a man who was not so much handsome as imposing, his chiselled features lending him a composed, dignified air. Sally guessed he was little older than her, mid-thirties, perhaps. 'Why did you come here?' she asked.

'I wanted a date, a date with you. I saw your ad in the paper, your photograph doesn't do you justice, I must say, but it captured my attention in a big way.'

'So that's what this charade is all about?'

'Absolutely.'

'You are an actor?'

'I am, with *The Gallery Theatre Company*.'

'I think I might have seen you in something quite recently, Laertes in *Hamlet*?'

'Yep. Was I any good?'

'Na, rubbish, still, I thought you should have been given the lead.'

'I *have* been given the lead in the forthcoming production of *A Christmas Carol.*'

'It will be a blast, your portrayal of Scrooge certainly convinced me.'

'But I didn't faze you one bit, your performance was amazing.'

'Because I was totally *in the moment* by the end of it.'

'So, where would you like to go for dinner tomorrow? New York, the moon, Giovanni's in Fulham?'

'Better stick with Giovanni's for now.'

'Whatever my lady desires, farewell for the present.'

He took her hand and kissed it several times, then, with a flourish and a deep bow, Jake Grenville plucked the remnants of Scrooge from the floor and was gone. Sally regarded her reflection in the large picture behind her desk and smiled broadly.

A FAIRY TALE IN FULHAM

How many times had Sarah's parents warned her about the perils of online dating? Had she listened? Of course not, what did they know? They met at school, fell in love whilst still at university, and married in their early twenties. They were sickeningly happy, and still embarrassingly romantic. Life just wasn't like that for most people.

Sarah's older brother, Oliver, was tall, dark and exceedingly handsome; he only had to glance at a girl to have her falling at his feet. Oliver was, however, highly principled where girls were concerned, where people generally were concerned. Girlfriends came and went, but strictly one at a time, and when a break-up was imminent, he was sensitivity personified. Oliver didn't need to go *online* to get a date; girls practically stood *in-line* to capture his attention. Sarah could only dream of meeting a guy like him.

Sarah was petite; she had fair hair with auburn lights in it, and soft, natural curls that danced about her neck, as if in play. Her hazel eyes were full of mischief, reflecting her bubbly personality. She knew exactly why she was frequently overlooked in the *dating game*. At nearly nineteen, she looked not a day over fourteen.

If she happened to pass the local boys' grammar school when the sixth formers were in the playground, a cacophony of whistles and saucy remarks hastened her on her way. She was after a man, not a boy. It was all so very depressing.

This online date, Simon, said he would meet her in the lounge bar of the 'The Smugglers' at eight. To avoid embarrassment later, she had arrived early in order to produce the ID she knew would be requested. Simon had sounded promising: educated, and funny; he looked pretty fit, too.

By eight thirty it was clear he was not going to show up. Sarah finished her wine and headed for the door just as it was thrust open by a gang of Chelsea supporters bemoaning a crushing defeat at *the bridge*. Oliver was amongst them.

'Hey, Sarah, what are you doing here?'

'Being stood up.'

'He's a bloody fool, whoever he is.'

'Bless you, Ollie.'

'Have a drink with me and the gang, who knows, one of them might take your fancy.'

None did. In twos and threes they left, but Oliver made no attempt to follow them. 'Are you hungry, Sarah?'

'Yes, starving.'

'Let's finish our drinks and head off; I know a place, cheap, but good; it's where all us interns hang out. I'd offer you something fancy, if I could afford it, you know that.'

Yes, Sarah did know that, *that* was part of the problem. Oliver had been blessed with a big heart and a generous spirit. She remembered when he'd arrived home from school on one particularly cold day without his coat and told their mother he'd given it to a tramp. She'd berated him roundly for his foolishness and told him he had to replace it with his own money. 'I know, mum,' he'd said, giving her a hug. Next morning, she went to town and bought him a new one.

Sarah had been so moved by this selfless act of benevolence she could not help comparing every male she met thereafter with her wonderful brother, but they had all fallen short, so far. 'I made such an effort to look my age tonight, Ollie.'

'Sarah, you are seriously gorgeous, a true sweetheart, inside and out; just concentrate on being yourself. You'll be grateful for your youthful appearance one day.'

'You are my brother, and just a teeny bit biased.'

Oliver took several swigs from his beer glass, and then a couple of deep breaths before saying, 'Sarah, I'm not, actually.'

'Not what?'

'Your brother.'

'What *are* you talking about?'

'I was waiting for the right moment to tell you; I think this might just be it.'

'Ollie, tell me what?'

'That I was adopted.'

'Adopted! How long have you known this?'

'Since last Monday, after my visit to Cambridge on the weekend, something Grandma said stuck in my head. She told me I was the baby that died.'

'Which kind of proves how advanced her dementia is. Why did it get to you?'

'Can't say exactly, anyway, I decided to talk to mum about it. Actually, I got the distinct feeling she was glad of the opportunity to offload, to share a very sad and difficult time in her life… There was a brief hiatus when she and dad first got married, apparently. He'd been a bit *over friendly* with one of her friends, so she went on a date with a chap she knew from uni. They both got helplessly drunk and one thing led to another…'

'She got pregnant?'

'Yep.'

'Bloody hell!'

'She couldn't bear the thought of an abortion and dad

agreed to accept the child as his own; partly because he blamed himself as much as her for the rift.'

Sarah could hardly believe what she was hearing, 'I'm confused, Ollie, if you were *that* baby— '

'No, Sarah, that baby, a son, died before it was a month old. Mum believed it was retribution, a punishment; she had a nervous breakdown over it. They tried for another baby without success, so they adopted me a year later.'

'Then how did I come about?'

'Four lots of IVF treatment.'

Sarah remained perfectly still and silent whilst her brain computed this piece of news, then she said, 'The implications for us are enormous.'

'Aren't they? I've thought of little else all week.'

'This… this revelation isn't necessarily a bad thing… is it?'

'Certainly not as far as I'm concerned.'

'Mum and dad should have told us,' Sarah said, with a touch of bitterness in her voice.

'Maybe, but it might have made things a little tricky between us, don't you think?'

'I suppose so.'

'I mean, as siblings go, we've been especially close.'

'Yes, yes we have, we are.'

Out in the cold night air, Oliver took Sarah's hand.

He'd done this so many times when she was tiny, his adored little sister trustingly toddling along beside him in the street.

The feel of her hand grasped firmly in his own now was… well, it was different, *very* different.

A ROYAL PRESENCE

'It's not quite what I'm looking for,' Albert told the shop owner.

'You asked for an inflatable doll.'

'I didn't expect it to look so, so plastic, so blown-up.'

'Sir, inflatable dolls *are* plastic and blown-up.'

'I suppose I was hoping for something more, well, life-like.'

'I see. I might be able to accommodate you; it all depends on how much you wish to spend. There is an exclusive, latex range available. I don't stock them, naturally, as they do not inflate, but I can show you the catalogue. There are some gorgeous-looking young females to choose from; I take it you want a female?'

'Absolutely, but not a young one.'

'Really!'

'She must be the very image of our dear queen.'

'Definitely not a young one, then.'

'Excuse me!'

'Sir, Elizabeth Two carries her age with extraordinary grace and could be easily taken for a much younger woman, but she is old, you must concede.'

'She's still a beauty in my eyes.'

'She has never failed in her duties to crown and country, and that's what really counts.'

Since the shop owner was clearly a staunch monarchist, Albert decided to confide in him.

'I am to receive an OBE at the palace for voluntary services to the homeless here in London.'

'Goodness me, congratulations!'

'Thank you. The thing is, when I was a boy, I had a dreadful stammer which was always accompanied by a bout of trembling. My entire body would shake most violently. It has taken me fifty years of therapy to rid myself of this affliction. I fear it might return when I am faced with the ordeal of kneeling before her majesty.'

'She would certainly understand, just think of her father's battle with his stutter. Still, I can certainly see why you would wish to avoid any embarrassment.'

'I thought, if I had an effigy of our queen in my home, I could practise being presented and the occasion would be as joyful and rewarding as it ought to be.'

'Leave it with me, you have allowed plenty of time for the execution of your request, I take it.'

'Oh, yes.'

'I will speak to the gentleman who runs the company, he's connected with Madame Tussaud's, quite an artist, I'm told.'

***

Elizabeth Two – in all her finery and sitting in the carver chair Albert had fashioned into a throne with a curtain of brocade fabric – was so authentic in appearance that Albert found it impossible to ignore her presence, even for a second. Wherever he went, her eyes seemed to follow him, it was extremely disconcerting. He tried covering her with a sheet before sitting down to watch television, but when a draught from the kitchen became trapped beneath it, and her majesty seemed to have started breathing, he hastily snatched it off in fright.

He took to talking to his guest. Ma'am was consulted on every domestic issue. In some ways it was like having Doris back. Albert's darling wife had been largely immobilised by a stroke and speech became so difficult that eventually she stopped talking altogether. Albert started speaking for both of them, relying on facial expressions and the gestures she made with her body to determine her needs and thoughts. When she died, he felt completely useless and redundant, and threw himself into the charity work that had earned him the title he was soon to receive.

Albert's friends, Stan, Charlie and Will were getting increasingly concerned about him, about the royal presence in his home. His speech had started to become stilted and slightly plummy, and he'd stopped swearing altogether. More worrying still was his inability to turn his back on her majesty when taking her leave. He wouldn't have caused himself quite so many mishaps had he not felt it necessary to bow umpteen times when in reverse gear.

'For God's sake, Albert,' said Charlie, shuffling cards for their weekly session of crib, 'you're going to break your bloody neck if you carry on like this much longer.'

'He gets his gong at the palace tomorrow,' reminded Stan.

'Fanbloodytastic, then he can dethrone Queenie and we can all get back to normal. That's if he hasn't already completely lost his marbles.' replied Charlie.

'She gives me the creeps, peering over my shoulder at my cards. Don't get me wrong, I consider myself a loyal subject and all, but this situation isn't natural. Albert, you are treating her as if she's real,' said Will.

'How are you going dispose of her?' inquired Charlie.

'You make it sound like regicide,' grumbled Albert.

'Well?' asked Stan.

'The man who got her for me will return her to the guy who made her, she will be re-formed, apparently.'

'Why, does she have a murky past?' Will's quip made all but Albert laugh, he was highly indignant on Ma'am's account.

'Will this man come and fetch her, Albert?' asked Stan.

'No, I will transport her.'

'What, not in the sidecar on your motorbike?'

'Of course.'

'It's 2018, Albert; that bloody old combination is sixty years old if it's a day, and it hasn't been out of the garage since you got your bus pass.'

'It is a fine machine, Stan, besides Doris loved it, I could never part with it. Still, if you are too embarrassed to help me put Her Majesty in it, and accompany me to the blow-up doll shop, I'll just have to manage on my own.'

'Nah, Albert, don't go getting all uppity, I'll help you; it should be fun.'

***

Albert was in heaven. Neither the hint of a stammer, nor a tremble had beset him on this special, special day. Everything had gone like clockwork. He thought about Doris, she would have been so proud of him. As he left the palace, he brushed a tear away and climbed into the taxi that would take him home.

***

They were in Wandsworth when the police pulled them over. Even when it was established that they had not abducted the queen or raided Madame Tussaud's, both they and the ancient combination underwent extensive searches, and then came the questions. Moments later the news teams arrived with their microphones and cameras.

***

'Stan, you look like a pillock grinning into the camera like that,' opined Charlie.

'It was my celebrity moment,' snapped Stan.

'And you completely blew it,' informed Will.

'You two are just jealous.'

The gang were sitting in front of Albert's new flat-screen television set. Albert had been reluctant to watch the local evening news; he felt he'd suffered enough humiliation for one day, but no excuse to leave the room would have satisfied his friends.

In the event, whilst Stan *had* made an ass of himself for the media, he, Albert Wilkins believed he had come across rather well. He'd made the whole – properly preparing oneself for an audience with the queen – episode sound totally reasonable. In a clear, confident voice, with a cut-glass accent he barely recognised as his own, he gave a laudable account of his actions.

***

Stan, Will and Charlie had gone home. Albert sat in his favourite chair waiting for the late night news, perchance the item was repeated. It was, *and* it had been slightly extended. The broadcaster announced that Her Majesty had viewed it. She'd asked one of her aides to contact the BBC commending Sir Albert George Wilkins for the extreme measures he took to receive his richly deserved award.

Albert promptly burst into tears and picked up his favourite photograph of Doris that stood proudly on the sideboard. 'Well, what about that, eh, Doris, love: Sir Albert George Wilkins, a knight of the realm, who would have imagined such a thing?'

A STRANGER
IN THE HOUSE

The Christmas of 1946 was different, very different.

My mother was always bragging about me, telling people how bright I was for a six-year-old. So why hadn't she credited me with enough sense to work out that the man who had crept into my bedroom with my stocking the previous Christmas Eve, when he was sure I'd be asleep, was Uncle Harry and not the real Father Christmas?

How did I know this? Well, Uncle Harry had a very bad limp, that's why he hadn't gone off to the war with my dad, his brother. Father Christmas was big and fat, but I was sure he didn't have a limp, not with all those chimneys to climb down and rooftops to clamber over.

I really don't know how my mum expected me to go to sleep when there were so many treats in store. My stocking would be filled with goodies: oranges, apples, nuts, small chocolate figures, hand-knitted socks and perhaps a balaclava – which made me look very scary indeed and frightened all the girls. Maybe, if I was very lucky, there would also be a comic or two, and even some crayons or a little toy car.

Being an only child could be a lonely business, but it did have its benefits; although money was very tight, I never went short of gifts.

A dim shaft of light spread out across the floor of my bedroom when my door was opened. I was very good at pretending to be asleep whilst peering through the slits in my eyelids, and I could tell it was not Uncle Harry coming into my room, but a complete stranger. This man was tall with dents in his cheeks and eyes too big for his face. Whatever he had stuffed up his front didn't make him look fat and jolly like a Santa Claus, in fact he looked exactly like my Grandpa had looked lying in his coffin in our front room. Everybody in our street came to view his body, like he was something in a museum. I didn't like that much.

I decided this person was a burglar. His big sack was probably full of our possessions and now he intended to steal all my books and toys. Well, he wasn't going to get away with it!

I slipped my hand under my pillow and grasped my long-handled metal torch while the thief was rummaging about at the foot of my bed. And then he did something very strange, he bent low over me, as if about to kiss me, and whispered my name, 'Oscar.'

However, I had quite decided he was planning to

murder me, so, quick as a flash, I leapt up and brought my torch down hard upon his head. He yelped in pain and fell to the floor. I firmly believed I had killed him and didn't quite know how I should feel about that.

There was blood everywhere, and very soon an ambulance pulled up outside our house. My mother was sobbing and asked if we could travel with her husband, my father, to the hospital.

My father had survived the war only to return and be slain by his son. I would go to prison, but worse than that: my mother would hate me until the end of time.

But my mother didn't hate me. She told me the doctor said my father wasn't going to die and I'd been very brave to tackle the stranger as I did. She said the attack was her fault because she hadn't told me dad was coming home; she'd wanted it to be a big surprise on Christmas morning.

Dad came home from hospital in time for Christmas lunch. The house was full of relatives and good cheer. My father hugged me tightly whenever I was near him and told me if I apologised for hitting him one more time he'd clock me.

It is now 1952. My dad and I still play with the train set he gave me – purchased at the cost of his great coat – and we add to it regularly. We are great buddies. But it is the love and the pride he showed me on Christmas day 1946 that I remember best of all. How could I ever forget? I have only to glimpse the scar in the slight dent just above his hairline to be reminded of it. Still, his cheeks have filled out nicely, and his eyes no longer look as if they belong in somebody else's face. He is the man in the wedding photograph that stands on my mum's bedside table, a bit older, of course. He is my dad.

AN ODD CONCEPTION

It was twenty years since my husband had left our two young children and me for a bimbo. This was the first unpredictable thing he had ever done. Incredulity rendered me without the capacity to function properly initially, but Edward and Lucy needed my attention, everything needed my attention: the mortgage, the bills, the temperamental boiler, the garden, the broken hinge on the front gate.

At the age of forty-six, alone, blissfully content, a grandmother, and in a very well paid job, I was able to look back at the previous two decades with pride. I could smile when I recalled believing a partner was essential for a full and happy existence.

'But what about sex, Barb?' my best friend, Rose, inquired, as we sat sipping coffee in Starbucks. 'Don't you miss it?'

'No, not at all.'

This was quite true. I wasn't missing it because I was having regular virtual intercourse whilst asleep; it was sublime and quite unlike the fumbling, excessively messy business I had endured with men who were of the flesh and blood variety. Of course, there was no way of trying to describe my *night-time visitations* to Rose, her brain wasn't wired up to receive such information

I ascribed my first encounter with my *night caller* to a dream, a truly beautiful dream, and one I most ardently hoped would return. It did return, return to fill me with an exquisite sense of completeness, of being loved, cherished and very special.

There were no smelly socks to pick up in his wake, no shirts to iron, no toilet seats to lower, no stubble-coated basins to clean. Only the essence of my virtual lover lingered when he was gone. It was absolutely perfect!

And then, one night, it was different, wonderful, as always, but different. Something profound had happened and I had no idea what it was until I paid my doctor a visit.

'Pregnant! That's not possible.'

'Why, because of your age? There are lots of older mums, these days.'

'Yes, I know that… Doctor, I haven't been with a man… not a real one, anyway,' I unthinkingly blurted out.

'Oh! I see.'

'I very much doubt that.' I walked out of the surgery before the doctor had the chance to recommend a visit to a psychiatrist.

The implications of my condition were so enormous

my mind could hardly process them. What was I to tell my family? 'Oh, bye the way, I was impregnated by a non-human being whilst I slept?' They would have me sectioned! No, a secret relationship was the only answer: I'd been *having it off* with a toy boy and too embarrassed to tell them. Edward and Lucy would think I was mad, of course, but nutty mad, not insane mad.

In the event, my daughter told me I had been totally irresponsible, but that she would stick by me because she loved me. My son simply said, 'Good for you, Mum, but what are you going to do with a baby?'

Yes, what *was* I going to do with a baby?

My child was born with ridiculous ease: Labour, one hour; stitches, none. I was so pleased I'd had a girl. Given the nature of her conception, I would have felt like a very sinful, non-virgin version of Mary, had I produced a son.

My new daughter was a cherub; she rarely saw fit to cry or inconvenience me in any way. She filled my heart with love and pride and soon became the darling of my friends, children and grandchildren. If they gave a thought to her absent, adolescent of a father, they never mentioned it to me.

I named her Roberta after my twin brother, Robert, who had died at birth. As she grew, I couldn't ignore the fact that she was the very image of the young man I had loved and lost. Philip Carson was with the bomb squad and never returned from active service.

Every year on the anniversary of his death I visited his grave, sat on the kerb of the memorial and wept bitterly.

I pushed the buggy into the cemetery. My seventeen-month-old daughter was clutching a pink and white posy of flowers. I positioned the buggy at the foot of the grave, but Roberta's eyes were focused on something behind it, something or someone *I* couldn't see. 'Da, da,' she squealed excitedly, blowing kisses off her tiny hands.

AT THE TOP
OF THE STAIRS

My aunt had an unfortunate penchant for ugly, antique furniture. This affliction was compounded by the fact that she was also possessed of an unnatural antipathy for empty spaces.

The mid-terrace Victorian house that was home to my mother, grandmother, aunt, brother and me was already bursting at the seams when a decommissioned hearse drew up in front of it bearing her latest acquisition: a huge, ornate, totally hideous sideboard.

My aunt had paid ten pounds for it at an auction – a considerable sum at the time. She believed she had bagged herself a bargain. The mode of its conveyance, however, cast a slur on the piece and, in her eyes, was suggestive of tat rather than treasure. And that is how the sideboard came to be located in an alcove on the landing at the top of the stairs, an area out of sight from general view.

The sideboard stood so solidly on its bevelled base that our cat, Lucifer, mistook it for a building and promptly moved in. This was not a very practical arrangement since it meant the doors could never be fully shut, but nothing would persuade Lucifer to quit his new-found lodgings.

When Lucifer passed away, an army of smaller residents took up occupation in the sideboard. Closed doors did not inhibit the access of these species, and I developed a profound and abiding regard for all eight-legged creatures.

It was at about this time that my aunt's interest in the art of ginger beer making peaked. It was to this end that our small back garden was turned over to some rather strange-looking plants that summer.

The process was messy and laborious and involved a lengthy period of fermentation. Once the bottles had been filled and corked, they required a suitable facility in which to be stored. The sideboard was it.

The spiders, having been suddenly provided with ample diversion within, rarely ventured out any more – to everyone's delight except my own. I was young; they were my playmates.

Somewhere, in the uneasy stillness of a frosty night, when the house was having creaky conversations with itself, and chill draughts danced in the curtains and sought exposed ears to nip, and the world didn't extend beyond the warmth of our beds, it started.

Initially, it sounded like the distant rumble of thunder,

then, more like machine gun fire. Then a cacophony of popping and fizzing brought us scurrying from our beds, draped in whatever had first come to hand: eiderdowns, mostly.

The activity was on the cusp of erupting. We could only stand and stare as the sideboard doors burst open and sodden corks shot out in every direction, peppering the flocked, floral wallpaper and leaving indents all over it. My brother's eyes glinted with mirth as one ricocheted off the wall and clipped his ear before merrily bouncing down the stairs.

In the bottles, the ginger beer sat festering, liquid genies about to make a bid for freedom. Then, out they tumbled, balls of froth gaining size and momentum until the entire landing was awash with pungent surf.

It swilled around our feet before surging towards the staircase. My aunt, with theatrical flourish, threw her eiderdown across the top of the stairs in an attempt to check its progress. This, alas, served only to create a build-up. The spume rose, like a great foamy cloud, and made my grandmother sneeze most violently. My aunt snatched up the eiderdown and tossed it down the stairs. Luckily, the cloud followed it into the hallway below, carried along on a bubbling tide. The gurgling liquid then slipped effortlessly under the front door, slid down the short garden path, under the gate and onto the pavement beyond. The road, we knew, would be very busy with early morning pedestrian traffic bound for the railway station and bus stop.

My grandmother's chagrin rendered her bereft of speech, but her expression spoke volumes. We hastened back to our beds and out of her sight perchance she, too, would erupt, would erupt to even more spectacular effect than had the ginger beer.

AURELIA
AND THE QUEEN

I don't always accompany Her Majesty on her engagements, but when I do, I travel in one of her many handbags. These handbags, as you would expect, are specially commissioned: best leather, softest lining, plenty of legroom. They represent executive travel in spades.

Her Majesty takes great care not to buffet me around, restrict my airflow, or leave me unattended. Her handbags contain very little; she doesn't require a passport or purse and has people to attend to her make-up and hair. She does, however, carry a number of soft lawn handkerchiefs to mop her brow or wipe away the odd tear when a poignant situation threatens to undo her emotionally – she may be the monarch and the essence of aplomb, but she is still human, when all is said and done. Anyway, these embroidered kerchiefs provide bedding and warmth; handbags can be draughty places, don't you know.

I clearly recall the very first time she spied me. She was sitting on her sofa watching Coronation Street; I was beside her on a cushion. I truly believed she was about to suffer a seizure. I am a very large spider, you see, and extremely hairy, but I have the prettiest face and the most winning smile. So I smiled my sweetest smile and told Her Majesty that my name was Aurelia and on no account must she be alarmed. I then attempted to perform a curtsy with all my legs at once and toppled over in the process. Despite herself, Her Majesty started to laugh.

'You are a spider!' she declared, peering through the small spectacles that had slipped to the end of her nose.

'I am aware of it, Ma'am.'

'But you can talk!'

'Indeed,' I confirmed.

'Your voice is rather charming, I must say.'

'Thank you, Ma'am. It is most gracious of you to say so.'

It transpired that Her Majesty had seen *Charlotte's Web*, the film they made about my mother, Charlotte. It told the story of how she saved the life of a little pig called Wilbur – destined for the table – by weaving webs with clever words written in them.

Her majesty was, quite understandably, of the opinion that real life had somehow become entangled with fantasy, for she said, 'One is currently suffering from some frightful delusional condition.'

'Oh, no, Ma'am, I assure you that is not the case. I would like to serve you; it is the reason I am here.'

'Serve me, how, may I ask?'

'I would guard your interests, be a sort of spy — if you like. I could position myself where no electronic surveillance device has ever been situated before. I would dedicate my life to your safety and wellbeing.'

'Um,' said Her Majesty, resting her chin on the back of her hand in thought. 'What about flies, I do detest flies?'

'As do I, Ma'am. They are loathsome, filthy creatures. No fly escapes my detection.'

'Very well, you may stay. Now, let me get back to my programme.'

I settled down again on the cushion beside Her Majesty, and presently felt her stroke my head very gently with her forefinger. At length I started to drift off to sleep (soaps don't really float my boat) and thought about my mother. She would be looking down on me now from heaven, whilst weaving beautiful filigree webs for the angels. She would be so proud of her Aurelia, living in Buck House, serving the Queen. Wouldn't any mother?

BEAUTIFUL PEOPLE

Leo Roxborough knows that Marrith Hudson, screen goddess and triple Oscar winner, would not have fallen for him had he not been so dazzlingly handsome, so perfect in form and feature. Of course, the image the world sees is not the man *he* sees when he looks in the mirror.

Leo does not love Marrith. She looks fabulous, wearing clothes and make-up or none, and is very accommodating in bed. She satisfies a physical need in his life and is a decorative accessory. That is all. He puts up with all the Hollywood hype surrounding them as a couple because, whilst he loathes it, it entertains him in a perverse sort of way.

Leo, the dynamic young entrepreneur, has become almost as famous for his business acumen as his father, the oil magnate. Hugh Roxborough is as rich as Croesus and has an ego to match his fortune.

The blockbuster movie ends, the theatre doors are flung open and those who were standing on the sidewalk when the stars arrived are still there, hungry for another glimpse of their idols.

Marrith's gown, a scarlet tulle, floaty affair, just about conceals her private life, but leaves enough flesh exposed to excite the fancies of those lucky enough to get an eyeful of it. Leo is the very epitome of sartorial elegance: black, pure wool over soft, snowy white linen against his olive skin, and just a few wisps of rebellious dark hair falling onto his collar. His long, lean body somehow manages to arrange itself in the most flattering positions without the least deliberation or effort. His flinty-blue eyes are rarely still, and a wry, knowing smile hangs about his lips and only falls away when he is troubled. At such times his expression becomes haunted and totally irresistible to Marrith who truly believes she has the power to spirit this lost look away, to banish it forever. She is quite wrong.

Marrith slips her hand around Leo's waist as they emerge from the theatre. The spectators whoop and cheer and push against the barriers as the couple pass. The press and paparazzi hustle for the best vantage point. A great shot, revealing interview, careers are made and lost at celebrity events like these. This is premiere fever; it will peak, abate, be tomorrow's news and next week's history. For now, though, it is a moment in time sprinkled with stardust. It belongs to the dream makers and those who dream.

The first of a convoy of gleaming stretch limos glides

to a halt alongside the swathe of red carpet that runs from theatre door to kerb edge. The drivers of Manhattan respond in typical form by filling the night air with a cacophony of honking and beeping. The chauffeurs know their idling vehicles are creating a major obstruction. They do not care. This is *The Big Apple*, a crazy place where anything can happen.

A few blocks away, one of the oldest and grandest hotels in Manhattan awaits the arrival of the stars. Staff and management fuss and tweak in nervous anticipation – nothing must be found wanting. The hotel has a proud reputation to uphold. Supper tables groan under the burden of an outrageously extravagant array of finger food.

In the ballroom an orchestra is tuning up; the discordant sounds totally belie the prospect of harmony. Then the conductor gets his cue, raises his baton, and the warring instruments resolve their quarrel in glorious melody.

Leo moves among the party people, pecking the cheeks of the older women, hugging the younger ones, shaking hands with the men and issuing compliments aplenty. Silly women simper and say things they will deeply regret later. Husbands and escorts look at each other in complete mystification and, when he is gone, ask themselves what makes Leo Roxborough so bloody special.

Leo tells Marrith he has a headache and takes himself off to get a little fresh air. She should know by now that he is lying, but she sees only that for which she is looking.

In his absence she seeks out some female company. By the time he returns, the women are giggling, cracking dirty jokes and knocking back the juice like it's going out of fashion. He seizes the opportunity to inform her that he must slip back to her apartment for his pills and kisses her hard on the lips, too hard.

Marrith is so occupied basking in the glory that currently surrounds her that she forces herself to ignore what instinct is trying to tell her. Something is wrong, dreadfully wrong.

Leo walks three blocks before even thinking about hailing a cab. He needs space, a little time for reflection, but none for remorse. There is no place in his heart for remorse.

In uptown Manhattan – a district suffering from an identity crisis since its reputation as a ghetto was commuted to that of *an area of low employment*, Leo lets himself into his own apartment. His neighbours are dipsos, crackheads, hookers and no-hopers. They take his generous handouts and assume he is a porn merchant because he wears leather shoes.

The apartment is equipped with the basics: fridge, bed,

ancient sofa and microwave oven. The only concessions to modern living: a television set and music centre. Of course, Leo doesn't live here so much as *hang out*. He has a very large apartment overlooking Central Park, and a spread in Beverly Hills, but both feel less like home to him than this place.

He flops on the bed and thinks about Marrith. She will be trying to call him on his cell phone by now, she will want to know where he is. It is switched off. She might become more than a little concerned, but she will not leave the party. An actress never leaves the stage before the play is over and all the applause has died away.

He slips into the twilight zone betwixt sleep and wakefulness. This is when she comes: his mother. He can smell her, feel her breath on his face, hear her telling him how beautiful he is and how much she loves him, loves him enough to let him go. He doesn't want to listen anymore, but her voice just gets louder and louder, more agitated and upset. Now she is telling him that the American who visits sometimes, when he is on business in Mosul, is his father. She is saying that he is a very lucky boy because his father wants to take him back to the United States to live with him and his new wife. They have a lovely place in California and another in New York. Leo will have all the things every boy dreams of. He will go to school and university…

He awakes with a start, but the dream continues. He is begging his mother not to send him away from her and his brothers and sisters. He does not want to live with this American father with his big mouth, big dick and big wallet. The slap comes hard across his face but he doesn't cry. He can see in his mother's eyes that her pain is far worse than his own. He understands that she truly believes she is doing right by him, and, at the same time, saving his siblings from a life in the gutter.

For a stash of filthy American lucre, the beautiful boy is robbed of his name, his faith and his identity. He is given a lifestyle tailor-made for the son of a big shot: a person of discernment and enterprise. Leo becomes the young man he must become to survive and prosper in this plastic land. But he does not forget. He will never forget. And he will never, never forgive.

Leo stretches, gets off the bed and goes into the sitting room. He drops onto the sofa, flicks on the television with the remote control and looks at his watch. The minute hand moves towards the hour, and within seconds the news channel pumps out a bulletin. He switches on his cell phone. One moment later it rings. 'Leo, you are alive! My God, you are alive!

'Yes, Father, I'm alive.'

'You know about the hotel bombing, of course?'

'Sure, I just heard it on TV.'

'We thought you would be at the party.'

'I was, I had a headache and left.'

'Well, praise the Lord for that. Leo, what kind of sick-minded person does something like this? All those innocent people blown to bits to make some sort of point. I just don't understand how the world works any more, I really don't.'

Leo switches off his phone and tosses it onto the floor.

'You never did, Father. That's the problem.'

Leo raises the pistol to his temple. In the seconds before he pulls the trigger, he hears the gentle voice of his mother. She is calling out to him from the grave. And he can hear, too, the tortured wails that he knows will issue from his father when he learns of Leo's death, Leo's hideous crime.

BUMP

Donna wasn't a flighty young woman. She was sensible to the point of being considered exceedingly boring by her peers. She didn't drink, smoke, or do drugs, and she'd never had a sexual encounter. So, why in God's name had she been visited by this dreadful curse, pregnant whilst in her final year at University! It wasn't bloody fair. And who would believe she was still a virgin? Nobody, that's who.

The doctor had told her she was so lucky she hardly showed, even at eight months. Donna was forced to agree because it meant no explanations were necessary, and her friends just thought she'd put on a few pounds. She hadn't been sick or felt particularly tired, or had any cravings for certain foods. She had, however, saved an absolute fortune on tampons; that was some small consolation, she supposed.

Donna started hatching a plan, a plan that would only work if the baby arrived on its due day, a week before Christmas. Her parents were expecting her home for the holiday on the 21st of December.

The baby, a boy, put in an appearance on the 18th December. The whole process was over within three hours. Donna left hospital the following day, returning to the house she shared with five other students, all of whom had already vacated the premises for the holiday. She spent two days in the house with her baby, whom she called *Bump,* before setting out for rural Sussex where her parents lived.

The baby was gurgling happily away in his carrier on the front passenger seat of her car. She found herself talking to him, explaining the situation and apologising for not being able to keep him. He responded with a succession of quizzical expressions, as if he understood every word she said. 'You are the most agreeable little fellow I have ever met, Bump. When I have a child, through the normal means, I hope he will be exactly like you.' Bump closed his eyes and slept soundly for the rest of the journey.

*

The church was so quiet and peaceful now. The worshippers had floated out on a wave of Christian goodwill. The Reverend Pope stood at the great west door fumbling for the enormous key in the pocket of his overcoat.

He loved Christmas, the Christingle service, the carols, and especially the nativity play performed by members of the Sunday school. The little children could always be relied upon, in their innocence, to add a comical element to the enactment of the birth of Jesus.

He remembered last year's pint-sized innkeeper telling Mary and Joseph to *Bugger off!* when they knocked on his door, and the tiny angel, his granddaughter, lifting her white gown to admire her new shoes and finding a stray thread at top of her sock. The look of wonder on her face as the knee-length sock got shorter and shorter until it disappeared completely into her shoe was truly something to behold.

The Reverend Pope had ten grandchildren and never ceased to be charmed by their escapades. He was a man with a keen sense of fun, inexhaustible patience, and infectious enthusiasm. And his flock adored him.

He now reached up to switch off all but one of St Mark's internal lights: the one which illuminated the altar. The nativity scene, the crib and plaster animals around it – borrowed from the local butcher – looked almost as if it had been caught in the subtle glow of a full moon, much as it would have looked on *that night*, mused the Vicar.

Then he heard it, a sound from the crib: the unmistakable cry of a newborn baby. He'd watched his granddaughter carefully place the baby doll she'd been given for her birthday into the crib earlier that evening. And he'd seen her lift it out again when the service was over. So somebody had been lying in wait to replace it with a human version of the Christ Child when the church was bereft of a congregation, but not its Vicar. This was somebody who knew him and his routine.

The infant started to go red in the face, its tiny limbs thrashing about in its cocoon of snowy white swaddling, its wails getting shriller and shriller. The Vicar picked it up, tucked it under his coat, and hastily made his way down the aisle to the door.

Mrs Pope was in the kitchen putting the kettle on when the Vicar entered the rectory. 'Tea, Arthur?'

'No, formula, I think, Esther, my dear.

*

The reverend Pope was acting very strangely and his wife was becoming increasingly concerned. 'Arthur, we must call the police, that baby has been in the house for three days, we'll be in terrible trouble.'

'I'll think up a plausible explanation for the delay in informing the authorities, trust me, Esther.'

'What is it about *this* baby?'

'I believe he was sent to us for a purpose.'

'He wasn't sent, Arthur, somebody put him in the crib, a young unmarried mother, I daresay, a refugee perhaps; he does look rather foreign.'

'He's beautiful, isn't he?' The reverend's eyes started to glaze over.

'Yes, he is. He's a real little angel.'

'You are nearly right, my dear.'

'Whatever do you mean?'

'I believe it's the Second Coming of our Lord.'

'You had a vision?'

'I did.'

'Tell me about it.'

'I saw the world breaking to pieces on a giant screen, and then the image of this baby appeared, was superimposed upon it hundreds and hundreds of times, and it eventually became whole again.'

'What do suggest we do?'

'Offer ourselves as foster parents.'

'What, at our age? We will be refused.'

'I think not. Our Lord will facilitate the arrangement, if it is meant to be. Anyway, with our daughter still living at home, a highly qualified paediatrician, and showing no inclination to be married, I hardly think the agency would see fit to refuse us.'

'Well, that's all very well, Arthur, but we should at least acquaint Ruth with the situation.'

'You are right, my dear, I'll contact her directly.'

'She'll be returning from her holiday in Paris tonight, it can wait until then.'

*

Sally, another of the Reverend Pope's five daughters, was Donna's oldest friend and lived just two doors away from her parents' home. Sally was in the kitchen making coffee in her new machine when Donna came through the back door. 'Other women get jewels and expensive perfume for Christmas, look what Guy bought me!'

'Did you want jewels and perfume?'

'Not especially, but I didn't tell Guy that.'

'It's a fabulous piece of equipment, I must say.'

'Yes, it is, I love it, but I didn't tell him that either.'

'You are wicked, Sal.'

'I know.'

'How are your parents?'

'Well, to be honest something very odd is going on. Dad found a newborn in the crib after the nativity and... Donna, what is it?'

'I hardly dare tell you.'

'You can tell me anything, you know that.'

'I gave birth to that baby, and I put him in the crib for your father to find, I knew he'd do what was right for him.'

'Well, he and my mum want to become its foster parents, if you can imagine anything so daft: he's nearly seventy, and she's sixty-five. Ruth is going to have such a shock when she comes home from Paris tonight to find a baby in the house. Dad says it's a special child. I don't quite know what he means by that.'

'Oh, Lord! Oh, heavens! He can't be! This is so scary!'

'What is?'

'Sal, you know me better than anyone, how old-fashioned I am. I've been saving myself for *Mr Right*. I have never slept with a man, or knowingly, at least. I carried Bump, but he didn't feel like mine. I've been going nuts trying to work out what happened to me, how I got pregnant. I came to the conclusion that somebody had put something in my juice at a birthday party I went to.'

'Good God!'

'I'm not so sure about that now.'

'Donna, *an Immaculate Conception* in 2019, how absolutely amazing! *YOU* are the chosen one, my friend!'

'This isn't right, Sal, I'm just a very ordinary, conventional young woman; the whole thing is, well, it's impossible.'

'Nothing is impossible with God, Donna, it says so in the bible. And, remember, Mary felt exactly the same as you when the angel appeared. I think you were named Donna for a purpose: *Donna/Madonna, think about it.*'

Sally wondered if she should fall to her knees before her friend, given her newfound, divine status, but decided against it and unceremoniously plonked a mug of coffee on the table in front of Donna.

BURIED

The two stone cottages stood solid and squat at the end of the lane. Both were unoccupied and in a state of disrepair, but only the more dilapidated of the two had a *For Sale* sign planted at an angle in the front garden.

When Jim, my husband, and I were planning for our future after retirement, we decided on a project: a country property we could adapt to suit our needs. Our son was an architect, my husband a builder and a substantial home, with a large garden, our dream.

These cottages were begging to be united as a single dwelling, developed into a desirable residence. With a walled area enclosing the rear gardens and divided only by a flimsy fence, a space at the side for a double garage or workshop, views over pastures dotted with grazing animals in every direction, it was perfect!

Well, it would have been perfect had both cottages been for sale.

In the nearby village, the estate agent offered us a seat in his small office – a converted cottage, as it happened – and offered us a cup of tea that we graciously declined.

'So, you are interested in Clover Cottage?'

'We certainly would be, if the one adjoining it were also for sale,' said Jim.

'Ah, Ivy Cottage, I've had several enquiries about that one. You want to knock both cottages into a single unit?'

'Yes.'

'The gentleman who owns it is in residential care, he is very old and not in good health. He has willed the cottage to his grandson, I understand. I know little of this gentleman, except that he lives and works in London where he has a property, in Chelsea, I believe.'

'You have no contact details, I suppose?'

'No, Mr Stone, I'm afraid not. You aren't the first person to have asked.'

We discussed the issue at length that evening. Jim came to the conclusion that if Ivy Cottage suddenly came onto the market – which seemed very likely under the circumstances – both cottages would be snapped up by a local developer before we even had the chance to put in an offer. He felt we should take a chance and purchase Clover Cottage. I agreed with him. We sold our house in Richmond within a week, bought Clover Cottage and moved in. Jim made our new home habitable with a few basic alterations; we spent a good deal of cash and most of our energies landscaping the wilderness of a garden.

Six months later the old man died, and all our hopes of purchasing Ivy Cottage were dashed when its inheritor turned up with a couple of suitcases. Jim and I were weeding in the front garden.

'Hi, I'm Carl Grey,' he hailed pleasantly, before promptly disappearing through the front door.

We rarely saw him after that; he arrived late on a Saturday evening and was gone by Sunday lunchtime. We were desperately disappointed; if we had to have a weekend-only neighbour, couldn't he at least have been somebody willing to communicate more about himself than his name?

The lady who ran the village post office knew all about Carl Grey. She saw it as part of the service to acquaint customers with the goings-on in Barrow Cross when there was no queue.

'He was ten when he came to live with his granddad at Ivy Cottage; he and my daughter became great friends. He used to come to our house, always very polite and nicely spoken, but quiet. He talked to Sophie, told her things about his parents – stuff I'm not sure she believed, but we did. Apparently they were fighting and drinking all the time. Then, one evening, there was a terrible brawl and one of them threw a knife at the other and it caught Carl instead. He was rushed to the hospital and they had to give him pints and pints of blood. When he had recovered enough to be discharged, Alf, his granddad, took him back to Ivy Cottage, and there he stayed until he went off to boarding school. He was exceptionally bright and won a full scholarship. He's something big in the city now, and good luck to him, I say.'

'I wonder why he wants to keep the cottage, it's in quite a state.'

'Don't know, a retreat, perhaps?'

'Well, I wish he'd find his way into the garden, the grass is about to spill over the fence onto our side.'

The following Saturday afternoon, our neighbour could be heard attacking the grass with an industrial machine. He exposed a lawn in far better condition than it should have been, given its neglect. You might imagine my shock when I peeped over the fence the following morning to see it dotted with holes the size of dinner plates. 'Moles!' I screeched to Jim.

Jim didn't think moles were the culprits: the holes too big, too round, too evenly spaced and didn't have the telltale piles of earth around them. However, we were taking no chances with turf grown from the seed they use for the courts at Wimbledon. Jim removed all the plants from the flowerbed and dug a deep trench the length of the fence. He then installed a roll of fine-gauge wire netting, filled it with soil and replanted the flowers.

Ten more holes appeared the following weekend – yes, I was counting – and the plot thickened.

'Perhaps we are dealing with a different sort of mole here,' suggested Jim.

'What, a spy?'

'Who knows? Stranger things have happened.'

'Shouldn't we contact somebody, the police, or the Government?'

'And say what? "Our neighbour is digging holes in his garden". He might be just planting an orchard, cider apples or something.'

'I think we should make it our business to find out what he's up to.'

'How? We never see him, he must be digging during the night.'

'Which indicates some highly suspicious activity,' I concluded.

'Right, we takes turns to watch him next weekend.'

I took the first watch. Standing close to the fence, my legs astride a lilac bush, I peered through the peepholes Jim had drilled the previous day. My patience was eventually rewarded when Carl Grey appeared with a rake and long-handled shovel that tapered to a point and glinted menacingly in the moonlight.

I shivered a little in the cold night air and prayed that the tickling in my nostrils would not erupt in a violent sneeze. It did and, growling an expletive, our neighbour hastened indoors.

Carl Grey must have known we would not attempt to spy on him again that night because by morning his operation had been completed: all the previous holes and any new ones had been neatly filled in. We were left to theorise and speculate, with no prospect of solving the mystery of the holes. Mysteries for me are the ultimate irritation: the missing piece in a jigsaw, the empty space in a crossword, the unreachable itch. They drive me nuts!

Jim picked up the letter and handed it to me. It read:

Dear Mr and Mrs Stone,

I understand you wished to purchase Ivy Cottage and my arrival thwarted your plans. I am now in a position to offer it to you in a private sale. I have enclosed details and a contact number. I think you will consider the price acceptable. Ivy Cottage was, as you are no doubt aware, my grandfather's home and I spent the happiest days of my childhood there. You have already achieved much in the restoration of Clover Cottage and I would be delighted if Ivy Cottage were also in your ownership. I hope to hear from you soon.

Yours,

Carl Grey

So, our story had a happy ending. The mystery of the holes still nagged away at me on occasion, but the conversion of the cottages occupied most of my thoughts. My head was filled with colours, fabrics, furniture and fittings. Greystones was morphing into the most beautiful and much envied dwelling. Carl Grey would approve of the new name for the property, I was sure. I was equally sure he would appreciate an invitation to view it when all the work had been completed. I hoped he would feel, as I felt, the souls of a happy little boy and his granddad still lingering within its walls.

Jim and our son, Jack, were swigging beer in the garden while the grandchildren chased each other around with the garden hose. Ellie, our daughter, was sitting beside me on the new sofa in our gorgeous lounge. We were sipping spritzers when Ellie pointed to the television and asked, 'Isn't that Carl Grey on *The Antiques Roadshow?*'

Spread out on the table in front of the presenter and Carl was a vast collection of exquisite snuffboxes. The presenter was practically drooling over them. 'This a complete set, may I ask how you came by them?'

'They were my grandfather's. He and I buried them in the garden of his cottage when I was still a boy. He didn't want anybody but me to get their hands on them after he died. It was our secret. I dug them up about a year ago.'

'Have you *any* idea how much they would make at auction?'

'Oh, yes, an eye-watering figure, but I don't cherish them for their financial worth, they belonged to the one person who truly loved me and therein lies their value.'

The mystery of the holes had at last been solved. I lifted my glass in a toast, 'Good for Granddad,' I said, tears blurring my vision.

CONCRETE EVIDENCE

A Cornish Tale

'Mary 'ad a copper cow, she milked it with a spanner,
The milk came out in shillin' tins, and little 'uns, a tanner.'

May Tremberth started to laugh, 'Where did that come from?' she asked her husband.

'The girls at junior school used to sing it when they were skipping.'

'My, you're going back a bit, Esra'

'Regression, that's what they call it.'

'Is it, indeed. Anyway, I must say, it's nice to see our Petunia again.'

'Oh, she's a beauty, all right, May, and looks just like the original, now I've painted her markings on.'

Esra and May Tremberth gazed out of the cottage window at the concrete Friesian standing on their front lawn. The beast's head was bent low on the ground, as if she were nibbling the grass. Her right eye was fixed on the elderly couple and they liked to fancy she was winking at them.

Petunia had been the last of Tremberth Farm's dairy herd. When she died, their son took the farm over, completely restocked it, and Esra and May bought Rose Cottage for their retirement.

Ever since George Pengelly's friend, Esra, had asked him if he could reproduce *Petunia* in concrete, he'd been swamped with orders. He'd been making sheep, goats and pigs ever since he gave up hauling sacks of coal around for a living. Butchers, farm shops and agricultural attractions had provided him with a modest income to supplement his pension. Now, however, people wanted animals, not gnomes, in their gardens. A concrete lamb or two posing among the trees and shrubs seemed to have become the trend. The appearance of Petunia on the front lawn of Rose Cottage had forced people to think *bigger*. George only hoped he would not get a request for a dinosaur.

George had felt it prudent to create a small company and employ an assistant when business became more than a profitable pastime. A village lad called Tom fitted the bill nicely. He was not too bright, but strong as an ox, and keen to learn. With a bank balance he could scarcely have dreamed of in the hard days of his youth, George was able to indulge his wife, five children and twelve grandchildren, and they were by no means reluctant to let him.

Petunia had been in residence at Rose Cottage for just five weeks when she disappeared. Esra's feelings about this crime were stuck somewhere between mystification and outrage. How could an item so large and heavy be spirited away in the middle of the night without the couple hearing a sound? The audacity of the offence was almost admirable.

Esra had not shown so much interest in other people's gardens since he was a boy – an apple scrumper of considerable enterprise. Now, however, he was walking the legs off the dogs every day, peeping through wrought iron gates, peering over walls into private spaces, and encountering a lot of *funny looks*. When out and about in his ancient Citroen, he found it difficult to concentrate on the road ahead. 'We're going to wind up in a ditch, Esra, if you don't stop trying to look over hedges,' May told him.

Esra eventually spotted Petunia in the barn next to Jonah Moon's shabby bungalow. The man had stupidly gone off and left the doors open. Jonah Moon had caught May's eye some fifty years earlier, but when she discovered how parsimonious he was, she quickly ditched him in favour of Esra. Jonah had the edge when it came to looks, but, poor as Esra was at the time, there was no end to his generosity. No human failing was more detestable than stinginess, in May's eyes.

Was it possible that Jonah still harboured a grudge? Was this the reason Petunia had been misappropriated? Well, the man hadn't got May, and he wasn't having Petunia either! Esra resolved to see justice done without delay.

The officer took Esra into a side room at the small police station. He wrote his name and address in a book then said, 'You want to report a theft?'

'I do. My cow, Petunia.'

'Stolen from your home, Rose Cottage?'

'Yes.'

'When was this?'

'12th October.'

'That was weeks ago, why didn't you report this sooner?'

'I didn't know who'd stolen her.'

'I see. So you now know who stole your cow?

'Yes, Jonah Moon, Petunia's in his barn.'

'You've located both the cow and the thief?'

'Correct.'

'Can you be sure it's your cow?'

'Yes, I painted her myself, she's a Friesian with very distinctive   markings.'

'Is this some kind of wind-up, Mr Tremberth?'

'Not at all. George Pengelly made her for me, a replica of my old milker, Petunia.'

'A concrete cow?'

'Tes. I'd have taken my rope and led her home if she'd been real.'

'That would have involved trespass, Mr Tremberth.'

'But Petunia is my bloody cow!'

'That's as maybe, but you could be prosecuted if you were found trespassing on Mr Moon's land. He lives in Skeet's Lane, off Cobble Rise, doesn't he?'

'You know him?'

'Not really, I've met him in the pub a time or two.'

'The bastard trespassed on *my* land to steal Petunia!'

'Are there any witnesses to this crime?'

'No. But George would be happy to identify Petunia.'

'He makes a lot of those animals; that wouldn't hold much weight, I'm afraid. Anyway, he'd be considered biased if the case went to court.'

'So you can't help me?'

'We don't have a lot to go on. I will, however, question Mr Moon about your allegation.'

'Umph!' spluttered Esra.

'I'm sorry, Mr Tremberth. If you are able to provide more concrete evidence, we can take the matter further... CONCRETE EVIDENCE!' The officer started to roar with laughter, his guffaws bouncing off the walls of the small room. Esra's indignation began to rise so rapidly, he was not at all sure he felt safe in his own presence. He strode out of the police station in a state of high dudgeon.

May was violently kneading dough on the kitchen table. 'Don't go taking the law into your own hands, Esra; I'm too old to be a jailbird's wife.'

'That copper thought it was a joke, nearly bust himself laughing.'

'George popped in while you were at the police station, he said he'll make us another cow.'

'So that Jonah Moon can sneak back and nick that one, too? I don't think so, my 'ansome. No, there's a score to be settled here…'

George placed the lengths of timber side by side on his workshop floor. 'D'you think the trolley will hold her weight?' asked Esra.

'Without a doubt, I'll drive some rods through the timbers when I've bolted the metal struts in place, then I'll put the wheels on. I won't pump too much air into the tyres, we're going to need the exact amount of play to pull this job off.'

'How will we get Petunia onto the trolley?'

'I'm rigging up a hand-cranked hoist.'

'You're a good friend, George.'

'Ah, get on with you. I hate Jonah Moon as much as you do. The miserable swine would have sold his mother's false teeth, if he could have found somebody they fit. He was planning to sell your cow, course he was; what did he want with a concrete cow?'

'Revenge, George.'

'Notwithstanding that, I'll bet he has a buyer already lined up.'

May guessed that Esra and George were cooking up a plot to recover Petunia. They were spending every lunchtime at the pub, so she didn't doubt that Harry, proprietor of *The Farrier's Arms*, was involved, possibly some of the regulars, too. The small village of Poltiggen looked after its own when it came to a robbery within the community.

George, Esra and Harry sat at a round table in the corner of the lounge bar: a huddle of conspirators.

'Right,' said George, 'the heist will take place while Jonah is in here for his evening pint.'

'His evening pint only lasts as long as it takes for it to go down his throat, and the walk to get here from his place, well, three quarters of an hour at most,' said Esra.

'Ah, but I happen to know it's his birthday on Thursday,' informed Harry, tapping the side of his nose. 'He'll drink as many pints as are put in front of him if he doesn't have to pay for them. A show of generosity can be arranged, and Gloria is in on our plan, she'll see to it that he doesn't want to leave in a hurry. You've finished the hoist, George?'

'I have.'

'And have enough strong rope to reach from the end of Skeet's Lane to Jonah's gate?'

'Better than that, the cable on the pick-up is long enough. We can slowly winch the trolley in and tow Petunia away. It's a slight uphill gradient all the way, so she won't run into the back of us.'

'Let's hope the local constabulary have a proper crime to investigate on Thursday evening,' concluded Harry.

Jonah Moon decided to shave and comb his hair because it was his birthday. He'd contemplated having a bath, but the prospect of exposing his puny body to the horrors of his unheated bathroom in mid November was altogether too much, besides, the boiler was on the blink. He would wear a clean shirt to the pub tonight, and splash on some of the aftershave he'd picked up in the supermarket when he last ventured as far as St Austell – four miles away – in his tractor. That was in July, he recalled.

Jonah had met Gloria the previous evening when he'd gone to the pub for his pint. She told him she was a widow and, as her children and grandchildren were scattered far and wide around the country, had decided to sell her house in Gloucester and move to Poltiggen to be near her brother, Harry, and his family. She said she was used to bar work and was happy to help out at *The Farrier's*.

Jonah thought he wouldn't at all mind getting to know Gloria better. She was a good-looking woman with a cleavage a man could happily get lost in. He decided he'd buy her a drink, perhaps even two, in a bid to win her favour.

Esra, George and Harry were in the back room of the pub. They were waiting for their cue from Gloria. At half past eight it came. 'Here he is, then, the birthday boy!' she hollered. Esra and his accomplices slipped out of the back door and into George's pick-up.

'How did you know it was my birthday, dear lady?' Jonah inquired, approaching the bar.

'Brian told me,' said Gloria, winking at the barman who was currently pulling pints for the pub's darts team. She banged a pint on the bar in front of Jonah and smiled beguilingly.

'Thank you, Gloria, thank you very much.' Jonah drew closer, rank with the cheap aftershave, and Gloria had to turn away before she could draw another breath.

It was a star-filled, crisp night, the moon bright and full – perfect conditions for such a mission. George pulled the pick-up into the lay-by in Cobble Rise, opposite Skeet's Lane that led to Jonah's bungalow. The three men lifted the hoist from the bed of the pick-up and placed it on the trolley George had built to accommodate Petunia. As they tried to push it down the lane, they realised the operation they had undertaken was going to be much more difficult than anticipated. The lane was in a dreadful state. 'That old bugger's tractor has chewed this up good and proper,' said George, 'and now, with this cold weather, it's hardened into ruts the size of rail tracks.'

'It was a *mud nearly up to your wellies* job when I spotted Petunia in the barn, that would have been worse,' said Esra.

'Definitely,' concurred Harry. 'Anyway, let's get the animal loaded onto the trolley and out of the barn, then we can work out how to manoeuvre her along the lane.'

'We must try to even out the surface by knocking off the really high points,' said Esra.

'Better hope Jonah has some tools in the barn, then,' said George.

'I daresay he does,' said Harry.

'Yeah, every one stolen, no doubt,' added Esra.

The barn door was bolted but not locked. Once inside,

the men switched on the lamps fastened around their heads, set the hoist up beside Petunia and fastened a harness around her girth. Esra cast his eyes about the barn and saw several picks lined up against the wall.

Gloria ordered Jonah to a table in the far corner of the lounge bar – away from the other, more fragrant, patrons – and presented him with a vast pasty. 'There you are, get your gnashers around that.'

'Goodness me, this is a treat! Thank you, Gloria. I'm sure I won't be able to manage it all.'

'Try,' urged Gloria, a little more sharply than she intended.

'Oh, I won't waste it; I'll take home what I can't eat now, and have it for my dinner tomorrow.'

'I'll bring you another pint to help it down,' Gloria told him.

It was a well-known fact that Jonah was highly superstitious and didn't like walking past the church and cemetery at a late hour. He claimed he had seen a ghostly figure rising from a grave one night on his way home from the pub. Everybody knew that the *ghostly figure* was, in truth, none other than Dervil Moss visiting his late wife. These visits could be protracted affairs – depending on how much he'd had to drink – and he did have a tendency to lie upon her grave with his hands in a attitude of prayer: a sinister image.

However, Jonah would not be convinced that the figure *he* saw was Dervil Moss, and resolved thereafter always to be in his bed well before the witching hour. Brian and Gloria's best hope was that Jonah would be too inebriated to notice, or even see, the clock, by the time they had done with him.

It took the strength of all three men to turn the handle on the hoist. As they slowly raised Petunia from the barn floor, she tilted in the harness alarmingly and started to swing back and forth. It was some time before they were able to steady her and lower her onto the trolley. 'What time is it,' asked George.

'Nearly ten,' replied Harry.

'Running a bit late,' said George.

Jonah was getting edgy and beginning to slur his words. Gloria and Brian knew they could not detain him for much longer. The bungalow was the only dwelling in Skeet's Lane and situated in open countryside. It was a good hundred yards from Cobble Rise, the link road between Poltiggen and St Pew. He would be safe enough getting out of the village where the street lightening was good, but Cobble Rise was a sharp left turn after the cemetery and unlit. It meandered through fairly dense woodland before running downhill past the opening to Skeet's Lane.

Jonah always carried a torch in his jacket pocket, but his capacity to use it effectively would, doubtless, be hampered by his condition. 'We either try to keep him here until we get the call from Harry to say the coast is clear, then drive him home, or sober him up as slowly as we can,' said Brian.

'The latter, most definitely,' said Gloria. 'I'm going to make you a nice big mug of coffee, Jonah,' Gloria shouted from behind the bar. She promptly disappeared into the kitchen.

George was in his pick-up, slowly winching in the cable attached to the trolley. Esra and Harry were flanking Petunia, their shoulders pressed hard against her, knowing full well that she could topple and fall on either of them at the next rut. Eventually, they guided her over the last bumps in the lane and eased her out onto Cobble Rise. Harry looked at his watch. 'Five past eleven,' he yelled.

Harry got into the pick-up beside George, and Esra climbed onto Petunia's back as George reduced the slack in the cable to within a couple of yards of the vehicle. Petunia was on her way home at last. And the nearest police car was in St Pew dealing with a bunch of rowdies – friends of Harry's, as it happened.

Jonah's progress was slow. It took him twenty minutes to get as far as the cemetery. He would normally break into a run at this point, his gaze firmly concentrated on the pavement. Tonight, however, his legs were working independently of each other, the right, veering towards the kerb edge, and the left, straying onto the narrow grass verge in front of the cemetery wall.

His eyes, too, were playing tricks on him. Ghoulish shapes were dancing about in his peripheral vision, and, as hard as he tried to focus on the signpost indicating the turn-off to St Pew, it persisted in moving away from him. If only he could reach the signpost, he knew he'd be just a short distance from Cobble rise. He suddenly lurched forward, managed to grab the pole, and wrapped his arms around it. 'Got you,' he muttered.

The sound of a motor engine penetrated his senses. It was slowly labouring along Cobble Rise. He scanned the line of hedges that edged the road and fancied he saw the head and shoulders of Esra Tremberth bobbing along on top of them. And Esra was singing the old Cornish favourite, *Goin' up Camborne Hill, comin' down* at the top of his tuneless voice.

Except he'd changed the words to *Cobble Rise* and something about going home on his cow...

'Goin' up Cobble Rise, comin' down,

Goin' up Cobble Rise, comin' down,

On the back of my cow,

We're nearly 'ome now,

Goin' up Cobble Rise, comin' down.'

ECHOES

The bicycle was in its usual place: the recess under the stairs. I had taken my son, Ben, to the shop to choose it on his sixth birthday. It was raining heavily that day so he was not able to ride it around the pathways I had created in our garden. Instead he manoeuvred it up and down the long hallway of our Victorian home, and his joy knew no bounds.

This was the house my wife, Barbara, and I had purchased at auction the year before Ben was born. It was suffering from considerable neglect, hence the bargain price, but I knew that I was more than equal to the task of restoring it, given time and adequate funds. It was a project: the sort of thing you take on with a specific goal in mind. My goal was to give my wonderful wife everything I felt she deserved.

'You are really clever, Theo, you will make our home so beautiful we will never want to leave it,' Barbara had told me.

The house slowly started to take shape. I devoted every spare hour to its renovation. By the time our son had finished his first full year at primary school, it was finished. Barbara threw endless dinner parties so that her plethora of friends could admire our home. I allowed myself a level of smugness that did not sit comfortably on an inherently modest character like me. My gorgeous wife had changed me, but I was far too in love to see it at the time.

The week after Ben's sixth birthday, Barbara left with her lover and our child.

The bicycle is red with thick tyres and has a carrier behind the saddle. Ben's *Star Wars* helmet is strapped to it.

I move the bicycle once a week to mop the tiled floor of the hallway. Sometimes I guide it up and down, one hand on the saddle and one on the handlebars. I imagine Ben is sitting on it, I hear his laughter and feel his breath on my face. The pain of loss is as acute as ever.

Nine months pass, a lifetime, a moment. I work, I must work, what is there but work? My colleagues at the office tell me I am killing myself with work, but my sanity depends upon it. All day stuffing my head with statistics and all evening decorating rooms that do not need decorating. Memories of Ben are among the paint cans, timber and tools, I keep tripping over them. I try not to think about her, my wife, because bitterness rises in my throat like bile and threatens to choke me.

I ring the bell on Ben's bike. It makes a hollow sound that bounces off the passage walls: echoes of past, happy times. I know I will sell this house, now that the dream has died, but until I know where my boy is, that he is safe, I cannot even consider it.

I look at the bicycle, so shiny and new. Perhaps I should put it elsewhere, out of sight. I could donate it to a worthy cause, give pleasure to another small human being. To remove it from its current position, however, would seem tantamount to removing a headstone from a grave, perchance to forget what lies beneath. No, the bicycle must stay where it is.

The landline is ringing in the hall. I am running late and when I pick up the receiver my manner is unusually brusque. 'Hello.'

'Is this the home of Mr Brent, Ben's father?' My heart skips a beat.

'Yes, oh my God, yes, it is.'

'My name is Chloe Stanton, I'm calling from Perth.'

'Scotland?'

'No, Western Australia.'

'Give me your number, I'll ring you straight back.'

'It's okay. Your son wants you to come and get him, is that possible?'

'Of course.'

'Do you have an email address?'

'Yes.'

'Then give it to me and I'll try to fill you in on the situation   here.'

'Has Ben had an accident?'

'No, it's nothing like that. I found a note wrapped around a stone in my garden. It was obviously thrown from the house next door. It was from Ben. I will scan it and attach it to my email.'

'This is very good of you, Mrs Stanton. I've been out of my mind since my wife left with our son. I had no idea where they'd gone.'

'I have a daughter, Mr Brent, I can't even start to imagine how I'd feel if she were taken away from me.'

'I don't know how to thank you.'

'Come and sort out this business with your son, that will be thanks enough.'

Ben's note said: Dear lady next door, please could you phone my daddy in England and ask him to come and get me. Tel: 0117 8235612. I am very sad and lonely and miss him very much. Thank you, Ben Brent.

My boss is looking at Ben's note. 'Dear little chap, still, at least you know where he is now. Bloody hell, Theo, he must have had his wits about him, I mean, wrapping a note around a stone like that to summon help. And fancy him remembering the phone number! My word, he's a bright kid, my Godson.'

He picks up Chloe's email. 'She says your wife, the man she's with and Ben moved into the house a month ago and yet she hasn't seen woman or child since. He goes out in his car, but always alone and after dark. This is a rum business, Theo, and no mistake.'

'I can't wait to be on my way.'

'Only a few hours now. This Chloe Stanton, she must be a very decent sort.'

'Good-looking, too.'

'How d'you know?'

'Web cam, Cyril, we skyped, talked for ages.'

'Well, she wouldn't have thought that about you; you look like shit, my friend. You'd better get spruced up a bit, if she's going to pick you up from the airport. Is she married?'

'She and her husband moved *down under* from Cambridge. He was killed in an accident at work less than a year after they relocated. She has a daughter, older than Ben.'

'How dreadful, poor souls.'

'I hate to leave you in the lurch at such a hectic time, Cyril.'

'We'll manage, Theo, we'll manage.' Cyril didn't quite know how they would manage in Theo's absence, but had faith in his staff, even if all of them put together couldn't match Theo for efficiency. 'Take a month off, take two, but don't come back without our boy. By the way, I upgraded your flight, my treat.'

'Cyril, you really are the best.'

'Ah, get on with you, let me know when you have news.'

'I love you, Cyril.'

'Go, you silly sod, before I have you evicted!'

I instantly spot Chloe in the crowd, she is frantically waving with both hands, a wide smile lighting up her face. She is even prettier in the flesh, much prettier. 'Let's have a coffee, Theo, we need a plan of action.' She tucks her hand under my arm and leads me towards the nearest refreshment outlet.

It's so nice, even for a short time, to feel like part of a couple again. 'I've booked you into a hotel right next to the station,' she tells me, 'the trains stop just five minutes away from my house. We don't want to announce your arrival by booking a taxi.'

'It all sounds very cloak and dagger.'

'Unfortunately, I think it is. I have a feeling your wife and her, her – '

'Lover?'

'Whatever. I have a feeling they are planning to move on very soon, there has been more than the usual amount of activity going on in the house. I hear quite a lot but see very little, you understand. This is a big country, Theo, you've come this far, you mustn't let Ben slip away now.'

'Will I be required to kidnap my own son?'

'Perhaps. Isn't that what she did?'

'Yes.'

'And you didn't report her to the police?'

'I thought it was an aberration, what arrogance? I thought she would come back.'

'Perhaps she would have come back, had she been able to. She and your son are under house arrest, to all intents and purposes.'

'What a bloody mess!'

Chloe calls me at the hotel. '*He* has just gone out in the car, the boot was so full he had a job to close it. There is a train to Bloomboro in ten minutes, I'll meet you at the station.'

'I'll be there.'

We are sitting in Chloe's lounge waiting for it to get fully dark. Her daughter, Zara, is plying me with coffee and cake. She is a charming, friendly child with her mother's kind eyes and lovely smile. 'They are locked in,' she informs me. 'Even the windows are locked with a key before he goes out. I've seen him going around the house doing it.'

'You'll have to smash a window,' says Chloe.

'No, that will make too much noise. There is a grille in the side of the loft, it is only made of wire with plastic inside to keep out the rain, it's easy to remove.'

'How do you know that, Zara?'

'Because, mum, Jamie Fowler used to escape through it when his mum sent him to his room because he had misbehaved.'

'How did he get down to the ground?'

'He climbed down he drainpipe.'

'Well, Theo can't climb *up* the drainpipe to get in.'

'Of course not, he can use the ladder in the shed. I'll climb in, if you like.'

'You certainly will not, young lady,' Chloe tells her.

'I'll fit, won't I?' I inquire.

'Just about, you're skinny enough.'

'Zara!'

'Well you are, Theo. I daresay it's all the stress and worry you've had.'

'How old are you, Zara?'

'Ten.'

'Ten, going on fifty,' puts in Chloe.

'So it would seem,' I say.

I am accustomed to using ladders and steps, but Zara insists on sitting on the bottom rung to steady it; her mother is behind me to take the grille when I lift it out.

I slide through the aperture easily, and only realise I have no light with which to illuminate the loft hatch when my feet make contact with the floor. Before Chloe can stop her, Zara trots up the ladder and hands me a torch. 'You forgot something.'

'I did.'

'Theo?'

'Yes?'

'Just to the right, hanging on a nail, is a spare key to the front door. Jamie Fowler had it copied from his mother's, he didn't want to climb up the drainpipe to get back into the house. He used to sneak in when he knew she was in the kitchen.'

'You are a little star, Zara.'

'I know.'

A simple square of painted chipboard sits neatly in the hatch. I lift it out and am staring down into my son's astonished face. 'Daddy, you came!'

Tears spurt from his eyes. I gather him into my arms, my own tears running copiously down his small back. 'Please, Daddy, let's go before *he* comes back,' he whimpers.

'Where is your mother?'

'Downstairs. She's in the little room at the back, next to the kitchen; she's asleep or something.'

'Ben, I want you to go next door, to the lady who picked up your note, she's called Chloe.'

'How will I get out?'

'I have a key to the front door.'

I watch as Ben runs to Chloe who is standing in her doorway; she snatches him up and carries him inside.

Looking at the shrunken figure in the big, shabby armchair, it is hard to remember the beautiful woman I married. Her sallow skin is stretched across the bones of her face like clingfilm. Her eyes are puffy and dead in blackened sockets, and her hitherto glorious mane of auburn hair hangs damp and lifeless about her bowed shoulders. Her hand is tightly clasped around the gin bottle that rests on the arm of the chair. 'It eases the pain,' she says.

'I've come for Ben,' I tell her.

'How did you find us?' Her words are weary rather than slurred.

'It doesn't matter, I did, that's all that counts.'

She starts to cry and pulls the bottle into her lap perchance a drop of gin should be spilled as she slumps forward, her eyes focused on the floor. I don't want to look at her any more and walk towards the door. 'Theo, I am so sorry, so sorry for everything. Tell Ben, will you, try to explain, he always listened to you.'

'How do I explain, Barbara?'

'Tell him mummy went a little crazy, tell him she reached for the moon but it fell from the sky. A hard lesson, Theo, a lesson for us all.'

'You think *I* haven't already learnt that lesson?'

'I wasn't the moon, Theo, you only thought I was. I know I didn't deserve you.'

I open the door, but still don't turn; her voice trails after me. 'Please try to forgive me. Please.'

Chloe is quiet around me and gives me coffee whenever she thinks I need it. Every time she passes my chair, she touches my shoulder gently. It is a whisper of a touch, but I feel it only too well. I know I would make love to her if she gave me the least encouragement. 'Is there anything I can do, Theo?'

'I don't think so.'

'Are you still in love with Barbara?'

'No.'

'Could you love her again, in time?'

'No.'

'But you won't abandon her?'

'No, she's Ben's mother, and a human being.'

'You are a good man, Theo Brent.'

'You would do the same in my situation.'

Chloe is holding a large travel bag. 'I'll go next door and tell Barbara you are taking her and Ben away from that house. I'll put some of their things together then call you to start the car up.'

'I can sort out everything when we get to the hotel, when speed is not a priority.'

When Chloe returns she is as white as a sheet. She doesn't need to tell me what has happened. Zara gives me a look that is filled with an adult helping of compassion. She says nothing, just takes Ben's hand and leads him upstairs to her bedroom. 'How?' I ask.

'Hanging from the banister, she has slashed her wrists. There is so much blood, it's a horrible sight.'

'I must get her down.'

'I'll ring the police now, why not let them do it.'

'No, I must. She was always so dignified, she'd hate to be seen like that. Give me ten minutes.'

'Okay.'

'Chloe, I'm really sorry you had to see something like that. You must wish you'd never picked up Ben's note.'

'You are not a fool, Theo, you must know that isn't true.'

'Oh, Chloe…'

By the time the police arrive I have placed Barbara on the sofa and closed her eyes. Eyes that are wide with shock and confusion: the sort of eyes that awaken from a nightmare. She looks so very thin and small. And I am overwhelmed with pity. 'I forgive you, Barb, I forgive you,' I tell her.

He does not return that night, Chloe and I decide he will never return. He will lose himself in this vast country to cause heartache and pain elsewhere. Many statements are taken by sympathetic police officers. 'What do you know about him,' one young female asks me.

'Nothing. He damn near wrecked my life; that's all I know.' She shows Chloe a photograph.

'Is this him, Mrs Stanton?'

'Yes.'

'His name is Bradley Curtis,' informs the officer.

Ben knows that his mother will never again wake up in *our* world, but that's not quite the same as being dead, in his mind. I don't discuss arrangements and funerals in his hearing.

When the administration has been dealt with, I will organise repatriation and book a flight that enables me to be back in Britain when Barbara's body arrives. I will join her family for a service at the crematorium when Ben is at school.

I can think about a memorial stone later, somewhere to visit and place flowers; they'll want that, I'm sure. Ben certainly will; he'll need a place where he can feel close to his mother.

We are staying at Chloe's house for a further week. She and Zara are creating an atmosphere of normality in which Ben is steadily recovering from his ordeal. If Ben wants to talk about Barbara, Chloe and Zara know how to engage in the subject far better than I could.

Knowing that Zara's dad, is also in that *special place* seems to help him. 'Perhaps they will be friends,' he says.

'I'm sure they will,' replies Chloe.

'My dad will look after her, Ben,' Zara assures him.

I try not to think about the day we must leave. Chloe and I have become intimate. It seems the most natural thing in the world to share our loneliness in this way. I am trying not to question my feelings for her because the answer is too simple, too obvious, yet I have no idea how to handle it.

Airports don't lend themselves to fond farewells quite as railway stations do. No hanging from the window above the door for a last glimpse as those left behind fade to specks.

In the departure lounge Ben is sobbing. 'Don't you

love Chloe and Zara, too, daddy?'

'Yes, of course I do, but we must go home, Ben; there are lots of things I have to do.'

When I speak to Chloe on her mobile, I know she's been crying. 'Will you come back to the airport, I have something important to ask you?'

'So important that you'd risk missing your flight?'

'Yes.'

'I'm still at the airport, Theo, I wanted to watch your plane take off, do the whole *parting thing* properly, wallow in misery, it can be cathartic.'

'And this time?'

'Utterly devastating… Where will I find you?'

'Go to the information desk in departures and give them your name; a Quantas rep will meet you there and bring you through security. The airline has been wonderfully understanding; how could they resist helping a man whose future happiness hangs on just one word from the woman he loves with all his heart?'

EXCESS BAGGAGE

I gaped at Rupert's body on the kitchen floor. I could swear he was smiling. 'How could you die when I am house sitting, you stupid, selfish dog? I bet you did it deliberately.'

I hadn't been fond of Rupert when he was alive: a black slobbery article, always trying to shove his nose up your crotch, or having it off with the pouffe. Now that he was dead, and on my watch, I totally despised him.

My parents' friends, the Mortons, paid me very well for looking after their home and beloved pet while they were away on their travels. I'd always managed to conceal my feelings about Rupert in their presence, and assiduously attended to his physical needs in their absence.

The Mortons, much as they were devoted to their lump of a dog, always made it clear that they did not wish to be burdened with news of his demise or indisposition while away from home. When you have shelled out a fortune on a world cruise, or a month on and off piste in the Alps, this was understandable, I felt.

I stepped over Rupert's body to get to the coffee machine. A strong caffeine fix was called for.

I took my coffee into the lounge. With no lectures to attend today, I was at leisure to be a typical student and moon about the house like a slob. Except that I had Rupert to deal with. He was seriously old, had been around, like, forever, and would *go off* if I didn't apply some measure of haste to his disposal.

I thought about my dad, he would have sorted things out in a trice. Unfortunately my parents were in Cornwall visiting my grandparents; they had *gone home* as they put it, for a few days.

I fell into a deep reverie about my childhood days in St Mawes. I remembered my parents telling me about the budgie they'd looked after for an elderly neighbour while she was in hospital having her hip replaced. My mother had let the budgie out for its daily constitutional and it had become firmly attached to a sticky fly-catching card hanging in the window. My father had managed to extricate the poor little creature, but it arrested in his hand. 'Couldn't you save it?' I had asked, my six-year-old brain unable to countenance the notion that my dad was not possessed of extraordinary powers.

'Your father tried to give it the kiss of life, darling,' informed my mum.

'I did, Em. I put a straw into its beak and blew into it gently for quite a long time.'

'And it didn't get better?' I inquired, nearly choking on my tears.

'Naw, my 'ansome,' said my Granddad, his eyes glinting with mirth, 'just bigger, a lot bigger.' I didn't speak to him for a week.

Garreth Price was a guy I'd met at a party recently. There had been little by way of mutual attraction between us, a flicker, perhaps, but we'd got on really well. I knew he was a newly qualified vet working in a practice in Hounslow. I was sure he'd be able to assist me in my hour of need. 'Hi, Garreth, it's Emma, we met at Dave's party, remember me?'

'Of course. It's so noisy in the surgery, I'll take the phone outside, Emma, hang on… How can I help?'

'I am house sitting and found the owners' dog dead on the kitchen floor this morning. They won't be back for weeks and I have to dispose of the body somehow.'

'Can you get it to Hounslow West tube station at six, the surgery will be closed by then and I can pick you up.'

'That would be great. Will it be expensive, I'm a bit broke at present?'

'We have a pug to cremate, it can go in with that, neither owner will ever know. The other charges can wait until the owners get home. What sort of dog is it?'

'A big, black, 'orrible thing.'

'Ah, that's helpful. Well, see you later.'

'Yep, sure thing. Thanks so much, Garreth.'

Right, one problem: how was I going to get Rupert to the tube station in Hammersmith? A bin bag? Not strong enough. A holdall? Not big enough. A suitcase? Perfect!

The suitcase had wheels on it and would be, with a bit of pushing and shoving, sufficiently large to accommodate Rupert. I remembered how my father used to get large, heavy stones into his wheelbarrow when he was creating a garden feature. He would turn the barrow onto its side, roll the stone into it then yank the barrow into an upright position. Rupert didn't weigh half as much as a hefty piece of granite; it would be a doddle!

The thing is with granite, it does not lollop and spread out when approached.

Rupert's bones seem to have become disconnected. I'd managed to ease his trunk into the case, but his legs were sticking out in every direction. However many times I tried to turn his head to one side, it popped up again, his muzzle standing proud of the case by several inches. I needed to get his entire body onto its side if I was to succeed. Brainwave! Lift the handle side of the case until Rupert slid to the bottom.

Wow, it worked! The dead dog was in his fabric coffin

with only his tail protruding. I tucked it under his back leg and zipped him in before he could cause me further inconvenience.

It was a ten-minute walk from the house to the station. Pushing a seriously heavy suitcase around an air terminal is one thing, negotiating potholed pavements and road works is quite another. I briefly considered turning back, but then what, a burial under the old oak tree in the garden? Besides, I knew the Mortons would demand a death certificate, or whatever vets issue for a deceased pet.

The going got harder and harder and I was sweating like a pig. I even started eyeing-up metal clothing bank repositories as Rupert's final resting place, but I'd need assistance and would probably face some very awkward questions.

My heart was pounding out of my chest, and my breath was coming in short bursts by the time I stepped onto the platform. The train arrived seconds later; I hurled the suitcase onto it, nudged it out of the doorway with my leg, and collapsed into a seat.

As I got up to alight from the train, a young man jumped to his feet. 'Here, let me help you.'

'Great, thanks.'

'Shit, what have you got in here?' he inquired, heaving the case onto the platform.

Was I going to tell him the case was full of dead dog? I don't think so. 'Tablets, computer software, smart phones, I'm delivering them for a friend.'

'Is this friend meeting you?'

'Yes, but I'm early, he won't be here for a while.'

It's amazing how the suitcase became magically lighter as the young man snatched it up and sprinted out of the station. Garreth appeared seconds later. 'So, where's the dog?'

'It went that-a-way.' I pointed to the receding figure of the young man as he laboured down the street, his arms wrapped around the suitcase, his knees buckling under its weight.

FOGGY AND THE MILKMAN

Nora Sutcliffe opened her front door to bring in the milk and saw the inert body of her cat, Foggy, lying on the mat. Supposing him to be dead, she instantly gathered him up in her arms, buried her face in his dense fur, and wept bitterly. But Foggy was not dead, Foggy was breathing, rather erratically, but breathing.

The vet was hastily summoned; an examination revealed nothing conclusive, but the vet suspected food poisoning. 'I'll take Foggy back to the surgery for further tests,' he said. 'Has he eaten anything unusual, do you know, Mrs Sutcliffe?'

'Um… Well, I was making my husband's sandwiches this morning and there was a little salmon left over; I gave it to Foggy.'

'Better inform Mr Sutcliffe,' he advised, 'just to be on the safe side.'

Nora looked at the kitchen clock; it was nearly half past ten. Ken Sutcliffe started his early shift at seven and was ravenous by eleven. She grabbed her mobile and called the factory where he worked, *Jardin's*.

It was too late; Ken had already eaten all his sandwiches.

There was no hanging about in the waiting room for Ken; he was an emergency. Two nurses set about pumping out the contents of his stomach before he even had the chance to contemplate the horrors of the procedure.

Nora was pacing in the corridor – it was what she did when agitated – and she *was* agitated, big time! Her husband looked like a corpse, her cat was unconscious, and the supermarket was still selling contaminated tins of salmon to unsuspecting customers!

The vet called to say that Foggy was recovering nicely and purring loudly. Nora could collect him as soon as she wished, or the vet would drop him off on his way home from the practice. Nora didn't enquire about the cost of his treatment; she'd had enough shocks for one day.

Ken was sitting in his armchair with his feet up on a low stool. He was wearing his *long-suffering* expression; this was guaranteed to irritate Nora when she was not in the best of humours. 'I'll go to the supermarket and tell the manager about the salmon and then I'll pick Foggy up from the surgery,' she said.

'Okay, dear,' replied Ken, his voice as weak as it was woeful.

'You'll, be fine, I won't be long,' she told him.

'I'll manage,' he muttered, lightly pressing his outstretched hands against his stomach.

'I could ask Mabel to pop in for half an hour, if you like.'

'No! No, dear, I'll be all right on my own.' Nora knew the prospect of Mabel coming in to *Ken-sit* would sort her husband out in a trice.

At customer services, Nora was doing what she had no real talent for: complaining. Words she rarely used were tripping from her tongue with ease: compensation, legal representation, health and safety, on and on, until she ran out of breath. She found that standing up for one's rights was a purging, exhilarating experience.

When she had finished with the manager – something of a gibbering wreck by this time – she treated herself to a bottle of wine and three bars of Turkish Delight.

The milkman placed two bottles of milk on the doorstep, worked out what he was going to say, and rang the doorbell – before his courage failed him. Nora Sutcliffe emerged with a smile on her face, a very good sign. 'Good morning! Um…how is your cat?'

'Foggy? How did you know about Foggy?'

'Oh, I…perhaps I should explain. Yesterday morning I accidentally dropped a bottle of milk on his head. He is okay, isn't he?'

It took a moment or two for Nora to process this information, to register what the milkman had just told her. Eventually, she found her voice, the voice she had used when dealing with the manager at the supermarket. She'd be 'apology on legs' when she went back to tell him the wrong assumption had been made, based on the vet's suspicions.

She fixed the milkman with a menacing stare. 'Have you any idea what we've been through, young man?' The milkman was not given time to respond. 'My cat spent the day with the vet which cost me seventy pounds. My husband had to leave work and go to the hospital to have his stomach pumped out, and is too weak to make his shift today. Then I went to the local supermarket and had a go at the manager, and now I'll have to go back, grovel, and eat a great dollop of humble-bloody-pie. I'll probably be banned. I suppose I'll have to drive to Asda instead in future.'

'Why?' inquired the milkman.

'Why what?'

'Why did you do all that?'

'Because I gave Foggy a bit of the salmon I put in Ken's sandwiches. The vet suspected food poisoning.'

'I see…'

'Do you, indeed! If you had only had the courtesy to ring on the doorbell and tell us what had happened; it wouldn't have happened… all the other stuff, I mean.'

'Right. Well, in my defence, I know Mr Sutcliffe works at Jardin's and was on *earlies,* because he works with my dad. I didn't want to disturb him at four-thirty in the morning. Anyway, I thought Foggy was just temporarily stunned and would come around after a little while. I really am so very sorry. The cat *is* okay, isn't he?'

'Yes, he is okay. I suppose he was just *stunned,* after all.'

It was enough, Steve, the milkman was penitent, and Nora had assumed sufficient *attitude* to force him into an appropriate state of contrition. Just knowing she had the capacity to do this to another human being was…was *empowering.*

Nora noticed that Steve was trying not to smile. 'I suppose the whole business is rather comical,' she admitted.

'It's more than comical; it's hilarious,' said Steve, bursting into peals of laughter. Nora could not help herself and started to laugh as well.

'It'll make a cracking party story,' said Steve.

'Except, I doubt anyone will believe it.'

'I'm sure you'll convince them; you can be very forceful, Mrs Sutcliffe, I had no idea.'

'Neither did I. My Ken will have to watch his step from now on.'

GRAND LARCENY IN MICKLE MONKTON

In the greater scheme of things, the theft of an onion might not be considered a major felony. The onion in question, however, was no ordinary onion. It was the size of a football, the colour of mahogany, and had been buffed to rich lustre. The onion had been grown specifically for the annual village vegetable show by Reggie Seed, more commonly referred to as *Veggie Seed* for the truly prodigious proportions of his produce.

Reggie was a tiny, quiet, humble soul and did not at all fit the archetypal image of a local celebrity, yet that is exactly what he was. The effort he put into growing vegetables worthy of entry into Mickle Monkton's annual *Home Grown* competition had earned him the greatest respect within the village community. On the rare occasions he had not taken first prize in his chosen category, his failure was due to ill health. The poor man suffered badly from bronchial problems. This condition was greatly aggravated by contact with his plants, and the greenhouse became temporarily out of bounds.

Nobody seemed to resent Reggie for winning the prize of two hundred pounds and being re-awarded the cup so often. Indeed, the residents of Mickle Monkton well understood his need to keep warm during the winter months and the money contributed largely to the cost of heating his modest stone cottage. Not one among them would have allowed him to suffer for lack of fuel, but Reggie Seed was a proud, independent individual, and charity, anathema to him.

You might imagine the consternation in the community when Reggie's onion disappeared from his greenhouse the day before the show. It reappeared a week later in Lower Trewiggle, a neighbouring village, where it won first prize in *their* annual show.

Fury, condemnation, suspicion, and an intense desire for retribution combined to create a toxic atmosphere between the villages. Fortunately, Mickle Monkton was possessed not only of an expert vegetable grower, but Bert Cummings, an amateur sleuth of considerable talent. This gentleman did not intend to leave the smallest stone unturned in his search for justice.

There was little doubt as to the identity of the perpetrator of this cruel felony. Wally Bagshaw was Reggie Seed's closest rival in the business of growing outstanding vegetables, yet he had never won first prize in Lower

Trewiggle's annual *Home Grown* competition. However, Bert Cummings was certain that, while Wally Bagshaw was the instigator of the crime, he was not its executor. He was a giant of a man, far too large to squeeze through the narrow door of Reggie's greenhouse. No, one of his unruly, spliff-smoking, beer-swigging teenage sons must have been offered a pecuniary incentive to steal the onion. Of course, that by no means lessened Wally Bagshaw's guilt; indeed, it increased it considerably in Bert's eyes. Inciting illegal activity in a young person was abhorrent and totally immoral.

When the photograph of Wally Bagshaw appeared on the front page of the area's weekly newspaper, Reggie Seed became almost apoplectic with indignation. Wally Bagshaw was cradling the onion in the crook of his left arm and holding aloft the cup and cheque in his right hand. He was grinning smugly into the camera.

'We'll get the bastard, Veggie,' assured his friends. Reggie was in no condition to be placated. He aimed his fist at Wally's big, fat face, punching a hole right through the newspaper.

Bert Cummings, in various guises, infiltrated the social areas frequented by Lower Trewiggle's residents in order to glean information regarding Wally Bagshaw's habits: the pub, the café, the bowling club, the women's institute – he looked really very fetching in his sister's floral dress – and the church. Unexpectedly, it was the church that provided him with the perfect opportunity to confront the man and, by means he had not at this point determined, force a confession out of him.

*

Wally's ancient pick-up truck spluttered to a halt nearly a mile from the church. He looked at the petrol gauge: empty. Wally's wife, Myrtle, had used the vehicle earlier to go shopping and had obviously forgotten to stop at the petrol station on her way home from town. The family car was in the local garage awaiting a repair to the brakes and Myrtle wouldn't be able to come to his aid. Nevertheless, he groped in his pocket for his mobile; he had some serious steam to let off.

Myrtle was obliged to hold the appliance a full two feet from her ear. She might be deemed little more than a chattel in his eyes, but he'd do well to show her some respect. She waited until the tirade finally tailed off to a gruff squeak before informing him that she *had* filled the tank with petrol and had the receipt to prove it. She told him he'd better watch his step if he didn't want a repeat of the consequences of his last outburst when she had withdrawn *all* her services for a fortnight. He knew she meant it.

'Sorry, dear,' he muttered.

'Never mind the, *dear,* think on,' she told him firmly.

Of course, Myrtle knew exactly why he'd got himself so worked up. Every Saturday, well before sunset, Wally wound the church clock. He hated being in St Petroc's alone after dark, it really freaked him out. This fear was not supposed to be common knowledge, Wally believed it was a secret, but Myrtle was not stupid, she knew.

Apparently, when Wally and his brothers were boys, an aged villager by the name of Edna Biggins claimed to have experienced *an event* and firmly refused to enter the church thereafter. Her closest friends felt compelled to honour this decision even as she lay dead in her coffin. Hence, the mourners who had gathered at the cemetery for the interment were forced to endure a lengthy service in torrential rain, hymns and all, before she was eventually lowered into a very soggy grave.

*

The lights high on the walls of the lower belfry were angled into the centre of the area for the convenience of the bell ringers, creating pale pools on the flagstones. The bell chamber and platform on which the clock mechanism stood, however, remained in total darkness. Wally switched on his rechargeable lantern and slowly, quietly, mounted the narrow, stone stairway that flanked the walls of the square tower.

Overheard, the bells creaked against their supporting timbers as a stiff breeze whistled through the louvred apertures each side of the tower. Wally held the lantern at arms length to illuminate his ascent. With every step he took, shadows danced about maniacally on the stonework, as if mocking him, as if warning him against further progress.

'Shit,' he groaned, clutching the big, brass winding key in his sweaty palm. 'I have to wind the clock,' he intoned, 'I have to wind the clock, I have to…'

His breaths were getting more and more laboured, his pulse throbbing louder and louder in his head; he climbed the next stair, and the next, and the next until he was level with the clock mechanism. He thought he going to pass out or have a heart attack and cried out, 'God, oh God, please help me, please help me!'

'But you have been weak, Walter, you have transgressed.' The voice was velvet smooth and soft, but full of disappointment and condemnation.

Wally fell heavily to his knees; he was clutching his chest, his shirt was sodden with sweat so cold he shook violently.

'Thou shalt not steal, Wally.' The words, the voice, even more disapproving now, chased themselves around and around in Wally's head.

Bloody well confess, you useless pillock, thought Bert, sitting atop the frame that bore the immense weight of the bells whilst recording the drama unfolding just a couple of yards below. 'He who truly repents shall be forgiven,' he informed Wally.

Suddenly, Wally raised his eyes heavenwards and Bert tensed in alarm perchance he should be spotted. Wally, however, had his eyes tightly shut and his big hands, like bunches of bananas, together in an attitude of supplication.

'Lord, I stole Veggie's onion because, for once, I wanted to win a first prize in Lower Trewiggle's *Home Grown* show this year.'

At Last! Bert thought with relief. But Wally was not done with his exposition. 'I didn't steal the onion myself, but then, Lord, you know that. I was, however, the perpetrator, but then you know that, too. I misappropriated the aforementioned vegetable…

What is this, a confession or a chat? thought Bert. You cannot think God is more likely to forgive you just because you know some long words? My ass is numb, perched here on this bloody beam. Get on with it!

'Almighty God, my heavenly Father, I have sinned against you and against my neighbour in thought and word and deed, through negligence, through weakness, through my own deliberate fault. I am truly sorry and repent of all my sins. For the sake of your Son Jesus Christ, who died for me, forgive me all that is past and grant that I may serve you in newness of life to the glory of your name. Amen.

Wow, I had no idea our Wally was so well versed in the Christian liturgy, thought Bert. Still, he's done the job of confessing properly now; he's bound to be thinking about his evening meal and Myrtle's displeasure if he's late. Wrong!

'Our Father, who art in heaven…'

The Lord's prayer was the final straw, Bert tried to shift his weight a little and slipped off the beam and onto the largest of the bells below. He managed to grab the bell rope and cling on, but this set all the bells in motion, the clappers clanging in a discordant, reverberating, ear-splitting peal.

The sound of Wally's footfalls thundering down the stone stairway as he fled from the scene in terror echoed around the tower. And Bert just sat there, swinging back and forth, back and forth, as villagers were hastily evacuating their homes fearing some sort of impending catastrophe.

Wally's feet hardly touched the ground between the church and his home. He hurtled through the back door with such force that he knocked Myrtle off her feet, a saucepan of steaming vegetables in her hand. 'It's haunted, the church is haunted, just like old Edna Biggins said it was.'

The saucepan, mercifully, landed base down with a thud on the tiled kitchen floor; the vegetables, like small missiles, flew out in every direction, spattering the doors of the units and worktops. Myrtle had curled herself into a ball of resistance on the floor against the onslaught. Wally made no attempt to help her to her feet. He was sitting at the table, head in hands, sobbing and cursing by turns.

Myrtle didn't trust herself to speak, she rolled onto all fours, grabbed the back of a kitchen chair and slowly pulled herself up. She lifted the hot saucepan from the floor and held it menacingly over Wally's bowed head for a full minute before deciding he was not worth a gaol sentence. 'What the devil are you talking about, Wally? And you'd better make this good, very good.'

'The church is haunted.'

'By whom?'

'God, I heard his voice, loud and clear.'

'And what did God say?'

'Um…'

'What did he say?' she yelled.

'He made me confess…'

'For what?'

'For… For stealing Veggie Seed's onion, well, for getting our Sean to steal it. I wanted to win first prize in the *Home Grown* competition.'

'I might have guessed,' sighed Myrtle, 'I did wonder when I was chopping it up, you've never produced anything of that size before, anything edible, at least. You are a silly sod, what were you thinking of?'

'Don't shop me, Myrtle, please don't shop me, I'd never live it down.'

'I would if our Sean were not involved. That was a wicked thing to do; poor little Veggie Seed, he has nothing but his vegetables, they are his life.'

'I'll get his prize money back to him, Myrtle, the money and the cup. I promise.'

'You'll do much more than that. You have broken that dear soul's heart. That comes at a cost. You will write an anonymous note of apology, no, I'll write it for you, and you will pack it up with two thousand pounds in cash and the cup, and send it registered mail first thing tomorrow morning.'

'Two thousand pounds, have you gone mad, woman?'

'Don't you dare call me *woman*!'

'Let me tell you, Wally Bagshaw, I can get much madder than this, you'd better believe me.'

Myrtle took her coat from the hook on the back of the

kitchen door and thrust her arms into the sleeves. 'Where are you going?' inquired Wally.

'To the church, that din has to be stopped before my head explodes.'

'But it's haunted, I told you!'

'Yes, by God, you reckon; I have no reason to fear Him. Anyway, the church is *His* house, he's entitled to haunt it if he wishes.'

Moments later, Myrtle was in the garage revving up her vintage Triumph motor cycle. Wally had never ridden pillion as his wife morphed into something of a speed freak with such much power between her thighs.

Myrtle tripped lightly up the steps to the belfry, lighting her way with a torch. She had the key for the clock in her pocket; *somebody* had to keep Lower Trewiggle acquainted with the time.

She shone the torch full beam in Bert's face. 'Having fun?' she inquired.

'Oh, yeah, an absolute ball.'

'Did you siphon off the petrol in Wally's pick-up?'

'Guilty as charged, it's in my car, I'll reimburse you, naturally.'

'Why?'

'I needed to squeeze a confession out of your miserable excuse for a husband. I had to delay him, to be sure it would be dark before he arrived to wind the clock. I know he thinks this place is haunted.'

'How, it's meant to be a secret?'

'Nothing is secret when Wally is in the pub with his mates, totally hammered.'

'I see.'

'He confessed to stealing Veggie's onion, the evidence is in my phone, safe and sound.'

'Bert, I have adequately righted this wrong, he confessed to me.'

'How have you righted this wrong?'

'A note of regret, the return of the cup, and two thousand pounds.'

'Wow! The old skinflint can't be happy about that.'

'No, he isn't.'

'Well, I'll do my best to play it down in Mickle Monkton, he might do well to stay away from the village for a while, though. Veggie will be happy, that's all we really care about.'

'Right, I'm off, I have a kitchen to clean up.'

'Myrtle, Myrtle! You can't leave me here like this, every time I move I set the bells ringing.'

'And you expect me to help you?'

'We were close, very close once, weren't we?'

'And you jilted me for Jenny Pottle.'

'I had no choice, Myrtle, not after…'

'You had your wicked way with her.'

'Myrtle, for old time's sake, please. I can't hang onto this rope for much longer, do you really want my blood on your hands.'

'I suppose it would make a bit of a mess down there.' Myrtle shone her torch into the depths of the lower belfry. Okay, tell me what to do.'

'Grab the rope and pull it towards you, I'll try to jump onto the walkway beside you.'

The bell let out a single, final, thunderous *dong*, then eventually shuddered to a halt. Bert and Myrtle sat beside each other with their backs against the wall of the tower.

'Wally really thinks your voice is the voice of God, you know,' said Myrtle.

'Will you disabuse him of that notion?'

'I don't think so, a little humility and contrition will do him no harm at all.'

'Let's go,' said Bert. 'I don't think I'll be back in here anytime soon. I do feel rather wicked for what I've done, but I couldn't think of another way. I just wanted justice for Veggie.

'The object was worth the exercise, Bert, Our Lord will understand and forgive you. He'll be pleased for Veggie; if ever he had an obedient, humble servant, it's that dear little man.'

Bert got up and helped Myrtle to her feet, holding her hand in his own for a little longer than was necessary. 'I'm starving,' he said.

'Me too, and I won't be eating anytime soon; our evening meal is decorating the kitchen and the floor is awash with salty water.'

'Let's nip over to Upper Trewiggle for fish and chips,' suggested Bert.

'Oh, Bert, I don't think I'd feel right about that.'

'Don't be daft, my guess is that Wally will pay the boys to clean up the kitchen before you get back.'

'Okay, what the hell? I have to wind up the clock first, though.'

'Give me the key, Myrtle, my love.'

HAROLD'S REVENGE

Harold Gould believed there were many reasons why people went wrong in life, but he couldn't subscribe to the notion that this was because they were inherently bad. No, babies slipped, or were eased, into the world, innocent bundles of infinite potential. Nurtured, guided, disciplined, loved and protected from evil forces, there was a very good chance they would develop into decent, law-abiding human beings.

Mankind was deeply flawed by nature, of course, but had the capacity to conform to reasonable social and moral standards. Harold's Christian upbringing absolutely forbade any other philosophy.

Harold Gould lived in Winterdale: a small market town in the West Country, as quintessentially English as any in the land. His home was a substantial, detached property on the very edge of Winterdale. The large, well-tended garden and the meadows surrounding it enjoyed a rare, aesthetic union that pleased both his eye and his heart.

The location of the dwelling had suited the elderly gentleman's solitary mode of existence perfectly until recent times. Sadly, the world had changed, and by 1954 even quiet, sleepy Winterdale had succumbed to anti-social, disruptive, even criminal behaviour.

Harold's entire life had been devoted to the service of others, most particularly in the area of education. He had been a teacher for ten years before taking over the headship of the local primary school. That is where he spent the rest of his working life. A stalwart of the community, he was deeply respected by all who knew him.

These days he was at leisure to spend his retirement exactly as he pleased. He was a member of various committees, served the church as a lay preacher, visited people in hospital on a weekly basis, and several youths detained in the nearby remand centre, every fortnight.

Harold picked up the remnants of the two large flowerpots that had proudly stood one either side of his front door. The plants they contained had been trampled to pieces; they, at least, could be replaced. But the pots… oh, the pots! They had been made for him by his late wife the year before she died. She'd been so proud of her efforts in her pottery class at night school.

He went indoors and wept bitterly. And something deep inside him snapped…

An insistent chiming in the hall broke into Harold's reverie. Harold, in his usual, sedate way, which never played host to urgency, slowly rose from his armchair and went to open the front door.

Three witches and two wizards of junior school age screeched, 'Trick or Treat', and gaped at him hopefully.

He recognised all but one. 'Ah, Sarah, Cheryl, Holly, Ben, and?'

'Virgil,' informed the boy.

'Virgil! Really! Oh, well, you'd better come in; I'll see what I can find for you. Take your shoes off, if you would, please.'

The disappearance of the children was not reported nationally until late afternoon the following day. By this time it was clear they had not been engaged in some sort of prank.

At ten o'clock, as always, Harold sat down in his lounge to watch the news on television. As expected, the families of the five children were making impassioned appeals for the safe return of their beloved offspring – angels, every one, naturally. Harold's face broadened into a wide grin.

Just three days later, the names of two boys, last seen pushing a pram around the town with a pathetic representation of Guy Fawkes in it, were added to the list of missing children.

The endless speculation as to the fate and whereabouts of the children intensified to fever pitch. The townsfolk eagerly sought Harold's opinion whenever he was about his business in the town. He was always excessively solicitous and suitably scandalised, and declared that the world was no longer a safe place for anyone or anything.

The season rolled on towards Christmas. Two more sets of parents (having, seemingly, learned absolutely nothing from the incidents which had put Winterdale on the national map in such an unsavoury manner) managed to lose two eight-year-old carollers.

Nine youngsters, gone without a trace. And every avenue the police pursued led them on a wild goose chase, and then to a dead-end.

Sorrow, fear and indignation had filled the children when they realised they were being detained at the former headmaster's pleasure. This, however, promptly started to dissipate when it became clear he meant them no harm. He assured them, daily, that he did not intend to permanently separate them from their families.

They occupied comfortable quarters in his cellar – an area he had converted into a library – and enjoyed the wide and varied culinary treats he prepared for them. They scarcely even considered the awful prospect that the food might be *healthy!* In full acceptance of the fact that the old man was caught up in a bizarre sort of experiment they began to regard their plight as something of an adventure. Until, that was, he informed them that their school studies would by no means be allowed to fall by the wayside.

Harold instructed his young captives in the style of his own school days, indeed, his own teaching days. This made no allowance for bad behaviour. Somehow, Harold contrived to instil in them the idea that study was a worthwhile, noble occupation, and could even be enjoyable. The children chose to believe him, and very soon found that he was telling the truth. An adult telling the truth! That certainly gave them something to think about.

At night, when the children were settled on the airbeds placed in a semicircle on the carpeted floor of the library, Harold would tell them a story. His stories were wonderful. He could effortlessly transport them to a time long gone, a time for which his old heart still ached. He could describe an event in terms so eloquent it would almost gain substance. The children loved hearing his stories. They loved the fact that he made no attempt to conceal the mischievous side to his nature. As they perceived it, a child *could* do naughty things without being wicked.

Harold's stories always started with the words, 'When I was a lad...' and a hush would instantly fall on the company.

The time for release was nearly upon them. The children sensed it. Harold sat in his usual place on a low chair amid the airbeds.

'Mr Gould, did you build this cellar especially to keep us in?' inquired Josh.

'Good heavens, no. I wanted a library for all my books and somewhere to read, write and think.' And sometimes cry, he thought to himself.

'Why, exactly, are we here?' asked Virgil. Harold had quickly spotted the academic potential in this boy; he believed he would go far under proper instruction.

Harold moved about on his chair until he found the position that gave him most ease. 'Because the world has gone wrong,' he said at length. 'Don't you think so?'

'Yeah, lots of people are hungry, lots of people get killed with guns and knives,' said Sarah.

'And somebody stole my dad's motorbike,' informed Daniel.

'And our dustbin,' added Cheryl.

'And my mum goes next door when Mrs Perry is out, and she has sex with Mr Perry. I can hear 'em through the wall, they ain't 'alf noisy.'

Harold did not attempt to respond to this piece of intelligence from Louise. He just took on a suitably shocked expression. In truth, of course, nothing shocked him these days, saddened him, certainly.

'What bad things have happened to you, Mr Gould?' asked Matthew.

Harold cupped his face in his hands and rested his elbows on his knees. 'Well, last year, at Halloween, I was very poorly in bed; I had pneumonia – '

'My Nan had that… she died.'

'I am so sorry to it, Cheryl.'

'I'm glad you didn't die, Mr Gould.'

'Thank you, dear, it's sweet of you to say so. Anyway, I was upstairs in my bed, feeling very sorry for myself, when I heard children outside on the driveway…'

'I wasn't on your driveway last Halloween,' put in Daniel, rather too quickly.

'I am accusing no one, Daniel. When I had recovered sufficiently to go outside, what do you think I found?' The eyes of the children widened, but their faces remained blank. 'The paint on my car was peeling off; somebody had tipped a bottle of stripper all over it.'

A great deal of tutting ensued, but Josh looked decidedly uncomfortable. If the boy had not been a party to this offence, Harold was pretty sure he knew who was.

'Then, on bonfire night, while I was sitting in my lounge, still in my pyjamas and slippers because I remained very weak, somebody rang the doorbell, and when I didn't answer it… they… they pushed a firework through my letter box. I am sure you can't imagine what happened nest.' Not a single suggestion was ventured. 'My little cat, my darling Midge, jumped on the firework and swallowed it before it had time to go off, and she was blown all to pieces…' Harold tried to swallow the lump in his throat but failed, and he couldn't stop the tears from falling.

All but Virgil cried for the dead cat, but the boy's voice was full of compassion when he said, 'Mr Gould, I am so terribly sorry for your loss.'

'Thank you, Virgil.'

A suitable period for composure elapsed before Harold was able to continue his narrative. 'Quite recently, I opened my front door and found that the big pots, which used to stand either side of it, had been smashed to pieces. Margaret, my late wife, had made those for me…'

'Why was she late, Mr Gould, where had she been?'

'My wife died, Sarah, a long time ago. We sometimes say 'late' when a person has died.'

'But that wasn't as bad as the other things.'

'Matthew, that simply isn't true. The pots Margaret made for me can never be replaced, not by her, at least, any more than my Midge can be replaced with a different cat. Don't you see, this is my house, my home, everything I treasure is here, my memories, everything, each a small part of my life. Do you think it is right to defile and destroy a person's property?' Harold had worked himself into a state, and his voice betrayed it. He saw actual fear in the eyes of the children now. 'Don't be afraid, my young friends, I've upset myself thinking about my wife and cat, that's all.'

'Mr Gould, if we all promise, cross our hearts, hope to die, to try not to do any more bad things, not ever, and to tell all our friends not to do bad things either, will you be happy again.'

'More than you could ever know, Cheryl. Do remember, children, that nobody can do better than their best, and nobody expects it. We are humans, after all, and not designed to be perfect.'

'Will we be going home soon?' asked Ben.

'You will be going home tomorrow.'

'I wish I could stay here, it's warm and you cook nice food, and I like you lots, Mr Gould.'

'And I like you, Louise. I like you all so very much, but it is time you returned to your families.'

'I think they might put you in prison,' said Virgil.

'I'm sure they will. I have done a terrible thing. Your parents must be frantic with worry and grief.'

'Won't you mind being in prison?' asked Daniel.

'No, I don't think so. I wanted to hurt people because they hurt me. I wanted to teach Winterdale, perhaps even the whole country, a lesson. That is not Christian behaviour.'

'Why?' asked Virgil.

'Because my motives were wrong. In my case, the end can't justify the means, whatever the outcome.'

'But we've had a fantastic time, Mr Gould,' said Sarah.

'Yeah!' chorused the others.

God help and forgive me, so have I, thought Harold.

HORACE

My name is Horace. I am a mouse and I live in a…no, not a house, but a church: St Pirran's Parish church in the village of Pentwiddle, to be precise.

I am a very tiny mouse and rather skinny, a pygmy mouse, my doctor informed my mother when I was a toddler.

I've since researched the condition thoroughly, and come to the conclusion that it could render me prone to bullying. I, therefore, undertook an intensive search for a suitable property in which to settle. St Pirran's fitted the bill very nicely, as the small aperture at the bottom of the great west door provides access to nothing larger than insects and a tiny mouse.

I moved my belongings into my new residence and sorted out the domestic arrangements to suit my needs. Open-plan living is ideal for a creature of habit such as myself, and, since all the pews are exactly the same, one can relocate, should the desire for a change arise.

The church was currently being prepared for harvest festival. Foodstuffs of every description were being arranged in front of the high altar. I viewed the canned products with disdain, but the other provisions looked exceedingly tempting. When the volunteers and vicar had gone home for their evening meal, I hastened towards the banquet both hungry and very excited.

Excessively replete, I discovered I could hardly move. I decided to counteract the effects of over indulgence, specifically flatulence, by going for a long walk in the churchyard.

I laboured down the centre aisle to the door with my distended stomach brushing the dusty flagstones. Looking at my private entrance, in my panic, I decided it had shrunk. Then reality hit me.

So, what now? A diet, a gastric bypass, or Epsom salts?

IN THE STILL
OF THE NIGHT

It was the stillness that roused him, the stillness and the cold. Something had happened while they'd been sleeping, it was something bad; he just knew it.

He thrust out an arm and felt for his dressing gown. It lay in a heap on the floor between his brother's bed and his own. He caught a sleeve and, taking great care not to admit any unwelcome draughts, drew it slowly into the dwindling warmth of the bed. Then he fumbled about trying to put it on.

A few basic needs started to attack his senses, and the business of *getting up* became a matter of some urgency. He sat up and cast his gritty eyes about the room. The chalet had been cosy, bright and welcoming the previous afternoon when they arrived. Now it was an alien place, no more than a wooden shelter. The pure alpine air trapped within its walls was as palpable as fog.

He turned his collar up about his ears and knelt on his pillow. Fear gripped him as he drew back the curtains covering the window directly behind his bed. Gone was the fine view of the mountain gently sloping away and up to its summit. Compacted snow was pressed hard against the glass; not even a hint of daylight was able to pass through it.

And something else was wrong. Not a sound was coming from the bedroom next door. Why couldn't he hear Jack snoring? Jack could snore for England when he'd had a few drinks.

The coldness of the timber floor beneath his bare feet sent shock waves through his system and made him gasp. His brother, William, stirred, but didn't waken. He ferreted in his suitcase for a pair of ski socks, pulled them on, then darted to the bathroom.

The usual delight Edward derived from interrupting William's sleep – by sitting on him, more often than not – was replaced by something touching on fraternal concern. William was only nine, as his mother was constantly reminding him. 'Will, you need to wake up.' William opened his eyes, grunted, then closed them again.

Edward didn't want to infuse William with the panic he was struggling so hard to repress, but he felt he had to acquaint him with the situation. 'Will, we're completely snowed-in, and the place is freezing.'

'Tell Jack, he'll sort it out.'

'Jack and Mum aren't here. They didn't get back from

that restaurant in Schrevenhof last night. I suppose they are snowed-in, too.'

This piece of intelligence jolted William out of his sleepy stupor. He shot bolt upright, drew his knees up to his chest and wrapped his arms about them. Then he started to shake. Edward plucked the duvet from his own bed and pulled it tightly about his brother's shoulders.

'What are we going to do, Edward?'

'It'll be okay, I'll get the log burner going again.'

'What about her?'

'Her? Oh God! Harriet, I forgot about *her*.'

'I think you'd better wake her up.'

Edward and William had first encountered Harriet Olsen, Jack's daughter, at the wedding. It had taken place the day before they embarked on this honeymoon-cum-family skiing holiday. She was seventeen, a few months younger than Edward, disarmingly pretty and lissom as a young gazelle. Edward had found it easier to imagine she was *up herself* than to consider the possibility that she might be nice. He hadn't exactly treated her with disdain, but neither had he made any real effort to be friendly.

And now, here they were together, virtual strangers, holed up in this…this posh hut in the Austrian Tyrol. Edward tapped lightly on her bedroom door. Getting no response, he called out her name. 'Come in,' she muttered, a yawn distorting her words. Edward thought how very alluring she looked in the bed, her mass of tangled fair hair obscuring her face. 'What's up, Edward?'

'There was a terrible snowstorm in the night. Mum and your dad didn't get back from the village, and we can't get out.'

'So much for their romantic dinner.'

'I know. Thought I'd better let you know.'

'I guess you've tried your cell phone?'

'Yes. No signal.'

'Well,' said Harriet, 'I'm absolutely starving. Let's eat then we'll work out our next move. Jeez, it's cold in here!'

'I know, the wood burner has gone out; it heats all the radiators.'

'Can you get it going?'

'I think so.'

'Good. At least you are talking to me properly now, that's something.'

'Harriet, I'm sorry; I know I behaved badly. I felt awkward, it's a tricky situation: being thrown together like this.'

'Is it? Well, perhaps. So, now that it's us against the world, we'd better hope we get on.'

'I'm sure we will.'

Harriet hadn't behaved at all as Edward imagined she

would when she learned of their predicament; all girly hysterics and floods of tears. She was unflustered, grown up. An ally was exactly what he needed at present; he was sure she'd fill that role admirably.

By the time Edward had done his stuff with the log burner, and it was banging out some serious heat, Harriet had produced a cooked breakfast and a pile of toast. She was currently pouring hot chocolate into three mugs.

The atmosphere was charged with tension, but warm and replete, a sense of camaraderie fell on the small company. 'How long have you lived in Chicago, Harriet?' asked Edward.

'Six years, ever since my parents divorce. That's where Mom's boyfriend lived, so that's where we had to go.'

'Do you like it?' inquired William.

'It's okay, I miss London, though, my grandparents, friends… dad.'

'Do you mind that he married our mum?'

'No, William, I don't mind at all; I'm pleased that he's happy. Anyway, I really like Sarah; she's great. Do you mind your mom being married to my dad?'

'No, we think Jack's great, too; don't we, Edward?'

'Yes, we certainly do,' agreed Edward, smiling at Harriet.

Above the kitchen area was a mezzanine providing extra sleeping space. A sturdy set of bunk beds stood directly beneath a large skylight in the vaulted ceiling. Edward climbed up the fixed ladder to the mezzanine, leapt onto the top bunk and stood up. Because he was a generous six-footer, his head fell short of the skylight by just inches.

'What are you going to do?' yelled William from the kitchen.

'Open the skylight and get onto the roof.'

'You'll never manage it, the snow's too dense,' said Harriet.

'Won't know, if I don't try. We can't properly assess our situation from inside. I might get a signal out there, you never know. We must do something.'

Edward had no problem with heights and was adventurous by nature, but he was scared, very scared. Still, he felt he had a good deal of ground to make up with Harriet. If he wasn't exactly looking to become a hero, he wanted to show her that he wasn't a complete jerk.

Dressed in full ski gear and hiking boots, Edward wrapped his hands around the release bar on the skylight and jerked on it harshly. It clicked and the ice around the frame cracked. It opened slightly, admitting several wedges of hard snow. William and Harriet were now in the mezzanine, watching anxiously. Edward took hold of the release bar again and yanked on it with all his might. It swung open, propelling its load into the swirling blizzard outside.

'Edward. It looks absolutely dreadful out there, come down, please.'

'I'll be okay, Harriet.'

Without preamble, he grabbed the sides of the aperture, bounced several times on the bunk mattress to give him momentum, then braced his arms and hoisted himself through it. The snow was thigh deep as he stepped onto the gentle pitch of the roof. He had torn his salopettes on the metal strut of the skylight, and the snow quickly penetrated his lower leg.

The air outside was so bracing it hurt his nostrils, making him sneeze. He staggered, fell, but managed to throw his arm over the ridge to save himself. He could hear Harriet's voice calling out to him, shrill and desperate. And he could hear William crying piteously. 'I'm all right,' he yelled.

He regained himself and made his way along the roof to the chimney. He planted his feet squarely in the indentation created by the heat from the log burner and surveyed the scene, whilst clinging to the stack for support in the biting wind. The front pitch of the roof stood proud of the snow by a couple of feet and overlooked the village of Schrevenhof. But at the back, where the chalet was set at a sharp angle against the valley wall, it was impossible to tell where the roof ended and the valley began. He now crouched down behind the chimney and took his mobile phone out of his pocket. No signal, nothing.

Suddenly, the skylight opened and Harriet's head appeared. 'Anything?' she inquired.

'No.'

'What can you see?'

'The church spire, the shapes of the hotel rooftops, nothing else.'

'Come in, then, I'll make you a hot drink.'

'What are you standing on, Harriet?'

'A stepladder.'

'A stepladder on top of a mattress!'

'I pushed the mattress off, you twit.' Edward liked Harriet all the more for calling him *a twit*. Good-natured insults indicated a level of intimacy.

Before Edward quit the meagre shelter of the chimney stack, he cast his gaze about at the neighbouring chalets. There were half-buried dwellings dotted all over the valley, but none on higher ground than their own. The nearest was a good four hundred metres away, directly below. From the chalets that were occupied, smoke issued sideways from chimney cowls, only to be instantly torn to ribbons, whipped up and tossed about by demented squalls.

It heartened Edward to see that so many chalets were inhabited, though he didn't know quite why; the only thing the would-be skiers had in common was their isolation.

William, under Harriet's instruction, helped prepare an evening meal, but the log burner was left exclusively to Edward's ministrations. Luckily, there was still plenty of fuel indoors. Every now and then a clod of snow would find its way down the chimney and plop onto the burning logs making them spit and hiss. The fire was now too fierce to be easily extinguished and Edward was determined not to let it go out again – even if it meant setting his alarm for two-hourly wake-up calls throughout the night.

Resignation brought with it a level of calmness, an acceptance of the situation. Edward, ever the pragmatist, suggested a game of monopoly to pass the time. Soon they were placing real bets, and so utterly caught up in the diversion that midnight was upon them before they knew it.

Somewhere, in the murky place between sleep and wakefulness, Edward thought he could hear the sound of an express train thundering towards him. It got closer and closer, louder and louder—

The chalet began to shake violently. 'Avalanche! Avalanche!' Edward screeched, yanking William out of bed and dragging him across the chalet floor towards Harriet's bedroom at the far end of the building.

There was a deafening, almighty whooshing sound as the river of snow swept down mountain, shattering glass and splintering timber as if the chalet was constructed of nothing more substantial than matchwood. The biggest part of it disappeared into the abyss.

Harriet was so pale and still that, on first sight, Edward thought she was dead. A large shard of glass protruded from her arm as blood gushed out all around it. William screamed and Harriet roused. 'Don't try to pull the glass out, Edward,' she muttered, 'bind it very, very tigh…' Harriet's eyelids fluttered shut and she passed out.

'William, get the first aid kit and towels, lots of towels. Then bring one of those cans of energy drink.'

Edward looked at the smashed window beside Harriet's bed. He didn't want to run the risk of another shard falling out, so pulled the bed into the centre of the room. The walls of the only room left partially intact from the onslaught seemed to be doggedly resisting the weight of the snow packed against them, he could only pray that they, too, wouldn't cave in.

William heaped the pile of towels on the floor beside

Edward and opened the first aid kit, then he ran off for the can of drink. In this moment, Edward was so proud of his young sibling he wanted to weep.

When Edward was sure he had stemmed the flow of blood from Harriet's arm without cutting of her circulation, he put his arm under her shoulders, lifted her a little and let a small amount of the sugary drink pass over her lips. She opened her eyes and smiled, 'Thank you,' she whispered.

'We are going to get out of this, Harriet, I promise you.'

'I know, I trust you.'

The sky was an unbroken expanse of the sharpest, deepest blue. A rescue helicopter was circling overhead. There was a man in a helmet and heavy protective clothing dangling from the end of a long cable far below it.

'He's picking up survivors from down there,' yelled William, pointing towards to the wreckage of the chalet directly below them.

'Yes, he is. I must get his attention before he moves off. You stay with Harriet, try to keep her awake and warm.'

'Edward, take our long red scarves to wave about, then he is sure to see you.'

'Good thinking. You are a star, Bro.'

William beamed, Edward's approval was worth more

to him than that of everybody else's put together. He climbed onto the bed beside Harriet and nestled against her. 'Are you warm enough, Harriet?'

'Sure, I'm fine.'

'You are very brave.'

'For a girl?'

'For anybody.'

'So are you, William.'

'You are kind of like a sister now, aren't you, Harriet.'

'I suppose I am,' she agreed.

'I like that, but Edward won't.'

'Why?'

'Because he's really stuck on you.'

'Did he tell you that?'

'Na, I'm a fella, I know these things.'

IT'S MY LIFE

When I was young I wasted so much time, so many opportunities. I let life slip through my fingers because it had no *sell-by* date on it. There would always be tomorrow.

I am now eighty-six, with poor eyesight, partial hearing loss, creaky bones, and an unreliable bladder. These afflictions serve to remind me that my days are numbered. AND I DON'T INTEND TO WASTE A SINGLE ONE OF THEM.

If I shuffle off this mortal coil in pursuit of fun, excitement and fulfilment, then so be it. And if my well-meaning, but intensely irritating, sensible daughter, Monica, informs me one more time that I shouldn't be doing this or that at my age, I swear I will pin her to the wall with my walking frame.

She is currently sailing very close to the wind. 'Mother, I tried to dissuade you from getting on the back of a horse, but this: a flight in a hot air balloon, it's…'

I cast her a warning glare.

'I had a terrific time on *Flash*, I'm convinced the animal sensed I was a complete novice. I didn't even fall off when he broke into a trot.'

'No, but you did when he started to canter.'

'I didn't break any bones.'

'That's because most of them have been replaced or secured with metal.'

'There you go then, nothing to worry about.'

'You are impossible.'

'I know, dear.'

'I still can't get over the sight of you dangling from the end of a bungee jump rope and screaming blue murder because your teeth had dropped into the river.'

'Yes, but those nice police diver people found them very quickly, *and* we had our picture in the paper.'

'An image I'm trying hard to forget. Promise me this balloon flight will be the last of your escapades, that you'll settle for something less dangerous next time.'

'Fun usually involves some sort of risk, Monica.'

I don't feel the time is right to tell Monica about the parachute-in-tandem jump I have planned for the weekend. There are a few things I haven't told her

The evening is fine, the sky clear, and the breeze, light, if a little gusty. The pilot gives us all a glass of champagne when the balloon reaches its predetermined altitude. There is a camera attached to one of the cables holding the basket in place. Twelve happy passengers raise their glasses and smile broadly.

It is so very peaceful and pleasant floating across the sky with only the intermittent sound of the gas jets breaking the mood. Below, model villages and *Dinky Toy* cars glisten in the hazy light of the sun as it slowly dips behind the high hills of southern England. I am glimpsing paradise.

The balloon starts to descend quite rapidly as a sudden powerful squall hits the basket full-on. The passengers are thrown into each other's arms amidst squeals of laughter and shrieks of terror. A young man, with a chest the width of Ireland, holds me firmly in his grasp – absolute heaven!

We eventually come to rest atop a vast oak tree, its branches clutching at the basket and drawing it into its very heart. Twigs and leaves are raining down on us in abundance: nature's confetti. The pilot switches off the burners as a herd of terrified cattle stampede across the meadow below; the earth shakes and the great oak trembles.

The balloon deflates and settles over the branches like a tent. 'Oh well, must make the best of things,' opines the pilot. He produces a crate of beer and a case of wine from a receptacle in the centre of the basket and invites the passengers to *drink and be merry*.

It is fully dark by the time a huge, scary-looking piece of

plant equipment arrives at the scene to rescue us. Various levels of inebriation have been achieved which has given rise to much mirth and smutty humour. My young man refills my glass every time I take a sip or two of wine; eventually I fall against him in glorious oblivion.

George will have such fun hearing the details of my adventure. It is a shame the rescue mission is a bit of a blur, though I do seem to recall giggling a great deal. George is ninety-two and occupies the room next to mine at the retirement home. He is my lover. We are planning to marry very soon, well, what reason could we have to wait? I just can't imagine what Monica will have to say about it.

JAKE

Every class has at least one: the child with the walkabout mind. The child who becomes so lost in their own little world that they cause disruption and pandemonium without the least intent or effort. They are a teacher's nightmare.

Jake Sefton was my nightmare. He always acted on impulse because he had yet to grasp the concept of consequences. Still, though he drove me to distraction, I had to admit he was an extremely endearing little soul.

The children were crossing the road outside school, crocodile fashion, to get to the church opposite. It was pouring with rain and many were dressed in outfits for the nativity play that was to be performed that afternoon for the entire school and parents. Jake was looking in any direction other than the one in which he was going, and spotted a kestrel nesting in a tree in the churchyard. He stopped dead to give it his full attention, causing a domino effect of epic proportions.

Angels, wise men, shepherds, animals and even Joseph and Mary lay strewn about on the filthy road like so much human litter. Mary started to wail, not so much because her child had been catapulted from her arms, but because her pristine white dress was spattered with dirt. The baby Jesus had landed squarely in a big puddle, his shawl – a finely crocheted tablecloth that belonged to Mary's grandma – had sunk to the bottom. A few motorists leapt from their vehicles to assist, but most used their horns to express their impatience.

Everybody rallied, even the headmaster, who couldn't be described as *hands on* by any stretch of the imagination. Much use was made of wet wipes to remove the worst of the dirt from costumes and props, and those who had fashioned the crowns and wings did the best they could to restore them. The play might be a little late, but it *would* go on.

I sat in the second pew with Jake beside me; I was taking no chances! We were now just a few minutes away from the start of the performance. Jake was the very picture of contrition. He was comic book cute with straight, strawberry blonde hair gelled to peaks all over his head. His big, hazel eyes gave him a permanently astonished look and people tended to pat him on the head, as if he were a dog.

He now turned his gaze on me – a gappy gaze since he'd knocked out two front teeth walking into a door –

and I knew he wanted to tell me something. It would be something about his granddad's farm on which the entire family lived and worked; it always was. I lowered my head so that my ear was close to his mouth, hoping this gesture might indicate the need for a touch of discretion, as this was a holy place. I should have known better.

'Miss, our Steve left the gate of the sty open and the pigs got into the corner of the field with Granddad's bollocks,' he hollered.

Should I have tried to explain that *bullocks* was the name he ought to have used? No point, a wave of laughter had already washed around the church and even the vicar was tittering behind his hands.

It was a sad fact that this well-rehearsed play would be fondly remembered, primarily, for Jake's faux pas. He'd been given a small part in the play the previous year: the innkeeper. Unfortunately, he'd told the expectant couple to *bugger off!* when they'd knocked on his door seeking accommodation. I hadn't thought that even he was capable of topping that.

The secretary came into my classroom to explain why Jake was absent. Apparently, the seven-year-old had borrowed his grandad's forklift truck to gain access to the roof of the hay barn. To his mind, the icy surface on the corrugated panels looked perfect for a spot of tobogganing. He'd contrived to drag his small plastic sledge to the ridge *and* managed to sit on it before it hurtled down the steep pitch and into a huge pile of dung that, doubtless, saved his life. His left leg and right arm were broken in the incident.

I fully expected my class to burst into fits of laughter when I gave them a potted account of Jake's mishap, but instead it threw them into a sombre mood.

'Trust Jake! Good job he didn't kill himself,' said Max, my brightest pupil.

My classroom was a haven of relative quietude and study, where much learning was achieved and diversions were few. I looked at the small heads bowed over workbooks in concentration.

Without preamble, Jessica, who rarely opened her mouth, except to stuff an item of unhealthy food into it, broke the atmosphere by saying, 'It's really boring without Jake, Miss.'

'Yeah, it is' chorused the rest of the class.

Jake struggled with structured learning, his reading skills were poor, his comprehension of grammar, nil, and punctuation was what occurred when he rode over something sharp on his bike. It heartened me, humbled me a little, to see the depth of affection in which he was held. His needs demanded far more than his fair share of my time, and the capacity of his mind to wander certainly interfered with the smooth running of the class. A touch of resentment would have been understandable.

'It *is* boring without Jake,' I had to agree. 'Never mind, I am told he will be here on Monday, all plastered up and on crutches. He'll be just in time for our Christmas party.'

'Great!!!' rose the collective cry.

KEEP CALM AND CARRY ON

MONDAY MORNING

It was my first day as a post lady. I suppose the weather could have been worse: the rain wetter, the wind brisker, the temperature even lower. Still, I knew my round – had walked it several times previously with my son's rucksack full of pebbles over my shoulder – and believed I had prepared myself as fully as possible for the task ahead.

The process of sorting the mail, pre-delivery, took about half an hour; well, it should have taken about half an hour. Please don't forget that I was new to the job. Anyway, all the other post persons had left the sorting office before I finished filling my bag. I consoled myself with the fact that I had far more than my fair share of little white boxes to cram into my bag – fingers of wedding cake, obviously: tiny silver bells and hearts all over them. Quite how a bag stuffed with letters, bills and bits of wedding cake could weigh more than a rucksack full of pebbles remains a mystery to this day.

I threaded myself through the strap on the bag and heaved it onto my right hip – just as well I had a hip, I'd have fallen over otherwise – and set out on my round.

It was unfortunate that day had refused to break. The battery in my little torch had arrested and was about to expire, and my spectacles were so steamed-up I could hardly see anything anyway. Hey ho, these things are sent to try us.

In tones reminiscent of a funeral dirge, I repeated my favourite Mantra over and over: *keep calm and carry on*. How could this not be my mantra? It was plastered over any number of items in my kitchen. The bag gradually got lighter, as did the day, and everybody got their cake and mail – slightly damp, but intact.

TUESDAY MORNING

I awoke and was hardly able to get out of bed. My head hurt, my back hurt, and my nose had turned into a leaking tap. *Keep calm and carry on*. This is not easy when you are fumbling about in the dark, trying not to disturb your poor husband who has just fallen asleep having done a twelve-hour night shift.

I knew a fistful of tissues would not be sufficient to stem the constant watery flow from my nose, so opted for a toilet roll, a four-ply affair, the type favoured by cute puppies. I forced the toilet roll into my raincoat pocket, breaking the stitching on the welt, and looked out of the kitchen window with dismay. The wind was gusting at gale force, hurling sodden pieces of garden debris at the panes. I refused to be defeated and set forth from my warm, pleasant home with a will. *Keep calm and carry on.*

I was down to the last item in my bag. The addressee, an elderly lady, opened her front door in anticipation of my arrival. Her face lit up with pure delight as I handed her a large, stiff envelope. 'From my son,' she told me, 'it's my birthday!'

'Happy birthday! I hope you have a lovely day.'

'My dear, you are so wet and have a nasty cold, I see. Please, do come in for a little while.'

'I've finished my round and should be getting home.'

'Please, my dear, I'd love the company.'

'Just for a while, then.'

I wasn't exactly lost, just sort of misplaced. I knew my house was just a couple of streets away from the elderly lady's home; Dilys was her name. But I seemed to be going in the wrong direction. If our house was on an incline, why hadn't I noticed before? Then a familiar face loomed into view.

I started to giggle. 'You are my hus…'

'Husband?' suggested Derek.

'Yeah, that's right.'

'And you are drunk, Brenda.'

'Um, a bit…'

'I'll take you home.'

Derek was very patient. When I explained how I'd finished my round and Dilys had asked me in to dry out, then fed me toast and any number of toddies to warm me up, as well as to celebrate her birthday, he completely understood. 'I didn't realise I'd had too much to drink until I stood up. I'm sure I promised to visit again.'

'Better give me her address, in that case.'

'You are very sweet, Derek.'

WEDNESDAY MORNING

The day was bitterly cold but bright and dry. Hooray! My nose was completely blocked now, so at least it wasn't constantly dripping. However, my voice had gone which was more that a little inconvenient. I slipped a notepad into my bag, perchance I should need a means of communication.

Why must people send documents in a jiffy bag? A delicate trinket, perhaps, but sheets of paper! Humanity managed to bumble through life without bubble wrap when I was young. Newspaper kept your chips hot, lit your fire, soaked up the leaks in your shoes, and squares of it hung on a meat hook in almost everybody's outside loo.

And Velcro, almost as annoying as cling film in its determination not to co-operate. The stuff attracts jumpers like a magnet: my nice, smooth woollies morphed into mohair creations after sharing a wash with the gilet my daughter bought me last Christmas. I might resemble a sheep in appearance: skinny legs, ample blob of a body, gormless expression when confused, but being *fuzzed-up* in a fluffy garment does nothing to lessen the impression.

I hadn't realised how frosty the ground was until I sort of land-surfed the length of a garden path. A gnome stood grinning inanely beside the front door whilst clutching a fishing rod; he had no idea that his days were numbered. He toppled and crashed onto the concrete, shattering into a million pieces.

I reached into my pocket for my notepad. *Dear gnome owner, so sorry, accident, will replace. Postie.*

The front door opened, a man in pyjamas plucked his mail and the note from my hand, read it, then burst out laughing. 'No need to replace, the wife bought it, bloody stupid thing. Anyway, she probably won't notice, pissed, most of the time.'

It was a relatively trouble-free round after that. There was but one concern: the vast dog at number seven Rosewyn Close – some sort of hybrid species, a cross between a beast that was big, bad and ugly and one that was big, bad and totally hideous. The creature roamed free in the garden and had a bark that would cause timbers to shiver. I had, mercifully, no mail for number seven, a blessing indeed, for the dog eyed me with vicious intent. I wondered if it had ever occurred to the dog to jump the front garden wall, it wasn't really that high.

Never mind, Keep calm and carry on.

THURSDAY MORNING

It had snowed in the night, snowed so heavily that, when I opened the back door to leave, a considerable drift tumbled into the kitchen and instantly started to melt. My son, rarely seen before midday since losing his job for tardiness, gawped at it and carried on eating his breakfast. Since I had no voice, I could only glare at him in a threatening manner.

I yanked open the door of the broom cupboard, pulled out a bucket and mop and thrust both into his hands. My displeasure must have penetrated a small part of the lump of muscle that floated aimlessly about in his head; he grunted, got up, and dabbed at the large puddle listlessly. I wanted to kill him, so quickly pushed my feet into my boots and stepped out into the snow.

Keep calm and carry on.

Things were going well, I had sorted my mail in record

time and left the office with the rest of the posties. Early morning traffic had been reduced to a crawl, and haste was not an option in these dreadful conditions. Although it felt as if I had half a dozen cotton balls stuffed up each nostril, and I could not swallow without wincing because my throat was so sore, I was glad to be out of the house, away from my freeloading, idle lump of a son.

I drew the banded bundle of letters for Rosewyn Close from my bag and was horrified to see a communication for number seven: a bill, a final demand. How hadn't I noticed it when I'd been sorting?

Keep calm and carry on.

I approached the shabby semi and noticed that the gate was open. Good news, the beast must be within. Not so, it came hurtling around the side of the house, throwing up clods of snow, its teeth bared and saliva dripping from its jaws. Its fangs sank into the boot on my right leg; I felt the warmth of blood running down onto my anklebone. Men appeared, armed with shovels, spades, forks and hefty brooms. They valiantly attacked the monster until it released its hold on my leg and bounded off, licking its lips.

When I came around I was in somebody's small sitting room. My boots had been removed and I was lying on a sofa with my injured leg raised on a cushion. 'Hello,' said a kindly female voice. 'I am a doctor. The wound isn't deep, so won't need stitching, but I've dressed it and given you a jab, just to be on the safe side. Go to the hospital in a few days to have it checked out; I'll give you some antibiotics and tablets for the pain.'

'The doctor was next door with Mrs Curtis,' informed the lady of the house, 'wasn't that lucky?' I nodded, gave a small cough, and mouthed the words *thank you*.

'I'm Mrs Pearce, dear, and you are?'

'Brenda.'

'Glenda, got it.' I didn't have the strength to put her straight.

The police arrived just seconds after the doctor left and, it seemed, the residents of the entire close had crammed themselves into Mrs Pearce's home to put forward complaints about "the scum" that inhabited number seven. I was not their dog's first victim, apparently, and, as all previous warnings to the family had been ignored, the animal would now be forcibly removed from the property.

The company was jubilant and bottles of Mr Pearce's parsnip wine were cracked open. 'Glenda?' invited Mrs Pearce, holding a tumbler and bottle before me. I nodded enthusiastically. I didn't know how I was going to get home and didn't much care.

FRIDAY MORNING

My lower leg was almost black with bruising and very sore around the areas where I had been bitten, but I was determined to *Keep calm and carry on*. Derek told me I was insane, but this job had become a challenge, an endurance test, a mountain I simply had to climb.

Because my leg was so swollen, I opted for wellingtons with thick woollen socks beneath. The snow was still very deep in places although the temperature had risen noticeably.

Now, why isn't it a requirement by law that homeowners provide a letterbox of at least A4 size? Knocking on somebody's door at an unearthly hour is a delicate matter. A cardboard-backed envelope with '*Please do not bend*' writ large upon it does not guarantee a warm reception. Luckily, I had no such envelopes in my bag today.

I took two letters out of my bag for number nineteen Radley Street. I opened the letterbox and pushed them inside; they were instantly repelled. I tried again and the same thing happened. Then I looked at the frosted glass in the front door and saw what the problem was: coats hanging on the back of it.

What I didn't know was that a metal, spring-hinged draught excluder was being held in an open position by the sheer weight of the garments. I pushed my left hand into the letterbox to force a passage for the mail, but before I was able to pop it in with my right hand, the draught excluder snapped shut on my left hand, its sharp edge biting deep into my fingers. The pain was excruciating and I couldn't release my hand without ripping it to shreds.

So, there I was, hanging from the door, my bag like ballast, pulling me towards the ground. I couldn't scream because I had no voice; there was only one option available to me: I pressed the doorbell and didn't release it until I heard sounds of life from within.

Had the gentleman – I use the term loosely, for a more uncouth looking individual I had never seen – realised that the door and I were attached, I daresay he would have opened it with a tad more care. As it was, he wrenched it towards him so aggressively that I flew into the hallway knocking him over. The contents of my bag spilled out onto the floor. 'What the fu… Oh shit! You are stuck!'

To give him credit, he did release me without delay, and offered me a filthy handkerchief to stem the flow of blood from my fingers. 'Want a cuppa or summat,' he inquired.

I shook my head, pointed to my mouth, and uttered a hoarse, unearthly sound that I hoped would convey the message that I had lost my voice. It didn't; he darted off and returned with a rich tea biscuit.

I sat on the bottom stair and let the tears flow whilst stabbing at the keys on my mobile: DEREK, PLEASE COME AND GET ME. 19 RADLEY STREET.

DRUNK AGAIN? came the reply to my text. He was at the door, however, in no time at all, much to the tenant's relief.

Derek fussed over me like an old woman then, at my behest, completed my round. I am certain this contravened every rule in the book, but that was better than leaving a job half done, in my eyes.

With my new wounds tended and my stomach full of the curry Derek had made for our evening meal, I began to feel a great deal better. It was time to *Keep calm and carry on*. A look of incredulity crept onto Derek's face. 'You intend to do your round tomorrow, don't you?'

They tell me there is much less mail on a Saturday, I scribbled on my notepad. I thought my dear, caring husband would eventually lose his patience with me in that moment, but he didn't, instead he said, 'I am so proud of you, Bren.' I started to cry again.

SATURDAY MORNING

I eased myself out of bed and tiptoed to the bathroom. Derek was snoring softly. Our beloved son, Tom, was issuing the sort of sounds a bronchitic sow in labour might be expected to make. My hand hurt, my foot was still swollen and sore, and I knew that my voice would barely rise to a whisper if I tried to croak out a sound. But I was okay, well enough to *Keep calm and carry on,* at any rate.

I might have been able to save myself had I not caught my bad foot in the strap on Tom's football kit bag. He had, doubtless, flung it out onto the landing to avoid sleeping with the stomach-churning stench from his boots. I heard a loud crack and knew I had broken a bone in my, hitherto, undamaged arm. The pain made me feel dizzy and sick. Derek leapt out of bed to be at my side.

Tom, even as a baby, was too lazy to cry unless he was hungry. Derek would huff and puff about him, but never completely lost his rag. The time had come, was overdue.

Having settled me on the bed, with a pillow supporting my arm, he flung open our son's bedroom door. 'Get up, get dressed, and get down to the sorting office. And take your mother's bag with you.'

'What's up with you?'

'You threw that bloody football bag onto the landing again. Your mother's fallen over it and broken her arm. You are going to tell the postmaster that she's had an accident and apply for her position.'

'What!'

'You heard me.'

'A postie! You've got to be kidding!'

'Beneath you, is it? Well, you can apply for a managerial position when the opportunity arises, but in the meantime you get this job, or another by the end of next week, or find somewhere else to live.'

'You would chuck me out!'

'Gladly. I'm taking your mother to the hospital; if you want a lift, you'd better get your idle ass in gear.'

My arm was put in a cast and a sling and I discovered I could speak; well, squeak. Derek said he was due some holiday leave and would ring his boss to tell him he'd like to take it now.

'The job didn't beat me,' I peeped, as we were leaving the hospital.

'No, you deserve a medal, my love.'

'I wonder how Tom got on at the post office.'

'He's young, fit from running about on the football pitch, and agreeable, when he can be bothered. Are there any nubile female posties?'

'One, Ellie, she's gorgeous.'

'I suppose Tom might turn her head, if she's not already attached, he's a nice-looking chap.'

'Perhaps all he needs is the love of a good woman.'

'That's all I need, Bren.'

Tom turned up at the house shortly after us. He was bearing a huge bunch of flowers and looking very pleased with himself. 'Any luck?' asked Derek.

'Yeah, got a date for tonight, a postie, Ellie, what a looker!.'

'With the job!'

'The job, oh yeah. I'm on trial for a week, did mum's round, a doddle really. These are for you.' He thrust the flowers into my lap and my heart melted. 'The postmaster, Eric, sent them, said to give you his best wishes.'

Never mind, Brenda, I told myself, *keep calm*...

LAST OF THE COMMUNION WINE

The ministration of the Eucharist is precise in every detail. The fortified wine is usually red to represent the blood of Christ – if those who attend to the linen are not too precious about stubborn stains. Water is always added to the wine, to discourage an inclination towards hard liquor, one can only imagine, although I daresay a different explanation is presented within the liturgy.

It is generally accepted that when the giving and receiving of the cup is over and the congregation seated, the vicar will consume what is left in the chalice. The Holy vessel is then wiped with a small cloth: a purificator. A small rigid square is placed on top: a pall, and the chalice is covered with the chalice veil and shaped into what looks like a pyramid lacking an apex.

***

ONCE UPON A SUNDAY MORNING, when the sky was leaden with the threat of snow, and the congregation of St Bede's was severely depleted, the newly-installed Very Reverend Duncan Stott climbed the steps to the pulpit to introduce himself and give the first sermon of his ministry in the Parish.

He was an exceedingly small man and not designed for a church the size of St Bede's. Had he been a woman, people would have said he was petite, or dainty, even. When he mounted the pulpit only his shaven pate could be seen over the top of the huge Bible; it was shiny and rather flat, like the bowl on a ladle. A little tittering escaped from the mouths of some worshippers. One of the servers, embarrassed, rushed to the Vicar's assistance with a small stool for him to stand on.

The Vicar, with just his face now visible, smiled beatifically at his new flock. His true blue eyes were bright and full of mischief when he announced, in a surprisingly deep, clear, lyrical voice, 'I am Duncan Stott, but friends call me "Dinky"; I'm sure I can't think why. I am your new boss, and if you believe that great things cannot be delivered in small packages, think on, for I intend to disabuse you of the notion with all possible haste.'

There, he'd done it, he had his audience on side with his wit and self-deprecating manner; all the kindly, smiling faces told him so. He knew his address would be well received; it was full of hilarious anecdotes with profound messages barely disguised within.

When the Vicar stood at the steps before the high altar to invite people to the front of the church for the Eucharist, he almost disappeared into the scene depicted on the tapestry that adorned it, He was standing next to St Peter, who was addressing an animated throng in the street. 'See,' said the Vicar, 'I am very particular about the company I keep, you might want to bear that in mind.'

The congregation had lamented the loss of the old Vicar when he retired; they had been obliged to put up with some very unsatisfactory replacements in the interim. This new fellow was exactly what the parish church needed. It was the dawn of a fresh and exciting period in St Bede's.

When the celebration of Communion had come to an end and the people reinstalled in their seats, the Vicar slowly, very deliberately drank from the chalice. It had been overfull and took some time. The result was dramatic.

The Vicar swayed back and forth, then stood perfectly still in order to regain his composure. Shocked expressions registered on every face. Why would the Vicar imbibe from the cup if he knew the wine would have this effect on him!

The Vicar suddenly leapt from the altar steps, clearing the communion rail by at least a foot, and started to dance in the style of Michael Flatley. His small, nimble feet flew out in all directions, his hands clasped to his sides. his back ramrod straight. The performance was so accomplished that the congregation started to clap to the beat of his feet on the flagstones. When it was over cheers and whistles filled the great church, but the Vicar seemed not to hear them. He simply announced the next hymn and the service carried on.

The following Sunday saw a great increase in attendance, despite the appalling weather. The Vicar gave an inspired address that had a message in it for everyone. He invited the worshippers to approach him after the service if any matters, doctrinal or otherwise, were a source of worry to them. Then he climbed down the steps from the pulpit and moved towards the lectern for a hymn, prayers and readings.

The Vicar drank the last of the communion wine, and his flock sat in a state of frenzied anticipation. It was as before, he stood stock still as the liquid took effect, then walked to the edge of the altar steps with his microphone in his hand.

He moistened his lips with his tongue and the words of *Panis Angelicus* erupted from the depths of his soul on a wave of exquisite and perfectly pitched sound. Much dabbing of eyes and clenching of fists against breasts ensued. Could Pavarotti himself have evoked more emotion? It was truly incredible!

The Vicar, as if he were deaf to the rapturous applause,

simply gave out the next hymn and passed his gaze over the congregation. They looked so joyful in that moment; well, wasn't that what faith in the Lord was all about?

The following Sunday St Bede's was full to capacity, so full that people were standing in the side aisles. The service followed its prescriptive pattern and, too slowly, moved towards the moment the congregation had been waiting for.

The grand piano that stood in front of the Lady Chapel was used mostly when the choir was staging a special performance, including secular songs for which the organ was deemed unsuitable.

Having consumed what remained in the chalice, which had been refilled five times – along with the paten: the small plate that held the host – to accommodate the needs of the worshippers, the Vicar assumed a sort of swagger as he walked towards the piano.

Without ado, the infectious tones of several Scott Joplin classics rang out around the church. The Vicar's rubber fingers darted over the keys as *The Maple Leaf Rag* and *The Entertainer* caused many in the congregation to rise and clap so hard their hands hurt. The magic of these ragtime pieces seemed to hang in the air and echo around the ancient rafters and pillars.

The Vicar stood up, pushed the piano stool back in

place and waited until all signs of earthly pleasure fell from his face and he was again himself: a devoted servant of the Almighty.

Much work was done with the money generated by the weekly collections: repairs to the roof and stained glass windows and large sums given to good causes in the local community and Christian aid overseas. The very Reverend Duncan Stott was an extremely happy man.

***

One Sunday morning there would be no wine left in the chalice after communion. The Vicar could pretend to drink from it, but by that time he suspected nobody would notice, or even care whether he did or not. St Bede's was the house of God, and those who entered it, and those outside, were clearly reaping the benefits of its benevolence, and of being part of something so much bigger than themselves. If people chose to believe he was possessed of special talents through the power of the wine, or some other magical element, then so be it.

He thought about his pals from his old life, the men twice his size he could drink under the table with incredible ease. He remembered the band members he'd jammed with in pubs and nightclubs, and all the artistes he'd accompanied in recording studios around the world. *Riverdance* had eluded him because he was far too short, but, in any case, entertaining those who frequented the churches in which he served was far more spiritually satisfying. After all, didn't some of the worshippers enter a zombie-like state when listening to words they had recited a million times before, and actually fall asleep during a tedious sermon?

The very Reverend Duncan Stott had the wherewithal to change all that because the top man had found his way into *his* corner.

Amen.

MEGAMOGGY

Edna and her two stone pet lived on the tenth floor in the flat directly above mine. She went about her business quietly and was, in every respect, a model neighbour. She was a sweet, rather timid little lady of seventy-two. She had never been married but, being the oldest of twelve attentive siblings, was by no means without support or companionship. I could not help wondering if she had always been of a retiring disposition, or whether that gigantic feline thug, Megamoggy, had bullied her into submission.

Megamoggy would not set a paw outdoors during inclement weather – outdoors being the small veranda area beyond the patio doors of our living rooms. Even his restroom facilities were located in the corner of the bathroom by the radiator.

He commandeered his mistress's electrically operated reclining chair, and adapted it to suit his own specific requirements by pushing his nose against the remote control. The fact that poor Edna was relegated to an inferior chair – in order to accommodate Megamoggy's notion of his standing within the home – was of no moment. If Megamoggy had an elevated sense of his own importance, it was she who had promoted it by pandering to his excesses.

Luckily for Edna, Megamoggy loved fresh air. When the weather was fine he could always be found draped over the veranda balustrade in careless repose. I say careless because, for a creature so brazenly devoted to the pursuance of luxurious living, this position seemed singularly ill-conceived, precarious even.

The day the unthinkable happened was glorious. With my elbows planted firmly on the balustrade of my veranda, and my chin cupped in my upturned palms, I gazed across Bristol, my city, with affection. Megamoggy was above me on his perch. Normally, when he caught me in this attitude, he would open one eye, emit a sound that was somewhere between a snort and a hiss, scrunch up his huge, baggy face and scowl at me ferociously. On this particular day, however, he was so far lost in slumber that the draught from his resonant snoring caused his whiskers to quiver. His long sable fur was shimmering in the sunlight; he looked like an overstuffed cushion, his tail and legs, elaborate tassels that twitched by turns.

Several small feathers floated onto my head, a mangled body dropped at my feet, and I realised that some innocent little bird had dared to invade Megamoggy's personal space. A thwack of a paw, a rasping yowl and another bit the dust. I heard Edna's patio door open, heard her shuffling footfalls on the veranda, heard her call, 'Mega…' then waited for the inevitable gasp of horror.

Megamoggy plummeted past me, a great whoosh of electrified fur and petrified limbs. During his descent he contrived to form himself into something akin to a small spacecraft: paws outstretched for landing, tail erect like an aerial.

He seemed to be caught in an updraught that not only brought his progress to a halt, but lifted him several feet. A moment or two later the air pocket shifted and he floated gracefully downward until he was level with a flat on the fifth floor. Then, just as a delivery van drew up directly below in the street, he dropped to earth at supersonic speed.

There was a tortured twanging sound as Megamoggy thudded squarely onto the roof of the baker's van and it caved in. Shrieking obscenities, the driver emerged crab-like from the back of the van. He was clutching a large tray of cakes and had a jam doughnut firmly attached to his nose. His glasses were thickly coated in whipped cream and his hair, bedecked with chippings of meringue.

I hastily quit my flat and joined those who had gathered in the street to view the spectacle. When it was established that the poor driver had sustained no injuries, people started to laugh at the sight of him turning this way and that in a state of utter confusion.

The driver was well known in the area for his cheery nature and sense of fun. Spitting out crumbs, spluttering and gurgling, he slowly set down his tray of cakes on the road. He removed his glasses, cast his eyes around his audience, took several bows to rapturous applause, and let out a series of hearty guffaws.

The owner of the convenience store, for whom the consignment was destined, rushed to his assistance with umpteen damp cloths and towels. 'What the devil was that?'

'No idea, didn't see it, most of me was in the back of the van when it hit. It just sort of dropped out of the sky like a thunderbolt!'

'Yes, it did. Perhaps that's what it was.'

'Well, unless thunderbolts have legs, you'd expect some evidence, some debris.'

'Um, yes, how very odd! It's a bit scary when you think about it. Still, your insurance will cover the cost of the damage.'

'Yeah, I'm going to look a right twit when I try to explain what happened.'

'You have plenty of witnesses; give me a ring if you need backup.'

'I will. It's such a bloody nuisance; I'll have to rent a suitable vehicle while it's being fixed'

I could have put him straight about the offending object, but decided against it as it would implicate Edna, and that was the last thing she needed right now. Dear Edna, currently prostrate on her bed in a state of extreme distress.

Anyway, more importantly, where was Megamoggy?

I opened my front door to find Gilbert, Edna's brother, standing in the gloomy corridor. He told me that she had agreed to spend the night at his house. He asked if I would be kind enough to phone him if I heard any news of Megamoggy, good or bad. I scribbled his number on my notepad, bade him good night, and decided on a large glass of sherry and an early night.

I couldn't settle. How could I settle when Edna was so distraught she'd quit her home, albeit for one night? I got up, pulled on a coat to cover my nightdress, and took out the torch I kept in the drawer of my bedside cabinet. I decided I would have a little wander around outside the building, after all, who else would be looking for Megamoggy?

In the wake of the incident there had been much talk of meteors, bits of wreckage from spaceships, rockets and drones. Not one word was uttered, however, about a morbidly obese, highly-opinionated, domestic cat.

I pressed the button to summon the lift then stood back with the torch raised high above my head, perchance an undesirable lurked within. The lift was empty. At least I thought the lift was empty until I heard a pathetic squeak coming from the corner. 'Good God!' I declared, the echo of my voice startling me as much as it startled Megamoggy. When he opened his mouth to issue a warning hiss, I noticed that some of his front teeth were missing. The hiss eventually came out as a pathetic squeak.

This was a Megamoggy I had never expected to see in my lifetime. He looked so deflated that one might have mistaken him for a doormat. Indeed, Bagpuss would have appeared more confrontational at this moment.

He followed me into my flat and then into the kitchen. Anecdotes of Megamoggy's relationship with food were the stuff of legend. His palate was so discriminating that nothing less than full-cream milk would satisfy it. Semi-skimmed from the supermarket was all I could offer him; it was take it or leave it time. I put a bowl on the floor and half filled it. He lapped up every last drop. Then I opened a tin of smart price tuna which he tucked into with equal relish, whilst I phoned Gilbert with the good news.

The night was still warm. I took my stool from the

kitchen, put it on the veranda and sat down, so relieved for my dear neighbour and pleasantly sleepy. The moon was full and bright, casting gentle shadows all about. At first Megamoggy crept into one of these shadows, still obviously dazed and confused, but presently I felt his fur against my leg.

I awoke at half past five clinging to the edge of the bed. I had spent many nights like this when my husband was alive. He was a very generous man in most respects, but downright stingy and selfish when it came to sharing our bed, and the quilt.

I turned to find Megamoggy's head on Bert's pillow, his face serene, his whiskers twitching with each sonorous snort. I shivered a little in the early morning chill and made to pull the duvet over me, but Megamoggy had dug himself a deep nest in it. Was I going to disturb him? Not a chance!

MOTHER

Hector Whittaker-James sits beside the huge marble fireplace in a faded wing chair. His face is scrunched up in a fierce scowl. He runs his hands through his thin grey hair and fiddles with his hearing aid, then tries to dislodge a piece of food from his bottom denture with his tongue, fails, exhales loudly, and gapes expectantly at his brother.

Godfrey Whittaker-James sits on the opposite side of the fireplace in an equally faded wing chair. He peers through thick spectacles at the printed document in his hand, mutters, tuts and draws slowly on his pipe.

Hector lets out a grunt of impatience. 'Well, what does the bally thing say? If you would be so good as to share its contents with me.'

'Mother wants a phone installed in her coffin,' replies Godfrey.

'A phone!'

'Yes.'

'What, a landline?'

'Of course, a landline, a battery operated appliance won't satisfy her needs.'

'Good God!'

'Indeed.'

'Why on earth would she want a phone installed in her coffin?'

'One can only assume she fears her doctor will misdiagnose the symptoms of death.'

'And she's afraid she will be buried alive.'

'Quite… Hector, must you always be so brutally blunt?'

'The privilege of old age, Godfrey. You know, Mother never did trust anyone's judgement but her own. Perhaps that's why she has contrived to reach the great age of one hundred and ten.'

'I don't doubt it. But the telephone is the least of it. She has drawn up a list, or a *statute* might more accurately describe it,' Godfrey waves the paper at Hector, 'affairs we must promise, nay swear, to studiously attend to.'

'If we are to inherit?'

'Exactly,' confirms Godfrey.

'I was speaking to her earlier; she seems to regard death as something of an inconvenience.'

'She always did; can't you remember how cross she got when her dressmaker was sadly taken, said she'd never find another so reliable.'

'She's only halfway through a veritable tome of a novel, and I can't imagine that even the grim reaper would dare deprive her of the opportunity to finish it.'

'She will not go until she is quite ready, Hector, of that we can be quite certain.'

'Then I suggest we give her the assurance she requires; it might hasten the process of her demise.'

'Really! You are so indelicate?'

'We have played host to her whims and wishes ever since we were of an age to comprehend them, don't tell me *you* are not looking forward to a little freedom, even at this late stage in our lives. I assume we are permitted to proceed with these *affairs* immediately?'

'Indeed, mother expects it. She is intent on overseeing the project, in order to approve it.'

'May I see the document?' asks Hector.

For the attention of my sons,
Hector and Godfrey Whittaker-James

1. *My coffin is to be made of oak, solid oak, and not less than two inches in thickness in any part. It is to be oblong in shape, but must not be referred to as a casket: a frightful term that evokes images of a box in which one might keep jewellery — if one does not have access to a repository at the bank. I daresay there are such unfortunates, even in England. My coffin is to be padded and lined with pure white silk — so soft on the skin — and heavily ruched, naturally. A cushion is to be placed beneath my head, a proper cushion of duck down, not a small pad. The lid of my coffin must be hinged and spring-loaded.*

This will ensure that the lightest touch from within will cause it to open automatically. I expect you to test this facility fully.

2. *A six-month period must elapse before my body is removed from the cellar in this, my home, Candleford House. It can then be taken to the family plot in the cemetery. Please examine my remains for signs of decomposition before this takes place.*

3. *You will engage the services of Mr Albright to make ready the cellar for my occupation. The installation of appropriate lighting, subdued and wall-mounted, and a complete makeover – I believe it is called – will be required. Pale lilac, a most flattering colour, will do nicely.*

4. *I have acquainted the Vicar with my wishes regarding my funeral service, and informed Mr Scown, the undertaker, of the arrangements thereafter. Mr Scown ventured to tell me that he felt they were somewhat unusual. I reminded him that it was his business to do precisely as I asked, and mine, as the client, to decide what that business ought to be.*

5. *My coffin will be placed upon a pedestal – this will be made by the undertaker to accommodate my coffin. I wish to have set beside me in my coffin: a torch, a bible, a box of tissues, several bars of dark chocolate, a bottle of your father's best brandy, and a rich fruitcake, sliced, wrapped and stored in a tin. It would be a dreadful thing to awaken from a death-like coma and find oneself without a drop to drink, or a bite to eat.*

6. *THIS IS OF THE UTMOST IMPORTANCE. You must check the answer phone for messages daily, six o'clock in the afternoon would seem a reasonable time. I will not be selfish and expect you to remain exclusively in the house for six months, perchance I should call you and summon assistance.*

7. POSTSCRIPT. You were excessively tedious as children and in truth, seemed to have improved little since then. Still, you have been good, obedient and caring sons and I am happy to leave my estate in your capable hands. It grieves me that I will leave you in your dotage without wives or children. I daresay you had your reasons for cleaving to each other for companionship, instead of seeking it elsewhere.

Mother

***

Dorcas Matilda Whittaker-James is by no means incapable of perambulating Candleford House under her own steam with no more than an arm to lean on. However, she considers the exertion quite unnecessary when she has a perfectly good wheelchair and a private nurse to push it. 'Boys, you must see that I cannot possibly risk quietus before I am able to thoroughly inspect the arrangements you have made on my behalf,' she tells her sons. 'When I am completely satisfied, you may restore me to my bed where I will die at my leisure.'

If Godfrey and Hector Whittaker-James imagine there will be any haste attached to their mother's period of leisure, they are to be sorely disappointed. Hector celebrates his eighty-sixth birthday and seven months later, Godfrey, his eighty-fourth.

Dorcas Matilda Whittaker-James reads *War and Peace* and *The Forsyte Saga,* and the services of yet another live-in nurse are engaged: number thirty-three. Number thirty-three: nurse Stafford, a no-nonsense former matron from an unpronounceable village in Wales is resident in Candleford House for just one month when the final curtain falls. It falls very slowly and with a sense of drama normally associated with Classical theatre.

Godfrey and Hector are at home by six o'clock every evening to check for messages *from the other side* on the answer phone. They have been too well trained to ignore their mother's wishes simply because she is no longer there in the flesh to oversee them. And they do not become blasé about receiving a communication. As long as she remains in Candleford House, *anything* is possible.

***

The six-month period comes to an end. The body of the deceased can finally be taken to the cemetery for interment. The brothers have put Candleford House on the market and booked a world cruise, but first, there is one final duty to perform...

Hector unlocks the door to the cellar, it creaks ominously as he pulls it open, 'Oh, dear me, oh, dear, dear me,' he says, grasping Godfrey's hand for support.

'I don't like the thought of this one bit,' says Godfrey.

'Can't we get somebody else to do it?'

'I think not, we did swear on oath...'

It is difficult to say who is more shocked, the Whittaker James brothers, or the tramp in a state of almost total recline – not to mention inebriation – in their mother's coffin. He is swigging brandy and stuffing clumps of fruitcake into his mouth with a very grubby hand. 'Gawd 'elp us, what you doin' 'ere?' he inquires.

'What are *we* doing here!' Godfrey nearly chokes on the words.

'This is our mother's coffin!' screeches Hector.

'She is to be taken to the cemetery for burial this afternoon,' explains Godfrey. 'What have you done with her?'

'In that bin bag in the corner,' the tramp waves his finger at a green plastic sack that has been tied at the top. 'Nothin' but bones, no need to get worked up.'

'How did you get in?' asks Hector.

'Cellar door at back, 'ow dya think?'

'It was unlocked?'

'How can that be?' inquires Godfrey, looking at his brother accusingly.

'Cuz ya dint turn the bloody key?' suggests the tramp. 'You oughta be more careful, mate, I mighta took them chocolate bars and the torch, nice bitta cake, though, moist, very moist.'

SECRETS

Aunt Maud loved her garden. Her garden responded to her devotion by producing every plant, fruit and vegetable that was commonplace at the time, and perhaps a few that were not – those containing health-giving properties that would be considered highly illegal these days.

What struck me when first I saw the photograph of her standing in front of her cottage, waist high amidst a sea of flowers, was that, having consented to pose for it, presumably, she saw no occasion to smile. On the back of the photograph was neatly printed: *Maud Crawford in her garden. Polton Cross. 1937.*

My mother, Aunt Maud's younger sister, claimed that, even as a child, when Aunt Maud attempted to smile, she contrived only to scowl and was strongly advised to quit the exercise. Her mother informed her, in no uncertain terms, that she was exceedingly plain and appearing to grimace did nothing to improve her looks. I imagine poor Aunt Maud felt she had nothing to smile about after that.

I wasn't blind or stupid. I could see that on a physical appeal scale of one to ten, my mother was probably nine and a half, whereas Aunt Maud was – without being too unkind – a good deal less than three.

Mother was a fair-haired, delicate creature, a blend of feminine wiles and helplessness – traits irresistible to men of my father's generation.

Aunt Maud, on the other hand, had the form, stance and manner of a rustic; she was well upholstered, her skin was weathered, her thick, dark hair, wayward, and, if she'd ever been acquainted with a cosmetic product, it was clear she had no idea what it was intended for.

Aunt Maud never ventured beyond the village church that was situated at the end of the main street. If her garden was her life, Polton Cross was the universe in which she lived it. Everybody knew her, everybody knew her Christian name, but nobody dared use it. There was just something about her that absolutely forbade familiarity.

But, if Aunt Maud could frustrate the advances of an army of cabbage snatchers with one of her *withering glares,* and reduce small children to tears simply because they happened along the lane in front of her cottage, she was always very pleasant to me. My birthdays – the one day in the year my father insisted that I, her nephew, should pay her a visit – elicited something touching on kindness. I found her attentions disarming, since my feelings for her were my no means fixed in my mind.

Aunt Maud never came to our home: a rather pretentious, stone house set a quarter of a mile off the main street, just where the village gave way to open countryside. To the best of my knowledge, she was never invited. Now a teenager, with a firm notion of how the world should work, I found this slight impossible to reconcile with socially acceptable behaviour. I became almost gallant in my eagerness to compensate by calling upon her every Saturday afternoon for an hour or so.

Not a great deal passed between us by way of general conversation, but if I posed a question of horticultural content, her face would light up and she would let out a sigh of pleasure. Her approval of my interest would manifest itself in the measures she took to provide me with sound and comprehensive explanations: charts, graphs, drawings, nothing was too toilsome to be undertaken.

As my passion for the natural world burgeoned, my affection for Aunt Maud increased. I believe I began to love her a little.

It dawned on me that I had attained manhood when I fell in love with the vicar's daughter; she broke my heart by falling in love with someone else. It was at about this time that I noticed my father's hitherto erect body taking on a slight stoop. My mother's appearance was registering the passing of the years by the lacklustre tone of her skin, and her need for reading spectacles. Aunt Maud's appearance, however, saw no perceptible change.

And then, without the least warning, Aunt Maud died. She died, and the thing I learned about grief was that I had no idea how to deal with it. It was such a painful experience, like nothing I had ever been subjected to before.

The village turned out en masse for the funeral; my mother, rather grudgingly, bought a new hat, and my father slipped into a very uncommunicative, sombre mood for some reason.

Aunt Maud left me her cottage and all contained therein. Her money went into a trust fund for the establishment of a garden on a piece of wasteland in the village. I was entrusted with the task of overseeing the entire project and its subsequent maintenance. Had I been given a knighthood, I could hardly have regarded it as a greater honour.

I had never been in any room other than the parlour whilst Aunt Maud lived. Now that she was gone, the prospect of examining the rest of the rooms in the cottage seemed tantamount to defilement. I sat in the chair I had always occupied: the large, grubby affair facing the fireplace.

I noticed immediately that the photograph of Aunt Maud had been removed from the mantelpiece.

After so many years of gazing at it – for want of something better to focus on, whilst drinking weak tea and nibbling over-baked buns – its absence struck me as singularly odd. I realised I had never given the least thought to who might have wished to capture Aunt Maud on film. My curiosity ran riot. I simply had to find it, hoping it would provide a clue.

It lay upon the large bed – this was where Aunt Maud had been laid-out, for those wishing to view the body and pay their last respects. This was something I could not bring myself to do.

Beneath the photograph was tucked another of exactly the same size, and in a matching frame. In this photograph my father, a respected actuary by profession, was standing among the flowers in Aunt Maud's garden. He was wearing a baggy shirt with the sleeves rolled up to his elbows, ill-fitting twill trousers, and a cloth cap pulled on his head at a jaunty angle. He looked carefree and content.

I instinctively knew that if I opened the wardrobe I would find these items of clothing, and probably more besides. I had no desire to do this, or to question my father about his relationship with Aunt Maud. He obviously wanted me to discover the evidence of intimacy between them. He wanted me to know the truth.

I picked up the photograph of Aunt Maud and drew it close to my face. Why had I never before noticed her dour expression on *my* face first thing in the morning, or the strong set of our identical jaws. And why hadn't I spotted the telltale bump in her apron as she stood among her daisies and dahlias?

I suppose I should have cared about my father's infidelity, but I did not. I took both photographs downstairs and placed them side by side on the mantelpiece: my parents, together. It was as I did so that I noticed how bulky each was, as if padded.

The letters were beautiful: my father's fine copperplate script professing his deep and passionate love for *Darling Maud*, her compact, upright characters returning her love for him, her *Secret Swain*. I carefully folded the letters and replaced them exactly as I had found them.

SOMETHING
TO TREASURE

Joanna Carter was the new girl in class. She was deeply tanned from the Californian sun and her long blonde hair was pulled into a ponytail and tied with a ribbon: red, to match her school fleece. With true blue eyes, she looked like she'd walked straight off the set of a family movie. Of course, it was her American accent that captivated her peers; all the children wanted to be her best friend.

She was bright, very bright for a seven-year-old, eager to please, her behaviour impeccable, and she looked exactly like me at the same age. I found her frequent quizzical gazes at me, her teacher, extremely disarming.

I hadn't really needed to check her date of birth because I knew instinctively that this was the child I had given away when she was one week old. She was my secret, my shame; she was the sadness that gnawed away at me, stealing all hope of complete happiness.

What cruel twist of fate had brought her back to Britain, to Cheltenham, to my school, my class? My only consolation in handing her over to the authorities was the knowledge that she and her parents were relocating to San Diego, her adoptive father's home. I believed I would never see her again, and in time would forget. Oh, the folly of youth!

I knew I would have to seek another position, this situation had gone on for two weeks now and was becoming intolerable, particularly because there was a growing coldness in my manner towards Joanna. I knew what was happening: I was trying to protect myself from emotional meltdown at her expense. She was a darling little girl in every respect and deserved, at least, the attention I gave my other pupils.

I put my son, Thomas, into his cot, sat with him until he settled and then went downstairs where my dear husband, Bob, was doing his stuff in the kitchen. When away from the office, Bob loved to cook; he made a far better fist of producing an appetising meal than I ever could. 'Debs, something is wrong,' he said, addressing whatever was in the wok.

'No, nothing, I'm tired, that's all.'

'Debbie?'

'Well, I'm thinking of applying for a position at another school.'

'You love your school; whatever the problem is, leaving won't solve it.'

I started to cry, to sob. Bob switched off the hob and pulled me into his arms; he held me fast until all my tears had been spent and his shirt was soaked. 'You can tell me anything, Debbie, you know that, please don't shut me out.'

'You would hate me if you knew what I'd done.'

'Hate is not in my vocabulary as far as you are concerned. Let's eat, then sometime, anytime, you can tell me what's on your mind.'

'Okay.'

'Promise?'

'Yes, but not today. Oh, Bob, I don't deserve you. I love you so much.'

'And I love you. Let's eat, I'm starving.'

'Better change your shirt first.'

Thomas awoke and started to yell, I put down my marking pen down and hurried upstairs to see to him. I lifted him from his cot and held him close. He was a nine-month-old bundle of dribbling warmth and melted in my arms, his tiny fists snatching at the neck of my blouse.

'Your mother isn't a good person, Thomas. I had another baby, one I never fed, or held, or changed, and she's sweet and so beautiful.' Thomas went limp; I put him back in his cot and started to weep again.

It was open evening for parents: a time for some unwelcome truths to be told, a lot of encouragement and assurances given and, mercifully, much praise to be heaped on those children who achieved, at any level. The Carters came early and Joanna was with them. They entered the classroom, mum and dad either side of their daughter, their hands linked. They presented the perfect image of a perfect family. A feeling of profound jealousy gripped me so hard I began to feel unhinged.

'Go sit in the reading corner, sweetie. Mom and dad are going to talk to your teacher,' Mr Carter told Joanna. The girl trotted off obediently and the couple linked hands as they approached my desk.

'Mrs Best, it's so good to meet you. I'm sorry we missed you the day Joanna joined your class; you were on playground duty, I believe.'

Joanna's mother had a lovely voice, so soft and measured: a bedtime story reader's voice. I extended my hand in greeting to each parent, 'I am very pleased to meet you both, please, do sit down. I brought a couple of chairs from the staff room; at the last open evening a father sat on one of the chairs the children use and it collapsed.'

'How embarrassing, poor guy,' said Mr Carter.

'Not as embarrassing as when I tried to help him up

and fell on top of him instead. Unfortunately he didn't seem to mind.'

'Oh dear, I bet he thought it was his lucky day,' said Mrs Carter laughing, a pleasant, tinkling sound against Mr Carter's throaty guffaws.

Quite why I chose to share this anecdote with the Carters I don't know, an attempt to conceal my nervousness, I daresay. 'Anyway, you haven't come here for an account of my awkward moments.'

'It's nice to know that other people have them,' said Mrs Carter. 'Has Joanna told you that she is an adopted child?' Bang! Mrs Carter was straight in there with this remark.

'She mentioned it in her diary, the children are encouraged to share their stories and experiences with the class.'

'I expect some of their revelations both shock and amuse you,' said Mr Carter.

'Yes, indeed they do.'

'Joanna was very happy in The States. All Jack's family live there, but my mother is now very frail, she has a heart defect, so we returned to look after her. It has given Joanna the chance to get to know her before it's too late.'

'She lives with you, Mrs Carter?'

'Yes, we have a very good carer who comes in when we are not there, and Joanna is more than happy to fetch and carry for her; we bought her a nurse's outfit, she quite looks the part and has a convincing bedside manner.'

'I can well believe it. She seems to have settled nicely in class, and attracts friends like bees around a honey pot. Her work is exceptional and her behaviour exemplary. You must be very proud of her.'

'We certainly are,' said Mr Carter, laying his hand lightly on his chest.

'I was pregnant with twins fifteen years ago, but developed an aggressive tumour and had to have the babies and my womb removed.'

This piece of intelligence nearly took my breath away. 'Oh, Mrs Carter, I am so sorry, that is heartbreaking!'

'So you can see why our daughter is so special, so important to us.'

My eyes had filled with tears and Mrs Carter reached across the desk and patted my hand. 'I shouldn't be burdening you with our misfortunes, but you are a person I feel can talk to, Joanna will do well in your class.'

Mr Carter stood up to leave, drew his wife gently to her feet and put a protective arm about her. 'Come on, Joanna,' he called, 'time to go see how grandma's doing.'

'I'm here already,' chimed Joanna, springing from behind her father. 'Bye, Mrs Best, see you tomorrow.'

'Bye, dear.'

When we'd eaten, I poured wine into two large glasses and told Bob all about Joanna. 'The same thing happens to hundreds of teenagers, Debs; why are you beating yourself up?'

'Because most mothers decide to keep their babies.'

'Yeah, frequently to be housed by the council and get benefits. That involves little integrity and even less selflessness. Maybe if your parents had given you encouragement instead of condemnation, you would have done the same.'

'I don't know; they didn't want anything to interfere with my education, I suppose they were putting my needs first. If I'd been more responsible it would never have happened; I can't blame anyone but myself.'

'Could you, at seventeen, have given Joanna a better life than she has now?'

'Not a chance. The Carters are the nicest people imaginable and they absolutely adore her. They must have suffered so much. Imagine losing two babies and all prospects of any other children to fill the chasm in your life?'

'Debs, you have given these people the greatest gift of all.'

'She might as easily have been placed at risk with the wrong sort of family.'

'Adoptive parents are vetted from here till kingdom come.'

'But I'm not comfortable around her, I don't know how to behave. I cannot pretend she is other than she is: my child.'

'Do you want her to know who you are?'

'Absolutely not.'

'Then take your lead from her behaviour towards you. The kids see you as their friend as well as their teacher, I know that much.'

'Yes, that's true. You think I can be her friend?'

'Love comes in all shapes and sizes, sweetheart.'

The children often brought me things: a bun they'd baked, a piece of fruit, and sometimes a bunch of flowers they had picked. As the children were about to leave that Friday afternoon, I noticed Joanna lagging behind. When her classmates had gone, she came up to my desk and presented me with a little red felt purse. 'Mommy helped me make it,' she announced proudly. 'It's got my name and your name on it.'

I took the purse and gently smoothed it flat on the palm of my hand. 'This is beautiful, Joanna, such a clever and wonderful gift, I love it.'

'Well, you kinda look sad sometimes, and I want you to look happy.'

'Yes, I have been a bit sad lately, but I'm happy now. Thank you so much.'

As I made to stand up, Joanna threw her arms about my neck. I got up and knelt on the floor so that my face was level with hers. I wrapped her tight in my embrace, as if to imprint the shape of her small body on my own for all time; then I held her away from me, tears pricking the back of my eyes. 'Have a lovely weekend, Joanna.'

'See you on Monday, Mrs Best. I'm real glad you're my teacher.'

'Me, too.'

I held the little red purse a while longer then slipped it into my handbag. I knew I would never use it, but would carefully wrap it in tissue. It must remain pristine because it was something of inestimable value, something to treasure.

SUPPER WITH A STAR

As a young woman, Gladys Doyle had been prone to attacks of blind panic that invariably brought her out in a dreadful, blotchy rash, caused her heart to palpitate wildly, and required the ministrations of her doctor. She had detested this dour little man with his bad breath and fumbling fingers, and resolved never to get worked up about anything again, ever.

This self-help regime had relied totally upon the avoidance of aggravating factors and rendered her life deadly dull. But a dull life was nothing compared to a face that looked like a map of the world, and a heart pounding like a steam pump. These afflictions would have certainly inhibited the advances of Walter Doyle, the object of her affection.

A lapse of fifty years saw the widow, Gladys, leading a quiet, predictable existence in Coombe Haytor, a sleepy village set deep in the heart of the Wiltshire countryside. Gladys was, at seventy-four, so resistant to change and upheaval that her only hope for the future was that it remain as much like the present as age and infirmity would allow.

The kettle was whistling merrily on the Aga whilst Gladys sat at her scrubbed kitchen table munching contentedly on a piece of thickly buttered toast. A blast of cold air from the back door heralded the arrival of the postman, Gerald.

'Ready for a cuppa?' Gladys inquired.

'Absolutely,' replied Gerald, dropping his bag onto the floor before edging his way around the table to the ancient easy chair in the corner.

'Toast?'

'Yes, please, Gladys. I've a bit to do before I'm finished today.' Gerald pulled off his jacket and made himself comfortable in the chair. 'Have you heard the news?'

'What news?'

'The Beeb are going to feature Coombe Haytor in a six-part period drama. Of course, it won't be called Coombe Haytor in the production. It will take months to complete.'

'Are you winding me up, Gerald Budd?'

'Not at all. The village will be running alive with cameramen and celebrities by the middle of March.'

'And celebrity spotters,' growled Gladys, hacking a piece of bread the thickness of Yellow Pages from the loaf she held so firmly in her grasp.

'I suppose so. Still, it might be fun. Think of all those high hats, frock coats, bonnets and heaving bosoms.'

Had Gerald noticed how agitated Gladys had become, he would have dropped the subject. As it was, he closed his eyes and was letting his imagination run riot. A lecherous smirk was drawing up the corners of his mouth, exposing teeth reminiscent of a miniature row of weathered tombstones. 'They might ask us to be extras. I rather fancy myself as a dandy; I wonder what the missus would say.'

Gladys didn't trust herself to reply. She picked up a small knife and spread half a pot of marmalade on Gerald's toast in the hope it would stick his jaws together.

Gladys couldn't sleep, she tossed and turned, itched and scratched. At half past two she got out of bed, came downstairs and lit the small gas heater in her sitting room. She rifled through her DVD collection until she found Pride and Prejudice. Part of it had been filmed in neighbouring Lacock. She hoped that watching it might help her come to terms with a similar project in Coombe Haytor; it might distract her a little, if nothing else.

Gladys had loved her Sundays with Lizzie and Darcy, but it was the characters she engaged with, not the people who portrayed them. She had a very poor opinion of actors: overpaid, puffed up show-offs, the lot of them. She was sure this alien species would create nothing but havoc in the village.

It should have occurred to Gladys that her pretty, detached stone cottage would be slap-bang in the middle of the action. Alas, it did not. She responded to a knock on her front door to find a very smart-looking gentleman on her doorstep. He was holding a clipboard and letting his gaze pass over the front of her cottage. He was smiling. Gladys was completely taken aback – not least because she was dabbed all over with calamine crusts. 'It isn't contagious,' she blurted out before he had the chance to open his mouth.

'Shame, it's rather fetching,' he said, smiling broadly.

'Can I help you?' she inquired, somewhat brusquely.

'You've heard about our adaptation of Jane Austen's *Emma*, I take it?'

'I have, I only hope it will be as good as *Pride and Prejudice*.'

'I'm sure you won't be disappointed. I'm here to discuss any concerns you might have about the BBC using your village as a location, and to offer you a contract.'

'A contract?'

'To film the outside of your cottage. We do pay, you know.'

'I didn't know.'

'In fact, if you would agree to giving us active use of your front door, the amount would be increased considerably.'

'Active use of my front door! What on earth do you mean?'

'For the characters to enter and exit. All the inside scenes are shot in the studio, of course.'

'But my front door leads straight into my sitting room.'

'That wouldn't be a problem; the props team would block it off inside for the duration of the scene.'

'But you surely don't expect me to move out?'

'No, no. We will be giving everybody in the village a filming schedule and asking them to keep sets clear while the cameras are rolling. We have security people to stop outsiders wandering into the area.'

'So, I could stay in my kitchen at the back, out of sight.'

'That shouldn't be a problem. You would not be able to make any noise whatever, or be tempted to peek out of your front windows.'

'Why would I want to peek out of my front windows?'

'To see what's going on?' suggested the clipboard man. 'I trust you've put your name on the list for extras?'

'Don't be daft, of course not.'

'That's a pity, you'd be a great character.'

'What, Mrs Blobby?' Gladys started to laugh and the clipboard man laughed with her. 'It's because you lot are here I look like this. A nervous reaction.'

'Oh dear, I'd better see if we can add a little compensation to your award.'

'That would be nice. I could certainly do with the money, my roof needs some attention. Now, let me sign this contract before I change my mind.'

Gladys was dozing in the easy chair when the sound of the front door slamming followed by a string of strong expletives roused her. She recognised the voice: it belonged to Thomas Channing, currently Mr Knightley, she'd been informed. When the cursing stopped the groaning started and she knew he had sustained some sort of injury. She tiptoed out of the kitchen and across her sitting room to where a square had been partitioned off around the front door to protect her privacy. She put her face to a crack in the corner of the chipboard. 'Are you all right?' she inquired.

'No, I'm not! I've taken a frigging great chunk out of my sodding finger.'

'I'm very sorry. No need to swear at me, though, it isn't my fault.'

A moment or two later a knock came on the back door. Gladys knew it would be him and, amazingly, felt completely calm when she opened it.

'Good afternoon, Mrs…'

'Doyle, Gladys Doyle.'

'May I call you Gladys?'

'If you feel that swearing at me like a trooper entitles you to.'

'Look, I'm really sorry about that. Not very gentleman-like language was it?'

'Not very,' agreed Gladys.

'It's just that I don't really *do* pain.'

'Oh, for goodness sake! I don't really *do* many things, but have to put up with them and try not lose my rag with other people.'

'Forgive me, Gladys, please, I didn't mean to offend you. I'm Tom Channing, by the way.'

'I know who you are,' snapped Gladys.

Shirtiness didn't sit well on Gladys. Thomas Channing had apologised and seemed genuine enough; besides, he was bleeding quite badly. 'I have a first aid kit,' she told him.

'Some medical attention would be much appreciated.'

'You'd better come in, and don't bleed on my clean floor.'

Thomas Channing headed straight for the easy chair and dropped into it heavily. He offered Gladys his injured finger for inspection. 'Um, nasty, how did you do it?'

'Shut the door on it.'

'Are the film people waiting for you?'

'No, we've packed up for the day; the light is a bit poor.'

Gladys cleaned her guest's wound and dressed it neatly in a proper finger bandage. 'Wow, look at that!' declared the actor, 'like a little stocking.'

'Mr Channing, you know as well as I do that it looks more like a cotton condom for a man without much to brag about.' Thomas Channing burst out laughing and laughed long and hard. What a breath of fresh air this little woman was, with her chubby cheeks covered in a blotchy rash!

'Fancy a cuppa?' inquired Gladys.

'Certainly would. Please call me Tom.'

Tom looked about the rather cluttered kitchen, so warm and full of character. 'This is really nice and cosy,' he said.

'It suits me well enough. I expect yours is all stainless steel and straight edges.'

Yeah, sterile and heartless. A bit like the wife, he thought, sinking deeper into the chair and letting his head rest against the wing.

Gladys suspected he'd drift off to sleep the instant he finished his mug of tea. The mug he held protectively between his palms, as if it were precious.

Tom slept soundly and Gladys set about making the pastry for the steak and kidney pie she proposed to have for tea. A small part of her hoped that one of her female friends would drop in to witness the unique domestic scene being played out in her kitchen, but that would dispel the magic, and she was glad when no callers turned up.

She popped her pie into the oven, sat down at the table and regarded Thomas Channing with a discerning eye. He was a good-looking fellow. No longer in the first flush of youth, early thirties, she guessed, and maturing nicely. His long legs were stretched out across the floor in his breeches and knee-high boots. His head suddenly lolled sideways and his dark hair fell about his face making him look vulnerable, childlike, almost. Thespian or not, Gladys decided she liked him.

The pie was browning nicely by the time he woke up. His nose started twitching. 'Oh, God, that smells so good.'

'We can share it, if you like, there's plenty.'

'Really! I would love to share your pie, Gladys.' Tom's response was charged with saucy innuendo and Gladys liked him all the more for it.

The last time Gladys had seen an expression of such utter delight on a man's face was when her son, Greg, told her Sarah was pregnant again.

'It's no big deal,' she said, placing his plate before him.

'My dear, Gladys, I beg to differ. It is a *very* big deal.'

Tom attacked his food as if he were starving. 'Don't they feed you actors?' asked Gladys.

'Yes, we're staying in that country park place, can't remember the name, just outside the village.'

'Hartington Manor. You need to take out a mortgage to eat there, or so I've heard.'

'Culinary art, Gladys, that's what they serve. Now this, this is real food, the sort that fills you up and makes you feel really good inside.'

Gladys smiled at her guest fondly; she was sure he would drop in again for a cup of tea and some supper before the production came to an end. Most of her visitors were old biddies like her. Greg and his family made the trip from their home in Plymouth at least once a month, and she made the train journey every year in order to spend the Christmas holiday with them, but generally she was pretty short on young, interesting company. Thomas Channing had brightened her day no end.

'Apple crumble and custard for pudding, Tom,' she announced.

THE BED

Marge Baker wasn't jealous by nature. She didn't take much notice of what others did or had or looked like. If people were friendly and pleasant she was drawn to them, regardless of their social or financial status. If not, she gave them a wide berth. She was utterly content with her life and everyone and everything in it.

But then her dear, thoughtful husband, Harold, took her to a country manor for the weekend to celebrate her sixtieth birthday and she came upon something that made her green with envy: a bed.

The gentleman of the house, who was also the owner and manager, showed Harold and Marge to their accommodation: a very large room with a view of the lake and the glorious countryside beyond.

'This is absolutely lovely!' declared Marge, gazing out of the window.

'It certainly is,' agreed Harold.

'And I can guarantee you the best night's sleep you have ever had in this brand new, state of the art water bed,' informed the manager.

'How exciting, I've heard about those!'

'Mrs Baker, this bed is a feat of modern engineering. It was designed, at considerable cost, specifically for this room. It is, as you see, queen-size with a cantilevered, remote controlled mechanism that allows it to rise to a height of six feet.'

Harold's expression posed the question in his mind. 'We have a hard-earned reputation to uphold, Mr Baker, cleanliness being at the top of the list. This bed cannot be moved; it will have to be dismantled when maintenance is required, for that reason access is essential. It is possible to vacuum beneath it, when extended to its full height, without even stooping; our cleaning staff love it. The mattress is thermostatically controlled to heat or cool as desired, and the base can be adjusted to almost any position. I hope to install one in every room eventually.'

'But how is it supported?' Harold wanted to know. 'I can't imagine it has been bolted to the wall, thick as the walls undoubtedly are.'

'Indeed not. No, instead of struts, a sheet of tempered metal has been locked into the floorboards, and the area around it raised with suitable panels of timber. All hidden beneath the carpet.'

'I expect you had to shave a good deal off the bottom of the door.'

'No, luckily, the gap was rather too large before.'

'Never mind all that,' said Marge. 'I can't wait to get in it.'

When the manager had gone, Marge arranged herself on the bed in a variety of attitudes. In terms of comfort, the bed was off the scale. Pure heaven! 'I want it,' she told Harold.

'What now! Shouldn't we think about having dinner first?'

'Not *that*, a bed, a bed exactly like this one, just imagine it, Harold?'

'But it's huge, it would completely fill our bedroom. Anyway, I bet it cost a bomb.'

'I don't think I've ever wanted anything so much in all my life,' murmured Marge wistfully. 'Still, you are right, not a sensible idea.'

Harold fell into a state of deep contemplation for several minutes, Marge could almost hear his brain ticking over. 'Bugger sensible, I'll look into it. If we can afford it, Marge, you can have your bed.'

All the furniture except for two small bedside tables had to be moved out of the room to make space for the bed. The people from the water bed company set it up and gave Harold and his son instructions on how to fill the mattress.

The yellow hose was attached to the tap on the garden wall; it snaked up the front of the house and disappeared in through the bedroom window. The neighbours were agog and full of theories: a fire of some sort being the most logical, if not the most perverse. Harold's son was at the top of the ladder holding the hose. He put an end to the speculation by trumpeting, 'Mum and Dad have a new water bed, viewing between nine and five, weekdays, and ten till three on Sundays.'

'Shut up!' hissed Harold from the bedroom, 'these are *our* neighbours.'

'I know. Nosey buggers.'

The family arrived en masse to see the bed during the evening. The grandchildren wholeheartedly agreed that Marge was *dead cool* because she owned such a fun piece of equipment. They bounced all over it, filling the house with squeals of delight. Perhaps grandma would acquire a super-sonic stair lift next. *Wow! Dead, dead cool!*

Putting a sheet on the mattress proved a much more challenging task than Marge had anticipated: it was akin to trying to dress a squirming hippo as it emerged from a water hole. She decided she would order a couple of the recommended stretchy fitted ones especially designed for the job. A lesson here: when you've nearly cleared out your savings account to buy a bed, you shouldn't stint on the linen.

Harold was engrossed in something on television Marge, however, couldn't wait to try out the bed. She carefully positioned her pillows and dropped back, rather heavily, against them. They were promptly catapulted into the air and landed squarely on her face. Undeterred, she repeated the procedure, this time holding the corners as she slowly lowered her head and shoulders onto them.

The bed seemed to swallow her up. When she tried to remove her slippers, her feet shot up and she was beset by a fit of the giggles so debilitating that she remained in this position – an upturned crab – for a full two minutes. Eventually, she regained sufficient composure to consider her next move. Rolling onto her side, she cast off the slippers and shied them at the wall. One got caught on the photograph of Harold's mother, completely covering her face, 'That's better,' Marge mumbled.

Marge now, more or less, on her own side of the bed, reached for her book that was on the cabinet. Easier said than done! When she contrived to get close enough to grab it, the bed gurgled merrily and thwarted every attempt with a succession of ripples. 'Ship to shore,' she said, starting to giggle again.

She managed to catch the corner of the volume between her thumb and forefinger and drew it towards her. It opened, the bookmark slipped out, the book disappeared into the gap between the bed and cabinet and she was left with the cover in her hand. 'Shouldn't be reading such filth, anyway,' she said, tossing the cover in the air and quickly falling asleep from her exertions.

Harold always enjoyed a pint or two when he was watching television. He never became in any way objectionable when mellowed with drink, just somewhat lollopy, as if his bones had been disconnected. He was a big, heavy man and this presented Marge, compact and five feet nothing, with a few problems from time to time.

Marge was sound asleep when Harold landed on the bed. His arrival created not so much a *gurgling ripple effect* as a *tidal wave* as Marge was unceremoniously ejected from her nest. Harold fumbled about the bed for his wife, then inquired, 'Where are you, Marge?'

'On the bloody floor by the radiator, you silly sod.'

'Oops!'

Because Harold was twice Marge's weight and then some, she kept sliding onto his side of the bed. She was, unfortunately, in no mood for carnal activity, the very thing, quite obviously, on Harold's mind. 'What is wrong with this bed?' she wanted to know. 'It isn't a bit like the one at the manor.'

'Needs more water to firm it up. I'll see to it tomorrow.'

'Talking of water…' Using Harold as if he were spongy

stepping stones in a stream, Marge clambered over him to access the bathroom.

The bed, now fully firmed-up, was so comfortable that Harold awoke with a start when the alarm went off. Marge didn't wake up at all. She still hadn't roused by the time he left for work.

Marge opened her eyes to look at the radio alarm. It wasn't there, neither was the cabinet. She rolled onto her back and found that she was so close to the ceiling that when she lifted her head her hair brushed against it. Shock jolted her brain into gear and processed the fact that she had accidentally activated the remote control by leaning on it. She swept the mattress with her arm to locate the handset, last seen beside her pillow, and found nothing. Her breaths now started to come in rapid bursts, for she was intensely claustrophobic.

Peering over the edge of the bed, she saw the handset on the floor. She was gripped by a panic attack so severe she truly believed a cardiac arrest was imminent. She lay back and took long, deep breaths and tried to organise her thoughts, form them into some sort of workable plan, but instead burst into tears and started to pray. 'God, please don't let me die up here, forgive me for wanting this bloody bed. Help me, please, please help me!'

Marge was in a sort of stupor when she heard the unmistakable sound of a ladder coming to rest against the windowsill. She burst into tears again. Then it struck her that this was not somebody on a rescue mission – who the devil knew she needed rescuing? – but the window cleaner. She crawled – commando-style – to the side of the bed nearest the window, threw out her right arm and grabbed the curtain rail for support, then ripped back the curtains with her left hand, before waving it around in a frantic attempt to convey the message that she needed urgent assistance.

Marge knew that as long as she lived she would never forget the expression on poor Mr Jarvis's face when he looked up and saw her there. For a horrible moment or two she thought he would topple off the ladder and fall to the ground. Mercifully, he managed to steady himself and demanded to know what the hell she thought she was doing scaring the crap out of him like that.

Then he reached into his pocket, drew out his mobile phone and shouted at her to give him Harold's number.

If Marge had been expecting sympathy from the family, she was to be sorely disappointed. The account of her traumatic experience elicited nothing but unfettered hilarity. 'If the bed hadn't risen to its full height I'd have been flattened, squashed to a pulp,' she told them indignantly.

'Ugh, gruesome, or what?' said one grandson

'Yeah, think of all that blood and guts spilling onto the floor,' said another.

'It would probably have been on the news. *Grannie had to be rolled up to fit in her coffin,*' said a third.

'Well, thank you all for your concern,' snapped Marge.

'Chill, Grandma,' advised Chloe, Marge's oldest granddaughter. 'It put your survival skills to the test and proves you are much tougher that you thought you were. You must think of it as a character building incident, an adventure.'

'Perhaps,' conceded Marge, wondering how she could have failed to notice that Chloe was no longer a whining adolescent, but a sensible human being.

'Can I write a story for school about what happened, Grandma,' inquired Kerry, Marge's middle granddaughter, 'it'll make everyone laugh.'

'Why not? You've all had a good laugh at my expense.'

'Mum, you would laugh like a lunatic if someone told you the same tale,' said Mark, Marge's son.

'You nearly wet yourself laughing when granddad sat in the old deckchair and the canvas ripped,' reminded grandson number one.

'Yeah, he got his ass stuck and dad had to saw the deckchair off, remember?' inquired grandson number two.

'I do,' said Marge, now shaking with laughter.

'Mum, you are not thinking of getting rid of the water bed?' asked Marge's daughter.

'Good heavens, no, I haven't slept like that since I was a little girl. I'll just make sure the fiasco I had today won't be repeated.'

'You can never be sure of that,' said Chloe. 'I mean, there could be a mechanical failure, or the batteries in the remote might run out – '

'Stop!' bawled Marge.

'I know, Granddad could fit a rope ladder to the side of the bed, just in case,' suggested Kerry.

'What about a parachute?' Marge glared at her youngest grandson, but chuckled just the same.

'Or a bungee jump rope?'

'Or a trampoline by the side of the bed, that would be fun?'

The ideas went on and on, getting more and more ridiculous, until everybody was doubled up with laughter. Eventually, Harold and Marge ushered the tribe out of the front door and climbed the stairs to bed, totally exhausted.

Neither noticed that the base of the bed was almost on the floor – the position from which Harold had pulled Marge, sobbing with relief, earlier that day. They threw themselves on the mattress and landed in a tangled heap in the middle. The mattress issued a succession of loud whooshing sounds with the impact, and reared up angrily either side of them in complaint. The duvet folded itself around them, and thus they remained until dawn.

THE COIN

Esther's granddad could give a laudable rendition of the old Flanagan and Allen classic, *Underneath the arches*. As a small girl she loved to hear him sing it, but the words always made her sad. When she was tucked up in bed, warm and safe, she would think of the people who lived on the streets with cobblestones for beds and pavements for pillows. Perhaps that's why she had grown up tolerant of the vagrants, beggars, homeless, dispossessed, junkies and alcoholics she encountered daily on her way to the office. They were strewn about the cold floor of the pedestrian underpass like so much human litter. Esther, however, thought of them as life's casualties.

More than once she had offered a pre-packed sandwich, or piece of fruit to a down-and-out, only to have it thrown back at her. On one occasion she had been lightly scalded by a violently rejected take-away cappuccino. She had learned the hard way that most of these people just wanted money. Money for the next fag, the next fix, the next drink, the next journey into oblivion. So she set aside a one pound coin that she popped into a deserving hat as she walked through the underpass. It made her feel better, a debt to society, perhaps. It was a fitting gesture for someone whose philosophy was, *there, but by the grace of God, go I.*

For the past few weeks, however, her benevolence had become selective; there was a new deserving cause on the block in the shape of a young man, an enigmatic young man. He was like every representation she had ever seen of Jesus, physically, and his eyes exuded love and compassion. And something else: extreme sadness. He never spoke, somehow he didn't need to. He was considerate, too, for he drew in his body to occupy the least amount of space: a concertina of long, lean limbs.

She knew she was wrong to favour him, unchristian, even, but couldn't seem to help herself. It might go against her when she *shuffled off this mortal coil*, but he was so beautiful! One smile from him put her in good spirits for the rest of the day.

Today was going to be different. Today, Esther intended to forgo the smile and give her coin to the derelict. He always sat at the far end of the underpass, and she frequently tripped over his outstretched legs when approaching the steps.

Esther was never grumpy when she awoke, even if Bill had disturbed her with his snoring. But this morning he had put her in a bad mood by morphing into a two year-old at the breakfast table. He was so distracted by an article he was reading in the newspaper that he overfilled his teacup. Then, instead of placing the teapot on the stand, he set it down on his bowl of cereal, cracking the bowl and soaking the tablecloth with muesli and chopped up banana. Esther could not face coming home to the mess, so quickly cleared it up before she left the house to catch her bus.

Esther was getting onto the bus when she realised she'd forgotten to take a pound coin from her 'poor pot'. She sat down and drew her purse from her handbag. She had only copper and the shiny, new pound coin her little granddaughter had given her in a card the previous weekend for her birthday. 'It my own money, Gamma,' the tot had proudly informed her.

Esther was unashamedly sentimental, but a visit to the bank would put matters right, so she transferred the coin to her coat pocket. Taking one's purse out in a public place was a risky business, these days.

She threw *him* a glance and marched purposefully on her way. She suddenly felt a gentle heat, clear and perfectly round, in the small of her back. She knew it was because he was watching her, but she hastened on.

The derelict thrust out his hand to snatch the coin from her grasp, but she couldn't let it go. 'Sorry,' she muttered, then ran back to *him*, dropped the coin in *his* hat and hurried away. He said something, a word, a foreign word. It was a blessing, she was certain.

The traffic was reduced to a crawl. The passengers on the bus were muttering and grumbling and then somebody's mobile stared to ring, and then another and another. The news spread about the bus in a trice: the road had collapsed onto the underpass in the city centre. The talk turned to bombs, devices and bloody terrorists, and the business of getting to work on time was of no moment whatsoever.

They finally reached their destination via various diversions. Esther alighted from the bus and walked towards the underpass. The area was cordoned off, naturally, but the devastation could not be concealed. An articulated lorry straddled the gap where the road had given way, but there appeared to be no other vehicles involved. A police officer was viewing the scene. 'I've been in the force all my working life,' he said, 'but I've never seen anything like this before. That artic! It's so well positioned it could almost be a bridge. And the traffic, where was all the traffic when the road collapsed? It's always teeming at that time of day.'

'What about the poor people in the underpass,' said Esther.

'Well, we won't know about pedestrian casualties until they've shifted that lot.' The police officer pointed at the huge pieces of concrete with bent, metal rods sticking out of them at all angles. Underneath was rubble, nothing but rubble. Esther had never experienced a more acute sense of desolation.

Esther had been a secretary-cum-receptionist – because Mr Bailey was too stingy to employ two people where one would do – to the funeral director for twenty years. Her husband maintained she knew more about dealing with the dead than Mr Bailey did. This was simply not true; Mr Bailey was very skilled in his work. It was the living he had problems with. He was not emotionally equipped for the task; he sadly lacked the common touch.

Mr Bailey didn't know it, and wouldn't have believed it anyway, but more than half of his business came because Esther was in his employ. She knew how it felt to lose somebody you loved, how the bottom fell out of your world and you believed you would never find a footing again. She knew how it felt to lose a parent, because to lose a parent was to lose one's past. And she knew, too, how it felt to lose a child. Oh, God, did she know how that felt! Esther was of an age where she'd been touched by personal grief in so many ways. But, through her own sorrow, she'd learned how to reach out to other people. That made her invaluable to the business. It was a pity Mr Bailey didn't see her true worth. Still, it didn't matter to her, she loved her work and as long as he paid her a reasonable wage, she would not quit her position in his office.

Notwithstanding this, today was a very bad day for him to chide her for tardiness. She hung her coat on the stand in the corner of her office, and turned to find him tapping the face of his watch. 'Good afternoon, Esther.' Esther hated sarcasm and she was upset, extremely upset.

'You are sodding lucky I'm here at all. If Bill had dropped me off on his way to work, you might have had the pleasure of dressing me in one of your tacky bloody shrouds.'

'Oh, dear, Esther, I can see you are in a state about something. What on earth has happened?'

'The road has fallen onto the pedestrian underpass in the city centre; why don't you switch the radio on?'

'My goodness, I had no idea; I am so sorry to hear that.'

'Never mind, you might get a bit of business out of the tragedy, you never know.'

'Esther!'

'I'm sorry, that was uncalled for.'

'Do you know somebody who is likely to have been hurt, or, um, killed, in this incident?'

'Maybe, I didn't exactly know him.'

'I'm really sorry, Esther. You would never be late without good cause, I do know that.'

'It's okay.'

'Would you like to go home?'

'No, I'd rather be here.'

'Very well, I have a bod… a person to attend to in the Chapel of Rest. Esther?'

'Yes?'

'Do you really think my shrouds are tacky?'

Nobody was able to comment on the incident in the city centre without throwing in the word *miracle*. Two lads had been rescued from a pocket of concrete in the wreckage, and neither had serious injuries.

But what had happened to *him?* The miracle left in its wake a mystery, a huge mystery. His clothes had been found in a neat pile beneath the rubble, but his hat was gone and so was he.

Speculation peaked and abated, and new, more pressing issues found their way into the local headlines. But Esther didn't forget. She found herself looking for him in shop doorways, the bus station, train station, parks, and in crowds. It was a bereavement of sorts, like losing something that was never yours in the first place.

The coin was on the little cabinet beside the bed, shining in the glow of the lamp. 'Is that your pound, Bill?' she inquired.

'No, it was on your pillow, I put it there.' Esther picked up the coin and noticed a tiny blob of Blu Tack on it, no bigger than a pinhead. She placed it in the palm of her left hand and wiped it clean with a tissue. Suddenly, she started to feel heat coming from it, gentle heat. She closed her fingers around it tightly. This was the coin Holly had given her, the coin she had given *him*.

The warmth of the coin gradually travelled up her arm and spread into her body, feeding her soul, filling her heart with an exquisite sense of peace. She could stop looking for *him* now, *he* was with her, *he* would always be with her.

THE FIX

When the weather is fine, I take the path through the arboretum that separates the village where I live from the one where I work in the small post office-cum-general-store. It is not only a short cut, but provides a wonderfully uplifting start to my day before being incarcerated for eight hours in my tiny glass-enclosed cubicle.

The early morning mist is rising from the lake like a filigree pall. Squirrels dart up and down the tall trees and rabbits scamper about in the long, dewy grass with only their ears betraying their presence. Nature is putting on a show. Its magic is not lost on me.

It is now five minutes past five and my shift is over. The sky is dark, ominous; I pull on my raincoat and make haste to leave the store. I zip up my coat as I walk briskly through the arboretum and ferret in my bag for my tiny, retractable umbrella, but I cannot outrun the downpour.

I hear him before I see him, the walker. His steps quicken as the rain suddenly starts to pelt down in the form of hailstones, pinging off the sleeves of my raincoat and stinging my bare legs. He stops beside me and smiles a sort of crooked smile, quite sexy, I think. 'Why don't you wait out this shower in my cabin,' he suggests.

'I beg your pardon?'

'My name is Sebastian, I am a security guard here. The cabin is well equipped, I can make us a nice cup of tea.'

'Okay,' I reply.

What on earth is wrong with me, have I lost my mind? Sebastian might work in the arboretum, and he might have a sexy, crooked smile, but he *is* a complete stranger.

The cabin *is* well equipped. It has two upholstered reclining chairs, a television set, a fridge, a cooker and a desk with all manner of surveillance equipment on it. 'You wouldn't believe how many people turn up during the night with picks and spades to steal our plants and trees,' he tells me. 'That's why they took on somebody to cover a six pm to six am shift; it's not everybody's cup of tea, but it suits me fine.'

He hands me a mug of tea and a huge piece of carrot cake – I absolutely adore carrot cake. I tuck into the cake with relish and sip the tea which is exactly as I like it, steaming hot and not too strong. Halfway through my tea, I start to feel a little drowsy, pleasantly drowsy, and rest my head against the wing of the chair.

I have somehow become detached from myself, I have left my body and floated into the corner of the cabin.

There is another *me* sitting in the chair now, fast asleep and looking extremely peaceful.

Sebastian has morphed into another being. His impossibly long fangs extend beyond his chin and red, piercing eyes, blaze from his ashen face, with jet black, slicked-back hair reaching well past the collar on his scarlet-lined cape. He is the scariest incarnation of Bram Stoker's Dracula I have ever seen, yet I am not afraid, just utterly fascinated.

I wait for him to lunge at the *other me*, to sink his fangs into the soft skin on my neck, but instead he very gently straightens my arm, inserts a syringe into a vein on the inside of my elbow and fills it with my blood. He then gently dabs the spot and holds a piece of gauze over it until it ceases to bleed. He then expels the blood into shot glass and drinks it. 'Ahhh… delicious,' he exclaims, dabbing his mouth with a tissue.

I find myself back in my own body, slowly coming out of the most blissful sleep. 'You are not dead,' I inform him.

'That's true.'

'But I thought vampires were corpses who rose from their graves at night to feast on the blood of the living.'

'That's just folklore, my dear.'

'I see. I'm Rachel, by the way.' I have no idea why I

felt disposed to tell him my name. 'What exactly are you, then?'

'I'm an authentic vampire, Rachel, the real deal, you might say. I require a small amount of blood merely to maintain good health. I store it in my freezer, but it is so much nicer when it's fresh, the perfect temperature. Every now and then, if the opportunity arises, I give myself a little treat; I hope you don't mind.'

'Uh…I don't think so… no… no, I don't mind at all. I've often thought about becoming a blood donor but never quite had the nerve. I must rethink the situation, I mean, the nurses won't look half as terrifying as you, I daresay.'

'No, indeed, angels of mercy, the lot of them.'

'Tell me, does it just happen, the change, I mean, or can you control it?'

'Vampires need blood, just like people with a headache need an aspirin or some other pain-relieving drug. However, I have the mental capacity to avoid transition, it's a matter of willpower.'

'Are you a regular guy when you accost would-be tree thieves?'

'Absolutely not, a sighting of me scares the shit out of them, they never dare return.'

'They could report you to the police.'

'And say what? "Oh, officer, while I was in the arboretum looking for a Tiger tail spruce to steal for my front garden, a vampire appeared and frightened me half to death." That might give them the impression you were either on something highly illegal or completely mad.'

'It would sound a little strange, I grant you.'

I had heard that vampires had hypnotic, sensual powers. Well, that must be true or I'd have been out of the cabin door and sprinting towards my home like athlete by now. Sebastian had a lovely voice, soft and soothing, so easy on the ear.

'Please tell me more about vampires?'

'Well, there are more of them about than you might imagine. You almost certainly pass several on the street every day and think nothing of it. They probably don't have the capacity to alternate from one being into another as do I, none-the-less, they still need a daily fix.'

'And could become persuasive, even violent, in order to get it?'

'I suppose so, if they were desperate for fresh blood.'

'Blimey!'

'I understand vampires were first conceived during times of plague and pestilence in European countries, when hundreds of thousands of people were wiped out, whole communities, sometimes.' Informed Sebastian.

'Some evil force had to be blamed, and the folklore of vampires was born. Those with vivid imaginations turned them into monsters with insatiable appetites. They were a gift to literature and the film industry. Would you care for another cup of tea?'

'Yes, that would be nice, then I must go home, my little dog will be wanting his supper.'

'I will escort you out of the park. I will naturally return to my human self before doing so.'

'That might be best. It's possible my elderly next-door neighbour will come looking for me, he sometimes does that if I'm late getting home, he worries so and suffers from palpitations.'

'He is right to worry, Rachel. You encounter some very weird individuals wandering about in the arboretum at times.'

THE SHED SQUATTER

She knew he was dead the instant she awoke. The coldness of his body had penetrated the mattress and spread to her side of the bed. She slowly sat up, but didn't turn to look at him. She didn't doubt that he would be wearing the disgruntled expression he had always worn. There was no reason to suppose that a visit from the grim reaper had given him cause for cheer.

She eased herself out of bed with all the haste her stiff, aged bones would allow, lifted her dressing gown from the hook on the back of the door and pulled it on, then pushed her feet into her slippers. Only now did she look at him, Arthur Cropper, her husband for sixty-two years.

His eyes were glassy beneath half-closed lids, his mouth set in the drooping crescent of a frown, his wrinkled skin, alabaster pale. With his hands clasped upon his chest he looked like a statue of himself.

On the landing, she took a couple of deep breaths before negotiating the stairs. The thought popped into her head that she could now sell this house, the marital home, if she wished. A nice little bungalow or flat somewhere nearby would suit. She wouldn't want to live far from her neighbours.

Her brain could not even start to process the fact that fate had pointed its withering finger at Arthur and not her. She didn't immediately phone the doctor, or notify the family, and she didn't cry; instead she went downstairs, put the kettle on and made a pot of tea.

Beryl saw the doctor's car arrive from her sitting room window. She made her way to the front door. 'Take your time, Mrs Cropper, don't risk another fall,' he shouted through the letterbox.

'I won't, Doctor.'

The doctor told Beryl how sorry he was for her loss, then went upstairs to the bedroom. He needed to confirm that Arthur Cropper was dead – people had been known to make mistakes when in a state of shock.

Beryl was in the kitchen by the time he came down. 'We will need to establish the cause of death, then a certificate will be issued. I imagine it was his heart, how old was he? I couldn't find any records for him at the surgery.'

'You wouldn't, he was never ill. He was a year older than me, eighty-one.'

'You have family?'

'Marcie in Canada and Robert in Australia. I wouldn't expect them to make the journey, they both work and have families.'

'But you have good neighbours, I'm sure.'

'The best, couldn't do without them.'

'Would you like me to inform anybody? It won't be long before an ambulance arrives, once I've made arrangements.'

'No, I will do it presently. Would you like a cup of tea? I made a fresh pot just before you arrived?'

'That would be nice, thank you. Would you like me to give you something to help you sleep tonight, Mrs Cropper?'

'No, I'll have a toddy or two, if I can't settle.'

'Well, ring me if you change your mind, I'll come as soon as I'm able. Shock has a way of catching up with you later.'

'I'm fine. You are a good man, Doctor, you've served me well since you joined the practice.'

'It's been a pleasure, not many of my patients are as easy to accommodate as you.'

'Arthur was a miserable bugger, you know.'

'Really!'

'I suppose I shouldn't speak ill of the dead.'

'Well, if it happens to be true.'

'Oh, it's true all right, by God, it's true. *Things are never so bad that they can't get worse,* that was his motto. Living with him seemed like a punishment, a sixty-two-year sentence. Perhaps it was.'

'I'm sure that's not true. Actually, my father said the same thing about my mother before he moved on to someone half his age. My mother still hasn't come to terms with the disgrace of it.'

'Perhaps *I* should find myself a toy boy?'

'Perhaps you should. I'd get the funeral over first, though, if I were you.'

The house felt so cold that Beryl decided to put a match to the fire. Perhaps she'd have central heating and double glazing installed, she'd always wanted it, but Arthur would not hear of it, the upheaval and cost absolutely forbade such unnecessary changes.

The prospect of being able to do whatever she liked now that she was on her own came to Beryl as something of a revelation. She hummed merrily as she put the kettle on. 'Perhaps I'll get the decorators in,' she said to herself, 'and a new kitchen and bathroom would be nice. I'll spend some money and have all the things I've always wanted. I am going to stay in this house and turn it into a little palace.'

Beryl looked at the coal scuttle, it was empty. The fire had been Arthur's province, not the cleaning, of course, that was a woman's job! She couldn't face coming home after the funeral and having to go outside in the dark to fill it from the bunker.

It was raining, just a steady pitter-patter, but the wind was swirling around within the high walls of the back garden. It was tearing at the plants and shrubs, tossing weak and dead foliage into the air where it was whipped away by angry gusts. Beryl padded towards the bunker, clutching the scuttle with both hands.

As she passed the shed, she thought she heard a sound coming from within: Margaret's cat, Squiggle, she didn't doubt. The animal was smart enough to find its way in for shelter, but not sufficiently enterprising to exit by the same route: a hole in the floor.

Beryl pulled the door open, and gasped in alarm when she saw the lad sitting in the corner with a couple of sacks pulled over his legs. 'What the devil are you doing here, boy!'

'I'm sorry, Mrs Cropper, I didn't mean to scare you.'

'How do you know my name?'

'Everybody from around here knows you. I'm Jamie Cook from Derby Street.'

'The bloody Cooks, I might have known, always up to no good.'

'I haven't done any damage or anything, I just needed somewhere to stay.'

'Stay! How long have you been here?'

'Only since Mr Cropper died, and only at night.'

'You've been sleeping in our shed for a fortnight?'

'Yeah, I'm *very* sorry.'

'And I'm getting *very* cold. You'd better come inside and explain yourself. Could you fill the scuttle and bring it indoors.'

'Yeah, course. Are you going to call the cops?'

'I don't know what I'm going to do.'

Beryl plonked a mug of hot chocolate on the kitchen table and Jamie wrapped his hands about it to warm them. The bruises on his face and neck were clearly visible now that he'd pulled back the hood on his fleece. He had an angry looking cut over his left eye, and the area around his right eye was as black as pitch. 'You hungry, lad?'

'Starving.'

'Beans on toast?'

'Beans make me fart.'

'Bacon sandwich?'

'Magic! Thanks, Mrs Cropper.'

The manner in which Jamie attacked the food suggested he hadn't eaten for quite a while, days maybe. Beryl threw four more rashers into the pan and buttered more bread. 'Got enough sauce, young man?'

'Plenty, thanks.'

Jamie finished his repast, sat back, patted his stomach and belched loudly. 'Sorry about that.'

'Better than a fart. Now, tell me who's been knocking you about.'

'Garth's son, Jude.'

'Garth?'

'My mother's new boyfriend, he and his thug of a son moved in a month ago.'

'Your mother can't have failed to notice what's going on.'

'She says it's time I toughened up. Jude is built like a brick wall, and with about as much sense, how am I expected to compete with that?'

'There's not much of you, I must say; I don't know about toughening up, you need fattening up. How old are you?'

'Seventeen.'

'Still at school?'

'College. I haven't been since I left home, though, bumming around the town during the daytime.'

'Somebody must have reported you missing, surely?'

'Dunno. Shouldn't think so, Garth wouldn't want the attention, too much to hide. I might send mum a text when I know what I'm gonna do.'

'What *are* you going to do?'

'Dunno.'

'Arthur would have called the police by now. I daresay they would have found you a safe place to stay, in a hostel or something. It's Arthur's funeral today, people will be coming here in an hour or so. I can't think about you at present, I have enough on my mind. You'd better stay in the shed until I get back. I'll give you some bedding, a couple of hot water bottles, a flask and some sandwiches, that'll keep you going. You must not come out while the mourners are here, understand?'

'Yeah, sure.'

'And if you need to pee, please don't do it on my plants.'

'Okay. I was sorry to hear about Mr Cropper.'

'Were you, Jamie?'

'It's what people do, isn't it, say they are sorry and that?'

'I'll bet you wouldn't have been sleeping in our shed if he'd been alive.'

'Not a bloody chance.'

Beryl's small sitting room was packed to capacity with mourners awaiting the arrival of the hearse and funeral cars. Thunderclouds rested on the rooftops of Beckford like a pall. Beryl gazed out of the sitting room window despondently, her immediate neighbours in the terrace, Shirley and Margaret, stood one either side of her. 'Bloody Arthur has put a curse on the weather an' all,' grumbled Margaret.

'I wouldn't have worn my best suit if I thought it was going to rain,' informed Shirley.

The hearse and funeral cars drew up near the plot where Arthur Cropper was to be buried, and the heavens opened. Umbrellas offered scant protection against the driving wind, the hail pinging off gravestones and turning the grass into a slippery mush. Numerous arms reached out to support Beryl as she slowly made her way to the site where Arthur was to be interred. The hole was already starting to fill with rainwater.

'The vicar needs to get a move on, or the coffin will float to the surface,' opined, Bert, Shirley's husband.

'Show some respect,' hissed Shirley.

'Typical Arthur, trust him to put the mockers on his own funeral,' added Eric, Margaret's husband.

'Shut up, you two, let's get through this with as much dignity as possible,' said Margaret, wagging her finger at the men.

The vicar might have been intoning the words of *Waltzing Matilda* for all the twenty or so mourners heard of them during the committal rites. Arthur was eventually lowered into the ground and those present bowed their heads for a final prayer, bowed their heads and thought of the food, drink and warmth awaiting them at *The Black Swan*.

Beryl knew that if she invited her immediate neighbours in for a post-wake drink, she'd never get rid of them. Try as she may, she couldn't get her uninvited shed tenant out her head. He hadn't looked at all well, and must be stiff with the cold by this time. 'You look so tired, Beryl', remarked Shirley.

'To be truthful, I am; it's been a long day.'

'Well, get in and put your feet up. Margaret and Eric can come into our place for a few bevvies. We gave Arthur a good send-off, didn't we?'

'Yes, we did,' agreed Beryl.

Beryl pulled on her raincoat, picked up her torch and let herself out of the back door. Jamie was curled up asleep in the blankets she'd given him; he roused when the draught from the door hit his face. 'Come into the house, lad, I've just built up the fire. Now, I'm sure it's the wrong thing to do, but you can sleep in my back bedroom tonight. If you murder me in my bed and steal my money, I will haunt you for the rest of your life.'

'Mrs Cropper, I wouldn't do anything to hurt you.'

'Well, let's hope that's true. I brought some nice food back from the funeral, you can have a bath and we'll have supper together. We can eat it on our laps by the fire.'

Jamie had had a bath and was sitting beside the fireplace in Arthur Cropper's armchair, tucking into a large plate of cold meat, sausage rolls and pickles. He was wearing a pair of the dead man's wincyette pyjamas, Beryl's pink dressing gown and her fluffy slippers.

He presented an image that was both comical and pathetic, but he looked so comfortable and happy in this moment that Beryl couldn't help but rejoice in his presence. They chatted easily for over an hour, making serious inroads into Arthur's Irish whiskey.

Beryl and Jamie had been in bed for over an hour. Beryl was trying to concentrate on the book she was reading, but Jamie was making funny snuffly noises. Beryl recognised the sounds: he was crying.

She settled back against her pillows. The tears she couldn't shed for her dead husband now fell thick and fast for the scrawny youngster in her back bedroom.

She got out of bed, shuffled to Jamie's bedroom door, and opened it just a little. 'Don't cry, son. You can stay here for the time being. If it works out maybe we can make it a permanent arrangement. You could help me about the house, we could help each other.'

'What, like a lodger?'

'Well, sort of, I suppose.'

'I think I have just fallen in love with you, Mrs Cropper.'

'That's nice to know; the doctor thought my idea of finding a toy boy had possibilities.'

Jamie's jaw dropped in horror and Beryl found it difficult to conceal her mirth. 'Um, when I said I thought

I had fallen in love with you...'

'So you didn't really mean it, you wicked fellow?'

'Yes, but... but I'm not... not sexually attracted to you.'

'Don't know that I fancy you much, either, Jamie Cook. It's the tall, muscular, rugged types with lots of thick hair I go for.' Beryl started to laugh and Jamie's face broadened into a wide grin.

'Bloody 'ell, you had me going there for a moment.'

'Let's try to get some sleep now we are both a bit happier, shall we?'

'Good night, Mrs Cropper.'

'Good night, son.'

'Mrs Cropper?'

'Um?'

'If you like tall, muscular, rugged men with lots of thick hair, how did you wind up with a little bald bloke like Mr Cropper?'

'He wasn't always bald, and, anyway, I was no beauty. He was a lovely dancer, Jamie, a regular twinkle toes; he made me feel like Ginger Rogers. I was very young, I expect I thought I could waltz my way into wedded bliss.'

'Right.'

Beryl wasn't going to tell Jamie there was a good reason, two good reasons in the event, why she'd agreed to marry Arthur Cropper: her twins, Marcie and Robert Arthur had never noticed how very like Bernard, his best man, Robert was: tall, muscular and rugged, with masses of thick dark hair. It wouldn't have occurred to him to suspect Beryl of a moral slip with a married man, she just wasn't that sort of girl.

THE SLEEP THIEF

It didn't matter how much make-up Beth applied, she hadn't been able to conceal the dark rings beneath her eyes.

She felt her boss's gaze upon her as she sorted his mail. She'd been in his employ for six weeks and was fast approaching the end of her trial period.

'Had a rough night, Miss Lawrence?' His words were perfectly enunciated, as always, his tone betraying nothing of the sentiments behind them.

'I am so sorry, Mr Chambers, I had…'

'You slept badly, I fancy.' Did Beth detect a hint of sympathy in his voice, or was that just wishful thinking?

'Yes, I know I look dreadful.'

'Not dreadful, Miss Lawrence, just very tired; you had a late night?'

'No, an early night, actually. I had a nightmare and couldn't get back to sleep.'

'You are prone to nightmares?'

'Not nightmares generally, this is a recurrent nightmare, precisely rerun in every detail. I wake up in a terrible state, trembling, shaking, crying and nearly choking with fear, and an overwhelming sense of sadness. The worst thing is I am terrified of going back to sleep in case it returns. That's why I'm so tired.'

'I sincerely hope this nightmare has nothing to do with your work in my office. I'm afraid I have rather come to rely on your efficiency.'

'Absolutely not, I love my job here.'

'That is a relief. I believe we suit each other rather well. Your dedication to your duties is admirable for one so young. You are you twenty, or thereabouts?'

'Twenty-four.'

Beth felt her eyes welling with tears of relief. She drew a tissue from her jacket pocket and dabbed at them, fearing they would mingle with the excess of mascara on her lashes and course down her cheeks, painting her face with unruly black lines, *not a good look for a newly installed legal secretary.*

'I will have your contract of employment drawn up without delay, Miss Lawrence.'

'Thank you, Mr Chambers, thank you so much. I promise your faith in me will be well rewarded.'

Mr Chambers smiled, it was a lop-sided affair, but lent him a certain attraction Beth had hitherto not noticed. 'Now, Miss Lawrence, perhaps you would care to skip across the street to Starbucks: bring me a large cappucci-no and a Danish pastry, and whatever you fancy for yourself. A little celebration is called for, don't you think?'

Beth gave her boss his change and placed his coffee and cake on the desk before him. 'Pull up a chair and join me, Miss Lawrence, or may I perhaps call you Beth, when there are no clients around?'

'Of course.'

'You know, Beth, I, too, suffered from a recurrent nightmare. It quite wore me down, especially when I was studying for the bar. I would find myself in a lead-lined coffin. My limbs were immobilised by manacles and my head entrapped in a sort of metal brace, somewhat like a nag's scold. As the lid was about to be lowered onto the coffin by four very shabby peasants – all eerily reminiscent of family members – and darkness descended, I would wake up screaming, and sweating profusely. My flatmates soon tired of this unfortunate affliction and I was obliged to seek alternative accommodation.'

'How horrible! Were *you* afraid to go back to sleep?'

'Petrified. I briefly turned to the bottle in desperation. Beth, my dear, please do not pursue that route.'

'Do you still have this nightmare?'

'No, I have thwarted the sleep thief.'

'How?'

'I sought advice from various sources. Regular dreams, pleasant or otherwise, feed on a fertile imagination. They can be triggered by anything floating about in the unconscious mind. Recurrent nightmares, however, are quite a different matter. It is the opinion of a lady I spoke to, one who is involved in spiritual matters, that they indicate a warning, a message, or a premonition. They are, in her view, ignored at our peril.'

'Did you find out which of the three was yours?'

'Well, for a couple of weeks I thought my death might be imminent and went to great lengths to stay out of harm's way. Then my mother asked me to accompany her to the cemetery where my Grandfather is buried; she wanted to put flowers on his grave, as it would have been his birthday. It had been vandalised, completely trashed.'

'That is so spooky!'

'Yes… Oh dear, I daresay I've put the fear of God in you, Beth. That was thoughtless of me, I'm so sorry.'

'It doesn't matter.'

'The other, more conventional, advice I received was to analyse the content of your nightmare very thoroughly, confront your fears and share them with whoever is willing to listen. In that way they become diluted, are dispersed, and finally consigned to the past.'

That night Beth employed Mr Chamber's nightmare-ridding technique with such fervour she gave herself a blinding headache. She took two painkillers and eventually fell asleep. She dreamt about her boss: James Chambers, the tall, ramrod-straight, slim barrister with kind slate-blue eyes. He'd been so tender and passionate in the dream; she could still feel his arms wrapped tightly about her when the alarm went off at seven.

Two nights later *he* was back: the sleep thief. The nightmare followed its usual pattern. They were on the tube during the morning rush hour, people packed like sardines in a tin, but everything was somehow clearer than usual. The faces of her fellow commuters were more distinct, the general hubbub much louder, the smells stronger. And the man was even more imposing than before. He was tall, broad-shouldered, well-toned and fragrant with expensive aftershave. His facial features were so fine and perfectly proportioned that people openly gazed at him in admiration, or envy, perhaps.

He was close, so close that Beth could feel his breath on her forehead, feel his lower chest against her nipples, nipples that were tingling with anticipation and excitement. And then he spoke, his words deliberate and sexy as hell. 'Meet me on Waterloo Bridge this evening, at seven.' She let herself fall against him, felt desire running through him like electricity. And then, then…

She put her hand around the knife in her chest and felt the blood running through her fingers, warm and sticky. She raised her head and looked into his face: a face that was hard and cruel, with demented eyes that pierced the very depths of her soul. She started to feel darkness descend as she slipped to the ground...

She awoke, thrashing about and gasping for breath, her heart pounding inside her. But she wasn't crying. She was angry, very angry.

Beth was on her way to work. She was bright-eyed and bushy-tailed having enjoyed a long, nightmare-free period of blissful slumber. The tube was even more packed than usual and she had to force her way into the carriage. She grabbed the handrail as the doors closed behind her.

She didn't see him immediately as he had his back to her, and she was occupied with an attempt to tuck her shoulder bag under her arm for safety. When he turned, she froze, it was *him*, the sleep thief. She was face to face with him.

She shook her head in an effort to clear her mind; she must be still in bed, asleep, mustn't she? The woman beside her trod heavily on her foot, the heel of her stiletto catching one of Beth's tarsal bones and grinding deep into her flesh. She yelped with pain. 'I am so dreadfully sorry,' said the woman.

'Really, it's okay,' Beth muttered, a great wave of shock and fear rising through her, making her feel dizzy and weak.

The doors opened and the woman alighted amid a throng of travellers. Small spaces opened up here and there, but the carriage was still crowded. He came closer, much closer, just like in the nightmare. He would smile and rub against her and she would gaze into his eyes and fall under his spell. *Confront your fear, Beth, confront your fear.* She let her body fall against his and raised her eyes to look into his face.

'Waterloo Bridge tonight at seven, is it?' She inquired, slipping her hand into the inside pocket of his jacket and extracting the knife. 'Carrying an offensive weapon is a very serious crime, I believe,' she told him.

A female officer phoned James Chambers to explain why Beth had not turned up for work, that she was helping the police with their enquiries. 'Gosh, what a great boss you have, Beth! He said he would finish up some business that needed urgent attention then come and collect you.'

'Wow, that *is* thoughtful.'

'I expect he felt you'd rather not face travelling on the tube so soon after the incident. He has a lovely voice, what's he like?'

'Tall, skinny, thick mousy hair, but wonderful eyes,

compassionate eyes.'

'How old?'

'Early-thirties, or thereabouts.'

'Married.'

'No.'

'Gay?'

'I don't think so.'

'Kind men are invariably gay, unfortunately,' lamented the officer.

By the time Beth had given her statement, checked it and signed it, her boss had arrived. He was full of concern. 'What on earth has happened, Miss Lawrence? You have injured your foot, I see.'

'I was trodden on, but I'm fine. A policeman took me to A&E to have it checked out and dressed.'

'Are you going to tell me why you are here?'

'Yes, absolutely, you are the one person I most want to tell.'

'I'll take you for lunch and you can spill the beans.'

'That would be lovely, Mr Chambers.'

'You might like to call me James, when we are away from the office. I don't imagine you'd consider that inappropriate.'

'By no means.'

When James had fully acquainted himself with every

last harrowing detail of Beth's ordeal, he said, 'So a man known to the police in connection with a number of crimes against women has been finally apprehended?'

'Yes, so it would seem.'

'And all thanks to you.'

'Not really, you were the one who told me I must confront my fears, and that my nightmare might be a premonition.'

'I'm sure the police wanted to know how you became aware this man was carrying a knife?'

'I told them it was because the train was so packed, that I could feel it in his inside pocket when I was thrown against him; I said I was afraid he'd either harm me or somebody else, and that's why I relieved him of it. The truth would have made me sound completely deranged.'

'You'll probably get a commendation or something,' James's face broadened into a wide smile.

'Don't be daft.'

'Seriously, you mustn't underestimate the courage it took to do what you did.'

'In the nightmare he killed me on the tube, with dozens of people present to witness the crime.'

'In your nightmare, terror caused you to hasten your imminent death in order to draw you from its grip, to awaken you. In reality, he intended to meet you on

Waterloo Bridge and take you somewhere else to...'

'Stab me, and throw my body in the river.'

'Well, he didn't, Beth. Thanks to your grizzly dream.'

'I'll still be afraid to go to sleep in case I have that, or another nightmare.'

'The worst part for me after my nightmare was waking up. It's such a miserable, lonely business with no one to comfort you.'

'It doesn't have to be, I suppose.'

'No, indeed it does not. Beth, would you care to have dinner with me this evening, and afterwards, afterwards…'

'Yes, that would be lovely, James.'

'I have to get back to the office now, but I want you to go home and get some rest.'

'I'll meet you in town at, say, seven thirty.'

'Yes, that'll be fine, but I insist you take a taxi. Where shall I find you?'

'Anywhere but on Waterloo Bridge, James.'

STUCK

Daisy was cradling the vanity case in her arms; it was heavy, stuffed with expensive cosmetic products, she didn't doubt. Room 708 on the seventh floor was right at the end of a long, thickly carpeted passageway.

A lady wrapped in a large towel with a small, matching one around her head eventually responded to her rapping on the door. She gaped at Daisy, then her eyes were drawn to the bag. 'What are you doing with that!' she inquired, not too kindly.

'I found it in the taxi that drove me here. It has all your details on the airline tag.'

'And you didn't think to hand it in at reception?'

'One of the porters might have got into trouble if I had.'

'As they should, that was a very serious error; they ought to have checked the taxi thoroughly before loading my belongings onto their trolley. Anyway, the bag might have contained a device of some sort, my girl, you could have put yourself and others at risk.'

'It was passed through the metal detector.'

'Oh, and how did that come about?'

'My father is a part-time doorman here, he had it checked.'

'I see. Well, the porter should still be held to account.'

'The bag was right under the seat, if it hadn't been for the handle, I wouldn't have noticed it. I'm sorry if I did the wrong thing, Mrs Bancroft.'

Daisy held out the bag to the woman and made to move off. 'Just a moment… I was… I was more than a bit brusque with you; you have done me a great kindness and didn't deserve that. Please, do step inside. Do you have time for a drink, a coke or something?'

'Yes, my dad's shift ends at six, he's taking me out to dinner and then to see a show.'

'Oh, how wonderful, what show?'

'He wouldn't tell me; it's a secret.'

'A special occasion, my dear?'

'My birthday.'

'Let me guess, fourteen?'

'Sixteen.'

'Sweet sixteen, and pretty as a picture. Do you think your father would object to us sharing a glass of champagne to celebrate?'

'No, not at all.'

'Well, you make yourself comfortable. I'll throw some

clothes on and call service. It's a long flight from LA, I live there for half of the year to be near my sister; she's even older than I am, if you can imagine, and not in the best of health these days. I really needed a long soak in the bath to ease my weary bones, hence my appearance.'

'I think you look fine, Mrs Bancroft, and you smell great.' You smell of extreme wealth, thought Daisy.

'Thank you, dear. Please, do tell me your name?'

'Daisy, Daisy Mullins.'

'Ah, I think I know your father, he's called Jim, isn't he? Such a nice man, always so pleasant and courteous.'

'Thank you, yes he is; he's a carpenter, that's his real job, but he works from our garage at home, so he fits that in with working here; he's the best, my dad.'

Mrs Bancroft smiled sweetly at Daisy and disappeared through one of several doors in the hotel suite. Daisy suspected Mrs Bancroft lived here most of the time when she was in England; she probably had a place in the country, or on the coast, as well, a lot of posh, rich people did.

The hotel would refer to her accommodation as a suite, but it was more an apartment lacking a kitchen, although there were, of course, facilities for making hot drinks and a small fridge.

The view over London was breathtaking through the wall to wall glass doors that opened onto a wide veranda.

Mrs Bancroft entered the lounge fully dressed but devoid of make-up. 'Wonderful view, isn't it, Daisy?' she said, coming up behind Daisy.

'Yes, I love central London. I wish we could afford to live here.'

'Where *do* you live, dear?'

'Tooting, near the hospital: St George's; that's where my mum died last year, she had cancer.' Daisy wasn't looking for sympathy; she just liked including her mother in conversation, it kept her close, somehow.

Mrs Bancroft now put her hands on Daisy's shoulders and gave them a gentle squeeze. 'I am so sorry.'

'Life can be a bitch, sometimes, Mrs Bancroft.'

'You've got that right, Daisy, you certainly have.'

The champagne arrived and Mrs Bancroft asked Daisy if she would like to pop the plastic stopper. 'It'll go all over the place, then I'll feel dreadful,' said Daisy.

'Do you know what I do?' Daisy shook her head.

Mrs Bancroft opened one of the glass doors and Daisy followed her onto the veranda. 'I think of someone I utterly despise and pretend to shoot them from all the way up here.'

'That isn't very environmentally friendly,' scolded Daisy.

'I know, dear, but it's so much fun.'

They both started to giggle as they sipped the champagne, and then Mrs Bancroft suddenly said, 'You will visit me again, won't you, Daisy?'

'Yes, if you want me to.'

'More than anything. I'll give you my card with all my details on it, just call to make sure I'm here.'

Daisy was waiting for the lift to reach the seventh floor. Her dad would be looking at the big clock behind reception and excitedly anticipating her arrival. She couldn't wait to tell him all about Mrs Bancroft and how well they'd got on, at least, once Daisy's good intentions had been established.

If Daisy had not been so preoccupied, she might have paid more attention to the odd noises the lift was making as it descended from the floor above, and chosen another instead.

The doors opened; there was just one male passenger within. When Daisy registered the identity of the man, her legs turned to jelly, her heart started to beat wildly, and she thought she might actually pass out. This was not the sort of meeting with her idol she had conjured up in her daydreams.

'Hey, you okay, kiddo?' He put is hands on her upper arms to steady her. 'You've gone kinda pale.'

He was so close she could feel the warmth of his body, could smell his aftershave, the freshness of his breath. 'I'm so sorry,' she spluttered.

'Why are you sorry?'

'I don't know.' Daisy muttered.

'Well, I'm Robert, friends call me Bob, care to tell me your name?'

'Daisy, Daisy Mullins.'

'It's great to meet you, Daisy Mullins.'

'Great to meet you…soooo great.'

'Now that the introductions are done with, we should get down to the business of working out what those weird noises are coming from up there.' He inclined his head and pointed at the ceiling. Daisy followed his gaze and listened intently. 'What d'you think?' he inquired.

'I think we should get out at the sixth floor.'

'Very wise, I agree.'

Unfortunately, the lift dropped several inches then juddered to a halt just before they were plunged into darkness. 'Fuck, fuck fuck,' shrieked Robert, 'God, sorry for the language, Daisy.'

'Is your fucking phone fully charged,' inquired Daisy?'

'Dunno, kiddo,' he said with a chuckle.

'Mine is, if I can find it in my bag, if I can find my bag, I put it on the floor somewhere.'

'Are you scared of the dark, Daisy?'

'No, I got over that stuff when I grew up.'

'I am. I s'pose I never grew up, that probably accounts for quite a lot. You might need to hold my hand.'

Daisy couldn't bring herself to believe he was serious, but wasn't going to pass up a chance like this. She thrashed around a bit, found his hand and grasped it tightly, whilst jigging about in a bid to locate her bag.

It was fifteen minutes before a source of subdued lighting kicked in. Daisy and Robert had found their phones by this time and switched on the torches.

'What are we gonna do when we need to pee?' inquired Robert.

'Let's wait until we do, then we'll think of something.'

'Like what?'

'No idea.'

Daisy could not believe this was happening. Was she really sitting on the floor of a lift that had broken down, shoulder to shoulder, hand in hand with the film star who crept into her wildest fantasies when her mind wasn't otherwise occupied? Robert B Kendrick was acting like a regular guy! He might be just two years younger than her dad, but he was the sexiest man alive, and here he was talking about peeing.

They had been in the lift for nearly an hour; it was hot and airless. Daisy had taken off her sweater and Robert, his jacket. Things were going on in the lift shaft overhead. There were voices, Daisy heard her father's raised voice; he never raised his voice. He was frightened.

'Could you lift me up, Bob? I think I might be able to shift that panel in the ceiling. It might be a service hatch or an escape exit. I'm not very heavy.'

'Are you kidding? My sister has a teddy bear not much smaller than you, but not half as cute.'

Daisy was able to easily push aside the square panel in the ceiling. She put her hands on the frame that held it in place, slowly forced her arms into a brace position and hoisted her body through the aperture. 'Go careful, kiddo,' Robert called, as she disappeared from view.

Daisy's father was standing in the open lift doorway on the ninth floor. Light was flooding into the lift shaft from, as Daisy recalled, a reception area for conferences and social functions. 'Why are you all the way up there, dad?'

'The men couldn't fit their machine onto any of the other floors, it's huge.'

'What sort of machine?'

'A sort of crane with a huge hook on the end of it. Somebody is going to fix it onto the lift so that they can safely lower you to the ground floor. It won't be long now, sweetheart.'

'Why did the lift stop, what's going on?'

'There's a problem with the cable, nothing to worry about.'

Daisy focused her attention on the cable and let her eyes follow it until they lit on an area a couple of feet from where it was attached to the lift. Most of the thick metal strands that wound around each other and gave the cable its strength had come apart, they looked as if they'd been cut, but that couldn't be right, could it? Still, the rescue team seemed to know what they were doing; she and Bob would be out of here in no time at all.

'Are you in the lift on your own?' Daisy's dad asked her.

'No, Bob is with me.'

'Who's Bob?'

'Robert B Fenwick.'

'Not that American, the film star chap whose mug you've got stuck all over your bedroom walls!'

'Yep.'

'Is anyone else in the lift?'

'Nope, just us… It's okay, dad, he's great, everything is fine.'

'I'll bet,' muttered Jim Mullins.

Daisy saw a man put his hand on her father's arm and gently nudge him aside; his leg then swung out and landed firmly on the top rung of the metal ladder attached to the wall of the lift shaft. 'You need to get back inside now, darlin',' he said, 'it's going to get pretty noisy and bumpy; you must prepare yourselves.'

The noise from the motor drowned out any further advice from above. Suddenly, a resounding thud on the top of the lift caused it to shudder violently.'

'Shit! What was that?' screeched Robert, as they skidded across the floor in different directions.

'The hook on the end of the hoist, I expect. They are going to fix it to the lift and lower us to the ground floor, we just have to sit tight.'

'I will definitely need a pee now.'

'Well, don't pee on my new bag, my auntie Steph gave it to me for my birthday.'

'When was your birthday?'

'It's today, I'm sixteen.'

'What! Why didn't you tell me?'

'Would you have arranged a lift party with balloons and a cake?'

'I could have wished you *Happy Birthday*, at least.'

'So, do it now.'

'Happy birthday, Daisy.' Robert crawled across the floor and planted a hot, wet kiss on her cheek. I might not have had the cake, thought Daisy, but I've certainly had the icing.

The lift started to descend without warning; it

descended very quickly and jerkily, until it bounced to a halt. Robert was thrown into a corner, but Daisy was hurled against the doors. She yelled out in pain, turned deathly white, and blacked out.

A great number of people were gaping at the lift as Robert emerged with Daisy in his arms. Her father pushed through the throng to reach her. 'She's broken something, her arm by the look of it, I heard it crack as we were flung about all over the place,' announced Robert with unmistakable concern.

'Is there somewhere a bit more private and quiet we can take her?' inquired Jim.

'Follow me, I'm acting manager,' instructed a voice, as its owner hastily approached the scene.

'Lead on,' said Robert, tightening his hold on Daisy.

When, Daisy, in her fantasies, entertained ideas of appearing on the front page of several national newspapers with her idol, she always imagined she would be, at least, conscious when the shots were taken. As it was, she looked like a corpse draped across Bob's arms.

Robert B Kershaw didn't need to pose to look totally gorgeous; he *was* totally gorgeous. With his shirt half in and half out of his trousers, his dark hair overlong and slightly curly with sweat, and his dark eyes filled with anxiety, he presented an almost seraphic picture.

However, the entrapment of a celebrity and a schoolgirl in the lift of a top London hotel was incidental to the main story: sabotage and attempted murder. Had the villain's plan worked, Mrs Matilda Bancroft would have been in the lift, and would now be lying on a slab in the mortuary.

It was two days after the incident. Daisy's father was sitting beside her hospital bed. Daisy felt a little groggy from the operation she'd had to stabilise the break in her arm with pins, but her mind was working perfectly. She'd read the sketchy news reports about the attempt on Mrs Bancroft's life whilst waiting to be taken to theatre, but there had been no details.

'Dad, why would anyone want to hurt Mrs Bancroft, she seems so sweet, well, when you get to know her a bit?'

'She's a very nice lady indeed, always has time for a little chat and a joke with the staff. Her husband was a high court judge. He passed down life sentences on three men from the same family a few years ago. They were convicted of the most obscene crimes against children.

'Six months later, Mrs Bancroft's husband was murdered in front of her, so she was able to identify the killer and he was found guilty. However, between being taken from police custody to prison, the van transporting him was intercepted and he escaped. He has been off police radar ever since; they assume he has been living somewhere overseas, until now.'

'Now?'

'He turned up outside Mrs Bancroft's door dressed in hotel livery. He told her somebody was waiting for her in the foyer, that he'd held the lift for her and would escort her to it. The plan was that she'd get into it and plunge to her death. He'd somehow managed to disable the lift, get into the shaft and cut through most of the main cable. The movement and weight of somebody stepping into the lift was supposed to rupture it completely. He'd secured himself with a rope attached to the ladder on the wall so that *he* wouldn't be a victim of the plot. Fortunately for you and Mr Wonderful, he didn't make a good enough job of it.'

'But why did he want to kill Mrs Bancroft?'

'He believed he had to kill her so that she would never be able to point the finger at him. He has a family, a wife and kids, apparently, I imagine he wanted to return to the UK permanently.'

'But how is he connected with the men Judge Bancroft sent to prison?'

'He is the son of one of them; they came out of the same mould, it would seem.'

'Retribution.'

'Exactly. Poor Judge Bancroft was murdered for meting out fair justice as punishment for appalling crimes. He paid a terrible price for his service to society.'

'Why didn't Mrs Bancroft go with the man when he knocked on her door?'

'He looked quite different after all this time, but she recognised his voice. She told him she'd pop into her bedroom to get her jacket, then slammed the door in his face, alerted the hotel manager and rang the police. They caught him climbing out of a window in the gent's toilets on the ground floor.'

'Wow!'

'Pretty savvy action for a woman in her eighties, eh?'

'Really cool; good for her! Have you seen her?'

'Yes, briefly. She was in shock, naturally, but much more concerned about you. She plans to visit you in the morning.'

'That'll be lovely. Have you spoken to Bob?'

'I have. He looked a complete wreck when he got out of the lift, poor fellow, I really felt for him. He seems nice, friendly.'

'He *is* really nice and friendly, dad.'

Jim Mullins put his hand in his pocket and drew out an envelope; he handed it to Daisy. From Mrs Bancroft,' he said.

'What's this?'

'Money, I imagine, she said she wants you to treat yourself to something special for your birthday as soon as you are discharged.'

'The envelope is pretty fat,' remarked Daisy, turning it over in her hands, but not attempting to open it.

'She's pretty rich, sweetheart... The hotel is moving her to a suite on the first floor; she told them she could manage just one flight of stairs, said she'd never get in a lift again.'

Robert was looking his usual suave self when Jim encountered him coming into the hospital; he was loaded down with bags. 'Hey, Jim, I've brought some stuff for my young friend.'

'You've brought yourself, Bob, that will mean much more to her.'

'How is she?'

'She'll be fine, she's in good spirits.'

'I'm off to do a bit of filming in Ireland tomorrow, I wanted to see her before I left.'

'I really appreciate that, Bob, as will Daisy. And the nurses, I daresay.'

'Do you have other kids Jim?'

'Yes, a boy and another girl, both younger than Daisy.'

'Are they like her? I mean, she's just so great, isn't she?'

'I think they are all fantastic, but then, I'm their father. I'm a very fortunate man, Bob, and I know it.'

'Daisy told me about her mom. That really got to me, you know. You are a terrific guy, Jim, and deserve every bit of good fortune that comes your way. I might be your daughter's idol, but you are her hero, one hundred per cent.'

'Thank you, Bob, you're not at all a bad guy yourself.'

'Tell me, which level is Daisy on?'

'Six, ward seven.'

'Right… okay… okay… I think I might just take the stairs.'

THE NEW VICAR

The parish church of St Cuthbert had a team of volunteers dedicated to its smooth running and service: readers, servers, ushers, welcomers, a Sunday school teacher, and Eve Barker, fondly referred to as *The flower lady*.

Eve could work miracles with a dozen blooms, a bundle of foliage, some wire and plenty of oasis bricks. Not a plant stand or windowsill was bereft of adornment by the time she packed up her small bag of tools and left the church on a Saturday afternoon.

She would never engage herself elsewhere on the eve of the Sabbath, no matter what the enticement. Her routine was as rigid as it was incomprehensible to those of a less altruistic disposition. They didn't know that she cherished the time she spent alone in St Cuthbert's with only the echoes of past generations for company.

Eve talked to God constantly, poured out her heart to him, and here, here in this lovely ancient building she sensed his presence keenly. St Cuthbert's was her spiritual home.

Eve was deep in contemplation when the vicar, the very Reverend Thomas Pane, entered by way of the back door. 'Eve, my dear, how wonderful the church looks, as always when you've been working your magic.'

'Thank you, Vicar.'

The vicar made his way to the front pew and sat down rather heavily. He fixed his gaze on the window behind the altar, the trinity depicted therein, then let out a huge sigh and said, 'I'm retiring, Eve, you are the first person I've told outside the family.'

Eve left what she was doing, moved slowly towards the vicar and sat down beside him. 'Oh, Vicar, I knew the time would come, but we will miss you so much. I will miss you so much.'

'Fear not, dear lady, Doreen and I have taken a cottage in the village and will continue to worship here.'

'But who will replace you?'

'A much younger man. His name is Samuel Carlisle and he can deliver an address that will make even the mice sit up and take notice. His words are passionate, but relevant. His installation in the ministry here will benefit the community no end; I'm sure you will like him.'

'I hate change, Vicar.'

'Yes, I know, but perhaps that's what this parish needs. Perhaps it's what you need, too, Eve.'

Eve awoke, felt the beat of her heart, and was forced to accept the depressing fact that she was still alive. She always ended her prayers with the words, *Lord, please take me when you want me, I'm ready*. She never doubted that he *did* want her, but obviously at his convenience and not her own.

Eve had her breakfast, washed, put on her clothes and a smile and left her bungalow for church. Today was the day when the congregation would meet the new vicar, the Reverend Samuel Carlisle. She was not looking forward to it.

There he was, the new vicar, at least six feet tall, but looking even taller in ecclesiastical attire. He stood at the church door welcoming parishioners as they entered St Cuthbert's. He took Eve's hand and shook it warmly, a smile softening his strong features. She imagined he could appear quite formidable wearing a frown, possibly enigmatic when feeling neither sociable nor sad.

He was designed to be looked at, there was no doubt about that. 'Good morning, it's so nice to meet you,' he said.

'I'm pleased to meet you, too, Vicar.'

'It will take me some time to remember everybody's name, but do tell me yours, anyway.'

'Eve Barker.'

'Ah, St Cuthbert's treasure! Your floral artwork is truly amazing.'

'Thank you.'

'I've heard all about you.'

Oh dear, thought Eve, then he will know that I'm deadly dull and might even discern that I have a death wish. The vicar had the kind of eyes that seemed to bore into you, large and flinty blue, x-ray eyes that one could easily fancy had the capacity to examine a person's soul.

'Nothing bad, I hope.'

'Absolutely not, I assure you, Eve.'

It shouldn't have mattered, but it did. The new vicar had called Eve by her Christian name. She felt sort of fluttery inside as she took her usual place in her usual pew and knelt on her usual hassock. It was extremely disconcerting, especially in church.

Samuel Carlisle was everything the old vicar had said he was and more, quite a bit more: direct, amusing and ardent. His words were entirely relevant in this age of cruelty, intolerance, persecution and confusion. He gave the congregation something to grapple with mentally, but at the heart of his address was hope. 'Despair is not in God's remit,' he assured his flock.

It was not until Frank Hiller started to intone the lesson with all the vitality of a corpse that Eve's mind started to wander. Was Samuel Carlisle married? How old was he? About her own age: fifty-six, she guessed.

Did he have children? What did he look like in slacks and a tee shirt? What did he look like in swimming trunks? What did he look like naked? Oh God! Where did these thoughts come from?

She coloured and shifted in her seat. Were any of the other women present, married or otherwise, having the same thoughts, she wondered? Of course they were, Mavis Bevan, also a spinster, for one, Gloria Owen, widow of less than a year, for another. She was having a perfectly normal reaction to the sight of a handsome man. The trouble was, Eve tended not to do *normal* these days when it came to emotions.

The new vicar mounted the steps to the pulpit and passed his gaze over the congregation before giving the blessing. Eve prayed he would not look at her, but he did. Helen Briar, sitting directly in front of Eve, turned and whispered, 'Isn't he yummy. All that thick grey hair, very distinguished, Richard Gere with bells on. And so much taller!'

'Yes, he's very nice-looking,' replied Eve, as casually as she was able.

Eve let herself into her bungalow and headed for the kitchen to put the kettle on. As she passed the mirror in the hall she stopped and looked at her reflection. She had a round, comely face and gentle hazel eyes that encouraged the sharing of confidences. She was of average height, with short brown hair and had an enviably trim figure. She had never stood out in a crowd, she knew this well enough. William had told her she was beautiful, but then he had viewed her through the eyes of love.

Eve wondered if the vicar would have paid her a visit had she not fallen from the stepladder whilst adorning the windowsill in the transept with an especially elaborate display. She was being uncharitable, of course he would, sick-visiting was part of his ministry. He was laden with offerings: an orchid, several bottles of fortified wine, a cooked chicken, a cooked ham and a basket of fruit.

She ushered him into the kitchen, hobbling along behind on her crutches. 'How kind of you to call, Vicar, and bearing so many gifts; it was not necessary, but I am very grateful indeed.'

'Nonsense, Eve, you underestimate your importance within the church community. How are you?'

'Well, very well. I've never worn a cast before, and the crutches are a novelty, of sorts, and at least I have no stairs to climb.'

'But your leg, what did the hospital say?'

'That the break was clean and should mend nicely.'

'Are you in pain?'

'A little discomfort, nothing more.'

'I am so sorry about the accident. I have examined the stepladder and it seems sound, but the flags are so uneven. I imagine that's what caused it to topple. I will make it my business to find a sturdier, adjustable replacement.'

'Vicar, I daresay I was careless, if anyone is to blame, I expect it's me.'

'You will still come to church on Sunday?'

'I'm afraid that will not be possible; I can't drive at present, I don't have an automatic car.'

'Good heavens, Eve, as if I'd expect it. I'll collect you myself, okay?'

'If you are sure, that would be wonderful.'

'All settled, then.'

'Would you like a coffee? I have some very nice cake my neighbour brought in.'

'Splendid, I'll put the kettle on, and you issue instructions, I've been told I would make a wonderful wife.'

Oh, God, please don't let him be gay, thought Eve.

The vicar was early, as expected, and Eve was by the front door waiting for him in a state of … of what? Apprehension, excitement, something unfamiliar, anyhow. And it suddenly dawned on her that she hadn't woken up wishing she were dead.

He marched down the garden path and escorted her to his car: a large, silver, expensive-looking vehicle. He relieved her of her crutches, threw them onto the back seat, pushed the front seat back as far as it would go and eased her into it. It was almost worth her current indisposition to receive this level of attention.

The Sunday rides to church with the vicar soon became the highlight of Eve's week. She began to dread the removal of her cast, of being capable of driving herself in her trusty little Honda. She was no longer fazed by Samuel Carlisle's bearing and position and found him very easy to talk to, especially when staring through the windscreen and not directly at him.

Eve's neighbour took her to the hospital to have her cast removed. The doctor informed her that her leg had mended like that of a ten-year-old and she'd be back to normal within a week. 'You are supposed to look pleased, Miss Barker,' he remarked.

'I am, Doctor, of course I am, you've all been very kind here. Thank you so much.'

The doctor was right; Eve suffered very little stiffness and no pain. She had no business feeling bereft, it was a sin, nothing less. The trouble was that her crutches and cast had identified her as a person needing care and assistance; now she was fit and able and would be left to her own devices.

She was searching in her handbag for her car keys when he turned up. 'Good heavens, Vicar, I didn't expect to see you here this morning! I can get to church under my own steam now, as you see.'

'Do you want to get to church under your own steam, Eve?'

'Well… I don't want to be a bother.'

'I'll take that as a "no" then.'

And things continued thus until Eve felt sufficiently emboldened to invite the vicar to share Sunday lunch with her. 'Eve, how could I possibly refuse when I have desired nothing more these past Sundays whilst eating my meagre repast: a sandwich, more often than not.'

'How miserable for you. I would have asked you sooner but didn't wish to appear forward. I didn't know if – '

'I had a wife at home.'

'Quite.'

'I was married, briefly, but she died, she killed herself. Have I alarmed you?'

'No. I don't think so…'

'I'll tell you all about it later, if you wish.'

'Yes, I do wish.'

'And, in exchange, you must tell me what gives you the haunted, defeated look that sometimes deprives you of your lovely smile. It's a look that makes me want to put my arms about you and hold you close.'

'Like a father comforting a child?'

'No, Eve, not at all like that.'

As they got out of the car and approached the bungalow, a fluttering sensation settled in Eve's breast, heat rising from her toes so that even her scalp tingled. She put her key into the lock and pushed the front door open.

When they were in the hallway the vicar said, 'You really don't know how wonderful and special you are, do you?' By way of response, Eve started to cry, and the vicar pulled her to him and held her close until all her tears had been spent.

They had eaten and now sat in the lounge drinking coffee and the vicar had, at last, finally stopped complimenting Eve on her culinary skills. 'This is a lovely property,' he remarked, casting his eyes about the large room.

'My parents bought it when my mother became too frail to manage the stairs in their previous house. She was ill for such a long time, my father was always the strong one. When he died suddenly, I sold my flat and moved in to look after her.'

'You had to give up your job, I presume?'

'Yes, I worked in the tax office, I loved it.'

'That must have been a wrench.'

'It was, but with no siblings there was nobody but me to care for mum. She was a wonderful lady, both my parents were wonderful. I have no regrets on that score.'

'I've glimpsed you from the rectory window putting flowers on a grave, theirs I imagine.'

'Yes.'

'On another, too, right beside it.'

'My darling William. He had a heart attack at our wedding.'

'Oh, Eve, I am so sorry.'

'We never had the chance to take our vows. I turned to look at him as he arrived at the west door; he was so handsome in his new suit, so proud, his eyes filled with such tenderness and love. And then he fell to the floor…I hitched up my dress and ran down the aisle to him, but I was too late. So, there you have it, Samuel: The tragedy of poor Eve Barker. Pity none of the great romantics thought to write a novel about me!'

'You were not wicked or wilful enough, I expect.'

'I daresay that's it. Now, tell me about your wife.'

'She was young and had a serious drink and drug problem. She was so fragile, a beautiful, fragile, lost little thing. I believed that love and constancy would bring about a recovery eventually. I thought, in my arrogance, that I had the power to save her from herself, to extract all the potential that I knew lay within. She died from an overdose as if to prove me wrong.'

'How dreadfully sad.'

'When you are humbled to that extent, you are forced to examine who you are and where you fit into the greater scheme of things. I had a totally unrealistic notion of my own power. Perhaps I thought I was God's sidekick, not his servant.'

'You must have been devastated.'

'Oh, I was, but my suffering was deserved because my love was more about my needs than Sophie's, whilst yours was selfless, I don't doubt. I am full of sin for a priest, Eve.'

'Your contrition erases past failings, I'm sure.'

Eve briefly disappeared into the kitchen and returned bearing a small tray. On it were two tumblers and an unopened bottle of Irish Whiskey. She filled each glass nearly to the top. 'I won't be in a fit state to drive back to the rectory tonight,' said Samuel.

'That is the object of the exercise,' replied Eve.

THE ONE UNDER

The train screeches to a halt and I am thrown onto the filthy floor of the carriage. 'Shit, not another bloody one under!' I screech. A man in a tracksuit puts his hands under my armpits and pulls me to my feet.

'I know, it is very annoying when you have to be somewhere. Are you okay?'

'Yes, thank you so much. What is it with The District Line and suicides? I'll be late; my first day in my new job and I'm going to be late. I can't even phone to explain why because I have no bloody signal.'

'I'm sure your new boss will understand,' reasons the tracksuit man.

'It takes ages for the underground police to recover the body parts, tag them, bag them and clear the line. Exactly the same thing happened last week. It must be a Monday thing.'

'Perhaps. I was on that train, too.'

'These people are so inconsiderate, just because they want to chuck in the towel, those of us who don't have to suffer. What's the matter with slitting your wrists in the bath, hanging yourself from a banister, overdosing, or jumping into the river? No, bugger up Sarah Parker's day, why not. She's only due to fill a position she's been after for, like, a hundred years.'

'Oh dear, Sarah, poor you. I'm sure it'll all work out fine, though.'

He's really nice, the tracksuit man, not bad looking either. I give him my best smile as I eventually alight from the train.

I am trying to pull myself into some sort of shape as I make my way from the station to the office block a couple of hundred yards away. Having been stuck in the stuffy carriage for over an hour, I feel sweaty and dirty. The sleeve of my best cream jacket has a mark on it, and my hair is hanging like a wet mop and starting to frizz, my make-up is running, and even my knickers feel damp.

It starts to rain so I quicken my pace, I am already fifty-five minutes late and my new shoes are pinching my toes. I start to prepare an apology speech in my head.

There are two police cars in the company's car park, but no sign of Matthew Crawford's BMW. Perhaps he caught the tube?

In the lift people are muttering about some sort of tragic event, shock and disbelief etched on their faces. My new office is on the fifth floor, one above the wages office where I have been working in ever since I left college and joined the staff of *Crawford, Maber and Strickland.*

The door of Matthew Crawford's office is open. His present secretary, Sheila Braithwaite, is dabbing her eyes with a wad of tissues. She is sitting at her boss's desk, staring blankly at a photograph of him with his family: husband, wife, two boys and a small girl. It is a happy scene set beneath a large tree. She becomes aware of my presence in the doorway, 'Oh, Sarah, I did try to call you.'

'I tried to call *you*, but I was on the tube and there was no signal. I'm really sorry I'm so late, there was a one under.'

'So, they have a name for those who throw themselves under the trains?'

'Yes, the railway police came up with it way back, apparently.'

'Well, I suppose it's apt.'

'Oh, my God! Was it Mr Crawford, or somebody connected with him?'

'It was Mr Crawford.'

'How dreadful, his poor family! I often saw him in the building, but had never spoken to him until I came for my interview. He always looked so carefree, so happy.'

'Yes, we all thought so. I've been in this office for thirty years, the last ten, the best ten, working for Matthew

Crawford. He was a gentleman, kind and considerate, the perfect boss.'

'You must be devastated.'

'Yes. You think you know somebody so well, but the truth is you never really know them at all.'

'But people aren't themselves when they do something like that.'

'No, perhaps not.'

'I feel so guilty, Mrs Braithwaite.'

'Why?'

'I was really annoyed when the train stopped, I knew what must have happened, yet all I could think about was the impact it was going to have on me and my life.'

'Suicides on the railway happen fairly frequently, sadly. They are mere statistics if the victim is unknown. Don't beat yourself up, I expect your fellow commuters felt the same. Go home and try to focus on something nice. I will be leaving shortly, just need to sort my head out before I get behind the wheel of my car. I'll ring you as soon as I know what's happening regarding a replacement for Mr Crawford. I'm glad I'm retiring, Sarah, serving another master would be altogether too much for me. Still, I'll stay until you have settled in.'

'Thank you Mrs Braithwaite; I am so dreadfully sorry this has happened.'

'You can call me Sheila, I expect we'll be friends.'

I sit on the train trying to fill my mind with pleasant things, but images of Matthew Crawford's dismembered body strewn about the tracks, his kind heart squashed beneath smashed ribs, create a scene so vivid in my head I can't push it aside.

I alight from the train, my shoes are really pinching now. I concentrate hard on the pain in an attempt to evict from my psyche the horrible pictures my imagination is conjuring up and wildly exaggerating: thousands of bodies littering the railway line with blood covering the tracks. I think about the joy of kicking off my shoes, the froth on my large cappuccino, lying in a bath full of bubbles until I turn wrinkly. The toasted ham sandwich I propose to have for lunch, washed down with a very large glass of wine.

I approach my flat and see Sean's car parked outside, I don't see my sister's, parked in front of it until I draw closer. My sister and my partner of six years, Oh, no, it can't be true!

They don't hear my key in the lock, or my footfalls as I creep up the stairs. Their discarded clothes are all over the lounge, and I can hear sounds of carnal activity. I'm not sure I want to see them in our bed. I decide I don't.

I scribble a note: *please be gone by the time I return.* I put it on the table under my engagement and eternity rings and leave.

Blisters have formed on my heels; they are bleeding, and my toes feel as though they are being crushed together by clamps. I find myself on a bench in the cemetery. If I take my shoes off, I will never get them on again. I take them off and hurl them into a nearby bin. I am suddenly overcome by tiredness, as if I've been drugged. I lie down on the bench, and close my eyes.

I am cold, so cold; it is growing dark and raining steadily. The stiffness in my bones makes it hard to sit up. I look at my watch and realise that I have been asleep for a couple of hours. The awful events of the day come rushing back. I know I am about to throw up so stagger towards a flowerbed and fall on my knees to empty my stomach of the bitter puke within.

Sheila Braithwaite calls me the following day and asks me to come into the office any time during the afternoon, she has news, she says. I haven't eaten, haven't been to bed, haven't closed the doors on the empty wardrobe, haven't shut the drawers in the chest we shared, haven't had the bath I promised myself. I am a wreck, I feel as if life has erased me, is this how Matthew Crawford felt?

Sheila Braithwaite looks at me, really looks at me. 'Sit down, dear, and tell me what has happened.'

'My partner and my sister are having an affair.'

'Oh, I am so sorry, Sarah.'

'Well, at least it's my flat, I was able to evict him. But my sister, my sister…'

'The ultimate betrayal, I can't imagine how that must feel. You came here with all this pain in your heart, I can hardly believe it.'

'I have to work, Sheila, rent to pay, that sort of thing.'

'I understand. Do you want to discuss your new boss?'

'Of course.'

'His name is Tim Gregson, he's currently with Robbins and Wilkes… Oh, my goodness, Sarah, what is it? You know him?'

'Life just keeps getting better and better, doesn't it?'

'Tell me.'

'I met him at a party, this was before I met Sean. He came onto to me, big time. He was a smooth talker and very persistent. I…I don't know what he put into my drink, but it wiped me out. I woke up hours later. I knew he'd raped me… I reported him to the police, I was examined at the hospital and there was a court case.'

'And he wasn't convicted?'

'No, he claimed it was consensual sex and the jury believed him.'

Suddenly, it is all too much, I run from the office, the building. I run as if I've been scalded by the very name: Tim Gregson, RAPIST.

I stand on the platform, a shell of a person drowning in the debris of a broken world, wondering what the hell has gone wrong.

I am drawn to the far end of the platform, just where the trains emerge from the tunnel. I feel nothing, completely detached from myself. I take one step, two steps nearer the edge, I cross the painted line. *Mind the gap, mind the gap*, the voice is playing over and over in my head.

The train is approaching, closer and closer. I make to leap, but somebody has flung their arms about my waist and is pulling me back.

'Sarah, Sarah! No!' Sheila Braithwaites's shrill cries penetrate my senses. We drop to the ground and I fall against her, sobbing so hard I feel my heart will break. She is shaking violently, her whole body charged with fear. And in that instant I think, somebody cares, I matter.

People gather, but she politely dismisses their offers of help and they slowly move away. She makes no move to stand up, she just sits there holding me in her arms until my anguish subsides. 'How did you know, Sheila?'

'I didn't, but I wasn't prepared to take that chance.'

'Tim Gregson was the last straw.'

'I know. However, that is a situation I can do something about.'

'How?'

'My late husband, Bill, founded Crawford, Maber and Strickland. It was just called Braithwaites in those days, a small concern he turned into a small empire requiring quite a large staff. When he died my younger brother, Gary Strickland, stepped into his shoes and took on Matthew Crawford and Frank Maber as partners. You have been with the company for a long time and been a loyal employee; you more than deserve this promotion. Gary will not see you robbed of it by bringing a lowlife like this Tim Gregson character into the company, I promise you.

'Twelve members of the jury didn't believe me, why do you?'

'Because I an excellent judge of character. As a matter of interest, were there more men than women on the jury?'

'Yes.'

'I rest my case.'

Sheila tucks my arm under hers as we slowly walk from the station. She tells me she is taking me home where she will cook us something nice for dinner, and we can pretend her best wine is water and drink as much as we like. She claims that even though great sorrow has cast a shadow over our lives, we still have much to celebrate. She is right, I have a new friend, a truly wonderful new friend.

THE PHOTOGRAPH

She is staring straight at me accusingly: the child in the photograph. Her huge, tear-filled eyes penetrate the very depths of my being and stir up feelings long since repressed.

My mother once accused me of being *shallow*. I wish she could see me now, at this exact moment. I wish she could experience the turmoil within me, the gnawing ache of it.

Images of children in desperate need are posted on notice boards or flashed up on our television screens constantly, and you know that somebody expects you to dig deep in your pockets. It is emotional blackmail of the most vulgar nature, but as necessary as any other type of advertising: selling a product, selling a dream, selling a charity, selling human suffering; what's the difference?

The difference is that I happen to be standing in front of an orphanage in Buenos Aires. I am beginning to feel uncomfortable under the scrutiny of the little Argentinian girl and make to move away, but find I cannot, she has fixed me with her tragic expression.

Beneath the photograph, on a scrap of card, is written: Juanita Gomez – aged 6. I really don't want to know the name of this beautiful, broken little person. Perhaps she is, even now, peering at me from one of the many windows in the orphanage, willing me not to walk away. I feel like a victim. I am a victim.

My husband, Charles, doesn't have a paternal bone in his body. We live exclusively, selfishly, some would say, for each other. How on earth can I explain what is going on inside me? How can I tell him that I want to adopt this little foreign stranger and make her our own? He will think I've been touched by some sort of temporary madness, that the heat has got to me.

But he doesn't. He tells me the little girl could keep me company when he is away on business. The thought flits through my mind that children of our own would have served the same purpose, but a family was never on the cards, I was forced to accept that from the start, or lose him.

Charles deals with all the red tape, he is very good at that sort of thing. Bureaucracy doesn't faze him at all, foreign or local. Charles is good at almost everything; it is a little intimidating at times.

I am not told how much money changed hands to effect a prompt adoption, but before we know it, Juanita is ours, and we are on our way back to our home in rural Sussex with our new daughter.

Juanita learns how to smile, to speak our language in her strange, exotic accent, to eat her food with a knife and fork and to play with other children, most of whom hold her in thrall. In no time at all she masters all the skills she needs to survive and prosper in her new country.

Charles never behaves in an overtly fatherly manner towards our daughter. He seems fascinated by her simply because she does not conform to his notion of the average modern child: the precious, indulged little so-and-so who drains your bank balance and tears your nerves to shreds. His regard for her cannot be questioned, but it leans much more heavily towards admiration rather than affection.

Juanita fills a huge void in my life, a life that seemed so full before I had to reinvent myself as a mother. I have to say that if the product is the sum of what it took to produce it, we are doing an excellent job. Juanita is a credit to us both; everybody says so.

By the time Juanita starts senior school she is popular, confident, bubbly and gracious. Our home has never heard the unfettered sounds of youth in such abundance, and I relish the constant unscheduled visits of her school friends.

Charles seeks the sanctuary of his study whenever a surfeit of hormones threatens to invade his personal space, but me, well, I just join in the party.

When I find Juanita trying on some of the cocktail dresses I had put by for the charity shop, I realise, with some alarm, that she is no longer a child. She looks alarmingly seductive. She is incredibly beautiful now. Her mane of sleek black hair tumbles in soft waves down her back, her waist is tiny, her thighs trim, and her breasts so well developed they cannot not help but draw the eye. Her face is, of course, as ever: huge dark eyes dominating every other feature, fired with passion or pathos, as the mood takes her. In a way I feel as if I am looking at a stranger. Other, natural, parents tell me this is not unusual. I find that hard to believe, but then, what do I know?

I force myself to think about a time when she will no longer be an active part of our small unit. She will attach herself to some totally gorgeous young man – of whom we will strongly disapprove, as a matter of principle – and the pair of them will create a unit of their own. And this unit will produce blood ties. How will Charles and I be able to compete with that?

***

Juanita attained the highest grades in all her exams and secured a place at university. As bereft as I felt in her absence, Charles seemed to feel it more keenly. Our home was still her home, evidence of her was in every room, cupboard and corner. I found the degree of his distress perplexing, and more than a little hurtful. Of course, I never questioned him about this. Other, natural, parents assured me that this, too, was completely normal, some even confessed to a measure of jealousy towards their spouses.

Then Juanita returned. First for the Christmas holiday, and then for the long summer break. She found herself a job in a supermarket stacking shelves. I was astonished when Charles, an inveterate snob, according to my mother, put forward no objection to her taking such a lowly position.

The supermarket shifts were truly dreadful: five until midnight, Monday to Friday, and ten until four every third Sunday. Charles raised no objection to these anti-social hours; this was surprising as it was he, at his own insistence, who turned out nightly to pick her up.

If there is one thing worse than being made to look a fool, it is the discovery that you *are* a fool, and that, being a fool, you deserve no less than to be fooled. My dear friend and neighbour tried to assure me that I was not a fool, but simply blind to all I did not wish to see. She said that I had somehow contrived to bumble through life believing that love and trust were bedfellows, and that neither, if genuine, were repaid by betrayal. A long-winded, if faintly touching, way of telling me that I was a fool, don't you think?

I did not apportion blame for the liaison. How could I? Was I not the author of my own fate?

I was a casualty of deceit, and the pain was so great it eclipsed all else. I slipped effortlessly into the twilight world of the mentally afflicted. What kept me from suicidal thoughts, I do not know, cowardice and my aversion to the sight of blood, I suspect.

Juanita went back to Oxford and shared lodgings with a female friend. I was pretty sure she would never return. I wanted to lay part of the blame for the liaison at her feet, but found I couldn't. Charles was always the one who called the shots, and his powers of manipulation were second to none. Had Juanita fallen for his charms? I couldn't bring myself to believe so. She had so many admirers of her own generation and had confessed to one particular favourite when we were engaged in some *girlie chat*.

Charles accepted an opening in his firm's Berlin office, and I returned to the marital home after spending two months with my long-suffering sister in Chicago. At length, I mustered the will to rid the house of every last trace of both Charles and Juanita. There emerged eventually, a very different me.

My friend, Carol, came upon this *different me* one gloomy afternoon as I hovered over the huge bonfire I had lit at the bottom of the garden. I had the orphanage photograph of Juanita in my hand.

'Don't,' she said firmly.

'Everything else has gone.'

'The only thing that has gone is *you*. You've built a wall of self-pity so bloody high that nobody can climb over it to reach you. Keep that photograph, Celia, some day it may serve to remind you that you once had the capacity to care about somebody other than yourself. You are not stupid, you know you are not the only victim in all this, think on.'

My friend left and didn't look back. I put the photograph in my pocket and went indoors.

I read the obituary in the paper. I didn't know how to feel about Charles's death. That night thoughts of my sexually depraved, late ex-husband crept into my psyche, stealing my sleep, unsettling what little equilibrium I had struggled so hard to regain. How dare he reach out from the grave to torment me. Bastard!

I got out of bed, sat on the floor beside it, put my head in my hands and wept. I wept tears so long suppressed they knew not when to cease. With the outpouring of grief came a soothing, heady sense of relief and liberation. A purging of all the darks forces festering within. I got dressed and drove to my mother's house, twenty miles away.

I had not seen my mother for over a year. I had pushed her away, shut her out. She hadn't given up on me, though, her weekly phone calls, so punctual every Sunday, continued unanswered, and hadn't stopped until very recently. And I had become too embroiled in the detritus of my miserable existence to even consider the possibility that all was not well with her.

The pallbearers were just bringing the coffin out of the house as I drew to a halt at the kerbside. A sizeable group of mourners followed down the garden path. I did not know whether I was going to faint or be sick. I got out of the car and fell against the low garden wall.

Eyes turned towards me, some registering sympathy, some, mild contempt. As everything became blurry and I felt my knees buckle, she was there, I felt her arms around me, supporting me. 'Mum, I tried to get hold of you,' she said.

'Oh, Juanita, I feel so ashamed; my poor old mum, my poor, poor old mum…'

'Grandma didn't suffer, she just went to sleep, she was so peaceful.'

'Was she alone?'

'No, I've been here for a few days, since she had a funny turn. It was her heart, a condition none of us knew about.'

'Oh, Juanita, what have I done? What have I done?'

'Got lost in the wilderness, that's all.'

Somebody brings me a kitchen chair to sit on and a glass of water. It is my mother's next door neighbour, Doris. 'Oh, Doris, I am so sorry, I should have been here for her.'

'She understood, Celia, she knew you far better than you realised. She always said you were like your dear old dad, lived in a bubble, felt safe there. Are you up to attending the funeral? It would be lovely for Juanita to have you there. She's a wonderful girl, Celia, best thing you ever did in your life was adopting her.'

'Don't suppose she has much of an opinion of me now.'

'She knows what that business with Charles did to you. How awkward that would have made things between you two, that's why she stayed away.'

'Yes, I guessed as much.'

'Anyway, she's a happily married woman with children now.'

'Oh God! Where was I when all this was going on?'

'In your bubble, Celia, in your bubble.'

***

My grandchildren: Sophia, four, and twins, James and Luke, two, take to me as if they know me, as if they had known me from birth. In this atmosphere of congeniality, I wonder how I am going to ask what I need to ask. It might just destroy this fragile moment, this potential reunion.

In the event, Juanita made it easy for me. 'You want to know about Charles and me.'

'The affair, yes.'

'It wasn't an affair, Mum, it was sex, recreational sex, as far as he was concerned.'

'Juanita, as far as I am aware, you never lied to me.'

'No, but I was economic with the truth at the time to spare your feelings, perhaps that was wrong. I loved you, love you, I didn't want to hurt you.'

'Did you love *him*?'

'I'm not sure I even liked him.'

'Didn't you mind this…this recreational sex?'

'Of course I minded, it disgusted me, but there was a debt of gratitude to be paid.'

'Oh, Juanita! You make it sound as if you'd been cultivated to provide sexual services.'

'I don't think it was quite like that.'

'Then, how was it, exactly?'

'Charles agreed to adopt me to divert some of the attention you lavished on him; he was stifled by it.'

'Is that what he told you?'

'Yes. It worked wonderfully until I became a young woman. If he had been bound by the constraints of a blood relationship, it wouldn't have happened.'

'He prostituted you, Juanita!'

'You think that hadn't happened before, just because I was a child?'

'Oh, God! My dear girl… I really have been living in a bubble, haven't I?'

'So it would seem.'

'I always believed he loved me as much as I loved him.'

'I'm sure he did love you, you were the perfect wife. He would have found another if he hadn't thought so. Trouble was you thought he was God, and he was just a man like any other.'

'How sad and pathetic I've been, Juanita. I never would have taken you from that orphanage to have you compromised, I hope you know that.'

'Mum, where do you suppose I would have wound up if you had left me in Buenos Aires, an Argentine with no family, no education, no prospects?'

'I really can't imagine.'

'On the streets, or dead in the gutter. Do yourself a favour and think about that, will you. Please?'

'I'll try, my darling girl. I'll try.'

Juanita's husband, Peter, helped me on with my coat. 'You will come again, Mum, won't you? May I call you Mum?

'Oh yes, I'd like that. And I will come again, as long as you promise to visit me soon, we've wasted far too much time already. You have a beautiful home and children, Peter.'

'And the most beautiful wife in the world.'

'And the most treasured, I hope.'

'You've got that right.'

The children stand at the edge of the driveway to see me off.

Sophia starts crying, real tears, big tears that roll down her cheeks and onto her clothing. And there she is again, the olive-skinned child in the photograph, my Juanita.

THE REUNION

She is smiling across the cosmetic counter at the man who has just made a large purchase. She hands him a crimson bag with the store's name emblazoned on the side of it in large, gold lettering.

I am almost certain it is Claire; I do not draw closer for she must not see me. It has been over twenty years and I've changed, naturally, but I'm sure she would recognise me, just as I have recognised her.

Her colleagues are very forthcoming; a few discreet inquiries confirm her identity. She is the new department manager, has been transferred from another branch, a promotion, apparently. She is currently demonstrating the art of salesmanship to a young trainee; the girl exudes an air of excessive boredom. She will not last.

Now I must find out where she lives; this is a nerve-racking prospect. I am not a confident driver and hate tailing people; I do it only when I am unsure of a specific location. As for trying to follow a bus! Forget it.

It is closing time; the sales workers file out through a door in the rear of the building. I am sitting in my car in the far corner of the large customer car park. She appears and I slide down in my seat perchance she should head in my direction. Instead, she walks briskly along Barton Street, directly behind the store; it leads to one of the inner city's residential districts. Great, she lives locally!

I get out of my car and, keeping a good distance, follow her for forty minutes or so. Her pace eventually eases, she turns and disappears through the front door of a large mid-terrace house. These homes, having once been occupied by Victorian gentlefolk, have been largely converted into flats and bedsits. I return to my car then drive past the house in order to take note of its number.

I intend to write to Claire in the first instance; I will try to explain everything and see if she is prepared to meet me. It will be a difficult letter, but now that she has turned up after all these years of not knowing her whereabouts, I can no longer ignore the need in me to contact her. She casts a long, dark shadow over my life, my marriage, my children, my peace of mind.

I hate the expression *closure* but that is exactly what I need, hopefully, she does, too.

She opens the door, shakes my hand and ushers me inside. The flat is very small but extremely neat with lots of small personal touches that make it feel homely.

She's a good-looking woman, Claire, my daughter. She

wears no ring, so I assume she is not married. Perhaps she didn't meet the right man? I was very lucky in that respect – the second time around.

She says she is pleased I contacted her, that she has often wondered about me: where I now lived, did I remarry, did I have other children? She offers me a glass of wine; I accept and start to relax. It all seems to be going rather well. Maybe we will become friends, or perhaps that's a bit of a stretch.

At nine o'clock I get up to leave. I thank her for welcoming me into her home, and reach for my coat which I folded across the back of a dining chair. 'I hope you understand why I left your father, Claire,' I say.

'Yes, he spent all of what little money you had on booze, fags and gambling, and when he was drunk he got handy with his fists.'

'In the end, I could stand it no longer and left; I didn't know what else to do.'

I push my arms into the sleeves of my coat and, to my surprise, Claire catches the collar and straightens it around my neck. Is she going to embrace me, give me a kiss?

Her hands move from the collar onto my throat, her fingers tightening, thumbs pressing against my windpipe. 'I don't blame you for leaving, mother, but why didn't you take me with you, I was five years old?'

I am scared now. The look in her eyes is scaring me; the increased pressure on my windpipe is making me feel light-headed.

'Did you even consider how he would treat me after you'd gone?' she asks. 'What kind of mother would leave their child with a selfish, cruel bastard like my father? He abused me, mother.' She is shouting into my face, her fingers pressing harder and harder. 'That filthy swine abused me until I was mentally and physically scarred. It was only then that somebody noticed. I was ten years old when they took me into care.'

Things are getting very blurry, totally winded, I slip to the floor. She does not release me, but holds me in a vice-like grip, her thumbs playing some sort of tune on my throat, a requiem, I wonder? 'You want forgiveness; you want to go back to your new family and tell them about me, about your terrible husband, about how you were forced to leave me, about how you've now seen me and we've been reconciled.

'You condemned me to the torments of hell, mother, you wouldn't want to tell your family that, would you? You wouldn't want your children to know that you once had another child and abandoned her, to know what sort of mother you really are? Forgiveness is mine to give, and I absolutely and utterly withhold it for all time. I hope you have a long life, mother.'

I am lying on the floor, gasping for breath nearly choking on my tears. She left, my daughter, Claire, left; she walked out of the door. I know I must be gone before she returns. I go into the tiny shower room and splash cold water onto my face. I catch sight of myself in the mirror above the washbasin. My neck is as red and swollen as my eyes. I bear the marks of my daughter's hatred. The marks will probably be gone within a day or two, but what about those on my heart?

I will not find closure, I will never find closure; what on earth made me believe I deserved it?

THE WAGER

Carne Lacey – ancestral home of the Bebe-Forresters – sits on the cusp of twilight. The house seems to quiver through a rippling, vaporous, ochre haze, cowering beneath a darkening sky. Restless clouds dance and swirl frantically, wrapping themselves around the tall chimneys and turrets. Do they know that someone within is dying; that the end of an era is nigh?

Four generations of Bebe-Forresters move about in the grounds; overwrought children chasing each other, knocking dead leaves and twigs from winter foliage. A rumble of thunder stops their play as it bangs out a sombre requiem for Lady Augusta Bebe-Forrester. Is it too soon?

Raindrops start to fall, hard, heavy and fast. The family make haste to get indoors for shelter. A streak of lightening splits the sky, filling the house with grotesque light, then another and another.

In the vast bed, Lady Augusta occupies but little space, her shrunken form appears to be drowning in the bedding. She wheezes and her poor bones rattle with the exertion.

Lady Augusta's doctor, solicitor, her domestic staff, friends and family wander around the house, their private thoughts and feelings as varied as their hopes and fears. Will the matriarch survive until the great hall clock has struck the midnight hour, until she reaches her hundredth birthday?

The bookmaker stands alone at the foot of the wide marble staircase. Not a single member of the family acknowledges him; he is *the enemy*.

The Bebe-Forresters have known about the wager for some time. They made their views regarding the situation quite clear when all five sons were summoned to Carne Lacey three months previously.

'Mother, what on earth were you thinking of; are you completely out of your senses, agreeing to something so ludicrous?' inquired Duncan, the eldest, and most stupid of her offspring, in Lady Augusta's opinion. 'This… this bookmaker fellow is obviously out to rob you of Carne Lacey. Two horses against the family estate –'

'Lame old nags, I shouldn't wonder,' put in Albert.

'Albert, your total lack of knowledge in equine-related matters only marginally exceeds your ignorance in the area of, say, bricklaying, or grave digging,' his mother told him. 'I'd shut up if I were you.'

'But the value of two horses could not possibly match

that of Carne Lacey,' opined her youngest son.

'Which, Stuart, shows just how much *you* know. We are talking about a stud sire and a mare in foal, they are extremely valuable animals.'

'Without being too indelicate, mother—'

'God forbid, Monty…'

'Without being too indelicate, what do you expect *us* to do with two and a half horses when you are…well—'

'Dead?'

'Yes, mother' said Edmund, who was clearly eager to wrap up this silly conversation and return to the golf course.

Edmund, the youngest sibling, unlike his brothers, had married into money; there was little chance of his family succumbing to the horrors of impoverishment.

'We are not all as fortunate as you, Edmund,' said Duncan, 'you will not be obliged to provide for your family should we be deprived of our inheritance by this scandalous bookmaker and his even more scandalous wager. It's a conspiracy, that's what it is.'

'What, to introduce you and your progeny to the real world where people expect to maintain themselves through gainful employment?' inquired Lady Augusta.

'I'm seventy-five, mother!'

'You weren't always seventy-five, Duncan.'

Lady Augusta was having fun. What sport her family provided when they were rattled about money. They were born believing the estate owed them a living, as was their father. It was *she* who had kept Carne Lacey going through frugality, good management, well considered investments, and, later, an innate skill at picking winners at the races. The place would have fallen about their ears by now had that not been the case.

'Boys, let me tell you, I fully intend to outwit my bookmaker friend, I mean to be the victor in this wager… Don't look so downhearted, only three months to go until my birthday, I'm sure you'll muddle through financially until then, and you don't even need to visit me in the meantime.'

'You make us sound as if we don't care about you, mother,' grumbled Albert.

'Is that so?' inquired Lady Augusta, raising an eyebrow.

The bookmaker now casts his gaze around the hall and up the staircase to where high balustrades encircle the upper floors, giving access to ninety bedrooms with bathroom facilities – the only concession in the house to modern living. Lady Augusta refuses to refer to them as en-suites – altogether too French.

The bookmaker tries not to imagine how wonderful this house would look when fully restored, but fails miserably. In his mind's eye he sees a fine hotel set amidst the glorious grounds, a restaurant for those with a discerning palate, a function hall for weddings, parties and conventions, a gym and health spa... He would relocate his stud farm here and provide facilities for riding and other outdoor pursuits; the possibilities were endless. Not least is the fact that the village would benefit hugely from such an enterprise. This is *his* village and he loves it with a passion. If fate should smile on him tonight, it could be so, even at this late hour. He looks at his watch, the hands are moving all too quickly.

Margaret, Lady Augusta's companion and carer, sits beside the bed in an easy chair, she is knitting a tiny garment for her new granddaughter.

Lady Augusta stirs, opens her bloodshot eyes, her vision dim but her brain razor sharp. She doesn't expend her strength in speech but tries to smile at Margaret, her true and loyal friend. Margaret puts down her knitting, takes her employer's wizened hand and smiles back in return.

Lady Augusta closes her eyes; she must strive to defeat the grim reaper, to defeat the bookmaker, she *must* hang on, she *must* hang on...

The bookmaker is sitting in the library. He knows every inch of this house, it's like an old friend. He desperately wants it for his own purposes, of course, but equally, wants to save it from the clutches of Lady Augusta's grasping, greedy, lazy and useless family. To see Carne Lacey gradually succumb to the rigours of time and ruin would break his heart, or worse, sold off to some conglomerate in the business of building theme parks.

He completely understands Lady Augusta's desire to *save the empire,* for that it how things have always been done here; that is how Carne Lacey came into her possession. *She* knows the Bebe-Forresters are a dying breed, but they are *blood,* when all is said and done.

What the bookmaker doesn't understand is that Lady Augusta's desire simply *to win* is far greater than her need to *save the empire.* Will her stubborn refusal to be beaten pay off? Are the finest Sire, Filly and Colt in the bookmaker's stud destined to occupy her stables, become the property of a bunch of total morons? Each animal has *future winner* written all over it; their potential is incalculable.

It is twenty-five minutes to midnight, twenty-five minutes to the date on which Lady Augusta was born, twenty-five minutes until she reaches her century and twenty-five minutes before either she or he, the bookmaker, win the wager.

The small army of domestic workers and gardeners are wondering where employment will found in the future. The doctor is hoping that somebody will see fit to settle his bills promptly. The solicitor has no such fears; he has power of attorney. Margaret has reached retirement age and knows she will survive on her state pension and a small monthly annuity. *Her* loss will be personal for, though austere and uncompromising, Lady Augusta is very dear to her heart.

As for the bookmaker, his mind is a conflicting jumble of feelings. He and Lady Augusta go back a long way. Their shared passion for horses and betting has formed a strong bond between them. Lady Augusta's diligence in studying form and performance has reaped great rewards for them both. He has never in his life respected or admired anyone more. He knows he will miss her good sense, her witty, clever conversation, her indomitable spirit, her very presence.

However, since she is destined to board the train to the great beyond imminently; he cannot help but wish she would oblige him by getting on a little early in order to spare him the agony of seeing his dreams turn to dust. After all, she will not live to enjoy the benefits of being victorious for longer than it takes her to finally be greeted by her maker.

At five minutes to twelve, Margaret calls the doctor, solicitor and the bookmaker to Lady Augusta's bedchamber. The trio reverently make their way into the room. The doctor and solicitor sit beside each other on the chaise longue – Lady Augusta maintains it is *a couch with a single armrest.*

Margaret beckons the bookmaker to the bedside. Lady Augusta's eyes flicker in recognition of his presence. The chimes of the great hall clock herald the arrival of the midnight hour.

'Gotcha,' she whispers, then smiles, and dies.

Lady Augusta is laid to rest in the family vault attached to the parish church of St Stephen. The Bebe-Forresters are effusive in their expressions of gratitude for the support and sympathy shown them by members of the congregation at this sad and difficult time. The bookmaker stands alone beneath an ancient oak tree. He wonders at their capacity to enact an almost theatrical display of grief, when his defeat must be filling their hearts with unfettered elation.

When the interment is over, Lady Augusta's solicitor places a card in the bookmaker's hand. It is a request for his attendance at the reading of her will at Carne Lacey the following day.

He is surprised and mutters to himself, 'Why?'

They have gathered around the table in the dining hall. The family occupying one side, the staff and bookmaker, the other. The family, expectant, everyone else, bemused

The solicitor opens a large, white envelope with the family crest upon it and plucks out the document inside. Without preamble, he starts to read.

One.

I, Augusta Celeste Mary Bebe-Forrester of Carne Lacey, in the village of Hambrook Ford, West Sussex, being of sound mind, do hereby revoke all former wills and testamentary dispositions made by me at any time and declare this to be my last will.

Two.

As sole executor of this, my will, I appoint my solicitor, David Martin Gollam of Fore street, Hambrook Ford, West Sussex.

Three.

In the event that I pass away AND SUBJECT to the payment of all my debts, funeral and testamentary expenses, I distribute my estate as follows:

To my staff of more than five years service, I bequeath the sum of one million pounds to be shared equally between them.

There is a loud gasp and not a few nervous giggles.

To my dear friend and companion, Margaret Sarah Duckham, I bequeath the sum of five hundred thousand pounds.

Margaret's astonishment manifests itself in a bout of uncontrollable sobbing which briefly focuses all attention on her.

To the adult members of my family, I bequeath seventy per cent of my monetary wealth to be equally divided between them.

To those who have not yet attained the age of eighteen years, I bequeath thirty per cent of my monetary wealth, to be shared equally between them, and held in trust until they reach the age of twenty-one.

The atmosphere in the room has reached fever pitch. Carne Lacey has not yet been mentioned and the Bebe-Forresters are squirming about on their chairs in anticipation.

To my bookmaker, Robert Charles Benton, I bequeath Carne Lacey, all the land attached to it, some one hundred and fifty acres, and all the horses in my stables.

I also hereby relinquish all rights to the sire, mare and colt I won legitimately in a wager between myself and Robert Charles Benton.

This bequest is made without impediment, restriction or encumbrance.

Dated and signed on the fifth day of September Twenty hundred and nineteen. 2019.

Outrage probably best describes the reaction of the family. The bookmaker, equally stunned, takes himself off to consider his situation. The Bebe-Forresters stare at the door in utter contempt as it closes quietly behind him.

The solicitor is certain the Bebe-Forresters will contest

Lady Augusta's bequest regarding Carne Lacey. They will claim she was coerced by the bookmaker whilst the balance of her mind was disturbed. This allegation would be disproved in less time than it took to make it, and the family exposed as a bunch of greedy fools in a court of law. But he suspects they are stupid enough to squander a large part of their considerable inheritance in pursuance of their objective: possession of the ancestral home.

Lady Augusta has been a prolifically successful speculator all her life, she's no more likely to be beaten in death than she was when alive; the family don't seem to have grasped that fact. Anyway, the solicitor hopes they will not be sufficiently stupid to suppose that *he* could be prevailed upon to represent them in any circumstance.

The bookmaker is sitting in his favourite chair beside the fireplace in the library. The door is locked. The noises coming from the hall outside indicate the presence of staff members, they probably want to congratulate him on his good fortune; he is very well liked in this house. Perhaps, also, they'd like to inquire about the prospect of future employment – hotels need a good and trusty staff, do they not? He knows he will accommodate them all, but such matters are not for today.

He looks at the well-worn armchair opposite him: Lady Augusta's chair. He thinks about the Bebe-Forresters; he has not one wit of pity for them. He and the solicitor alone are in a position to fairly accurately estimate the size of their inheritance. If the younger members of the family choose to join the ranks of the rather less privileged, they will be free from any threat of reduced circumstances or degradation in the future. As for those of pensionable age, well, unless they are totally reckless, they will have joined their mother in the family vault before their money runs out.

The bookmaker smiles as he considers in what sphere of employment Lady Augusta's grandchildren might prove themselves fit should the need arise. He wouldn't trust any one of them to clean his shoes perchance they'd polish his socks instead.

He closes his eyes and lets his head fall against the wing of the chair. When he opens them again, he fancies he sees Lady Augusta sitting in her chair, she is smiling, it is a wicked, wilful smile. He smiles back.

'Thank you m'lady,' he mutters, as he mops the tears from his face.

WATCHING

She is watching me. I am not looking at her, but I know she is watching me, glaring, scowling, her mouth set in an arc of disapproval.

She is old, my mother-in-law, very old, but, unfortunately, not old enough to die of the affliction. Her infirmities are many and diverse and serve to enslave me, body and soul. I am a lamb upon the altar of her discontent.

'Get me a milky coffee, will you?' She does not say *please*, or use my name; she just issues commands. I obey because she is my husband's mother and, much as I despise her, I love him with all my heart.

Die, you bloody old hag. The words play on my lips, but retreat to the safety of my mind where they can do no damage. One day, all the venomous thoughts stored so deep within me will erupt, will spill out all over her until she drowns in my vitriol. I know this is a fantasy, but it sustains me, for now.

She is a liar and sneaky, my mother-in-law. She tempers her behaviour when Bill is around, or our children and grandchildren travel from Nottingham to pay us a visit. On those occasions, she does not feign actual affection towards me, but slips into civil mode, as convincing to them as it is irksome to me.

Then, quite out of the blue, comes the chance of temporary release from her pernicious presence. Our daughter's third baby is due any day and my son-in-law is nursing a broken leg: he had an accident at work. Both he and my two grandsons will need looking after while Sarah is in hospital. I set off for Nottingham on the train with a spring in my step and a song in my heart.

Two days after my arrival, Sarah gives birth to a bouncing baby girl whom they name Natalie. Natalie is our first granddaughter. Our son, Simon, and his wife live in Australia, they have three boys.

Jonathan, my son-in-law, is a good man, just like my Bill. Despite being incapacitated, he helps me with the boys and the chores wherever he can, leaving Sarah free to recover and tend to the needs of the new baby. 'Mum, you are looking much better than you did when you first arrived,' he remarks, while Sarah is upstairs resting. 'It can't be easy, stuck in the house day in, day out, with the old girl.'

'I try not to complain; she's ninety-seven and frail.'

'Perhaps you should.'

'I might be like her, one day... if I live long enough.'

'You will *never* be like her, mum.'

'What are you trying to say, Jon?'

'You need to stand up for yourself more, you are not a doormat for her to wipe her feet on.'

'What is making you say all this?'

'I could see right through her from the moment I first met her; I could tell by the effect she had on you. She's a witch, don't pretend otherwise.'

'Oh, Jon, I've never felt able to share my load with anyone.'

'You can share it with me. You know that you will always find a welcome in this house when you need a break, and, mum, you do need a break from time to time.'

I sit down and start to cry. My grandsons, Marcus, six, and Jake, four, jump onto the sofa, one either side of me, and put their small arms about my neck, planting wet kisses on my cheeks. Jonathan hauls himself out of his recliner. 'I'll make a nice cup of tea for grandma,' he tells the boys.

'And chocolate degustives,' shrieks Jake.

'Those, too.' Jonathan smiles at me as he hobbles towards the kitchen on his crutches. 'Degustives, indeed,' I say, bursting into fits of laughter.

Bill opens the front door as my taxi draws up outside our house. I can't wait to tell him about our beautiful new granddaughter, show him the photos I took, and bring him up to date with all the news from Nottingham.

He puts his arms about me and pulls me tightly to him. 'It's so good to have you home, my love,' he says, and then, 'she's gone.'

'What?'

'She's gone, my mother.'

'You've put her in a retirement home!'

'No, she died two weeks ago. The funeral is on Wednesday, I've made all the arrangements.'

'Bill, why didn't you let me know?'

'Because you would have been torn between coming home to support me, and staying with Sarah and the family. I was able to manage things here; you were needed there. They must be so thrilled, they really wanted a little girl this time.'

'Yes, they got their wish, she's absolutely gorgeous and the boys are besotted with her; they can't leave her alone now they know she won't break.'

'We'll drive up north next weekend, so that *I* can have a look at my new granddaughter. I'll take Monday and Tuesday off', we'll make a proper little break of it, stay in a nice hotel, the works.'

'Oh, that will be wonderful, how exciting!'

I always thought Bill would be devastated when his mother passed away, notwithstanding her age, but he seems to have accepted her death with great calm and grace. As for me, well, I am so bloody pleased that I can hardly contain myself. I am finding it difficult to wipe the smile from my face, and when I am alone, I whoop and cheer like somebody deranged. I know I must pull myself together for the funeral and behave in an appropriate manner, but my relief and elation will be bubbling up inside me and making it extremely difficult.

The blessed day has come and the sun is shining. I slip on my new shoes, they pinch badly, hopefully badly enough to fix a suitably pained expression on my face for the duration of the service and committal. I take my black, long-sleeved dress from the wardrobe, hang it on the door and stand back to assess its suitability. It is, of course, entirely suitable, but I know I cannot wear it because it portrays emotions too far removed from the way I am currently feeling. I put the dress back and take out a navy and white, spotted creation instead.

The funeral is over. I contrived to adopt a sombre attitude and the occasion passed as it should, with dignity, and afterwards, with the consumption of a great deal of alcohol. We are now back in our lounge having an afternoon cuppa and some of the cake left from the reception at our local. Bill is sitting in the reclining armchair his mother usurped when she first moved into our home.

'I think we should get rid of this, Eileen,' he says, patting the arms of the chair.

'Why? It isn't stained or anything, the fabric just a little worn.'

'Mother didn't leave a fortune or anything close, but it was willed to be shared between whatever of her five offspring survived her.'

'And only you and Stan are still with us.'

'Yes, and Stan says it should come to us because we were the ones who looked after her for all those years. *You* were the one who looked after her.'

'That's very generous, I must say, good old Stan.'

'We can afford a few luxuries now, my love: some new furniture, replace the car and spend some money on renovating the house. When I retire next month, we'll go to Australia to see Simon, Kerry and their brood.'

'Oh, Bill, you can't imagine how I've longed to be with them again.'

'Eileen, why didn't you tell me how badly my mother was treating you?'

'She was your mother. Anyway, how did you find out?'

'Iris next door enlightened me.'

'I never complained to her, to anyone.'

'I know you didn't, you should have. Iris has a habit of popping in whenever the back door isn't locked, as you know. She heard mother say lots of nasty things to you whilst staying out of the way in the kitchen. I truly believe she didn't want to interfere, but while you were away she felt compelled to tell me about her abusive, spiteful behaviour. I would never have let her stay here had I known how miserable she was making your life. I should have been at home more to help you.'

'You wanted to boost your pension for our retirement, Bill, I understood that. Don't you give it another thought, it's just us now; we can do as we please. I'm glad you were the one to be with her when she died, she would have left the world in a very bad mood if it had been me.'

She wasn't exactly thrilled when I called time on her, thought Bill.

WHAT'S IN A NAME?

My mother gave me two things: life and a name, Portia Rosaline.

Before I was a couple of weeks old, I was adopted. Carolyn and Gerald Baxter were my parents, they changed my name to Stephanie Grace, and my life was a charmed affair. When, at the age of ten, I was told that I was not their biological child, I don't recall feeling even the slightest bit perturbed. I had a wonderful childhood, was loved to death, and my life stretched out before me like one big adventure.

It was only when I was shown my birth certificate that I became curious. My bio-mater, Eve Mae Howard, had given me the names of two Shakespearean characters and I wanted to know why. Was she a struggling thespian living in a rat-ridden garret? Was she a student of literature and fresh out of university without any means of support? Bio-mater had a story, and I was determined to find out what it was as soon as the opportunity presented itself.

I see her across the barrier, a woman tattooed and pierced to within an inch of her life. Spikes of puke-green, gelled hair rise like stalagmites from the very centre of her otherwise completely shaven head.

In my gut I know it is her, Bio-mater. She is absolutely not the sort of person I was expecting to find waiting for me at Heathrow. Do I slip back through the automatic doors of arrivals when somebody else is coming out, or do I rise to the challenge of meeting her?

She is holding up a huge card with PORTIA ROSALINE writ large upon it. 'Oh, God, this is a bloody nightmare,' I mutter. 'I am Stephanie Baxter-Cole, a respected lawyer from Boston,' I tell myself, 'and this frightful woman is no more than a biological truth. Take a few deep breaths – in, out, in, out…'

She spots me. Shit, why did I send her a photograph? And why didn't I ask her to send me one? She is waving her arms about so maniacally her nipples appear over the top of her stringy vest top. I cringe. 'Are you Eve Howard?'

'Yeah, darlin', that's me.'

I make my way slowly around the barrier and she runs towards me, arms outstretched. *Once more unto the breach. Stiffen the sinews, summon up the blood.* HELP!

Bio-mater is a great deal shorter than I am, and when she pulls me against her in a ferocious attempt at an embrace, the longest spike on her head stabs at the soft flesh under my chin making me yelp in pain. 'Sorry, darlin', you're so tall.'

'Was he tall, my father,' I blurt out.

'Dunno, can't remember.'

When you've grown up feeling special, chosen, and been given the best of absolutely everything, it comes as something of a shock to discover that you briefly belonged to someone so, so utterly... I'm sure there is an adjective to describe Bio-mater but it doesn't spring to mind. I suddenly feel like a bit of a mongrel, one who was plucked from the dregs of life merely because it was cute.

'Sid's in the truck outside waiting for us,' Bio-mater tells me.

'Sid?'

'The current, darlin', you'll like him.'

I daresay Sid is somewhere within his skin, although his skin could actually be a psychedelic lycra body suit. Bio-mater is positively unembellished by comparison. Sid is so heavily weighed down with hardware I'm surprised he hasn't developed a permanent stoop.

Bio-mater and Sid reek of weed and I am beginning to feel more than a little nauseous. 'Gotta drop this shit off at the garden centre,' he tells me. Is he talking about narcotics, I wonder? Then I see the truck is loaded with manure. A small, very old caravan is hitched up behind it. Please, please, please don't tell me I am to be accommodated in *that,* I think.

We travel three abreast in the cab, it's a squeeze. 'So, hon, you're married with two kids, Eve tells me.'

'Yes, Simon and Geraldine.'

'And the Baxters moved to the States when you were six?'

'That's right. My father's work took us there.'

'So, life's been good to you. Eve knew you'd be fine, didn't you babe?'

'Absolutely, Stan.'

'Life has been very good to me.' It only took a serious turn for the worse the instant I met up with you guys, I think. 'Do you still live in Kent?' I inquire.

'Nah, darlin' we move around all the time. We are camped on a site in South Wales at present,' Bio-mater tells me.

'Uh, um, right. Wales is quite a distance from here, I think.'

'Yeah, couple of hundred miles, hon,' confirms Sid. 'We hook up to electricity on site and there are showers and bogs in a block quite close by.' Stan tells me.

'How comforting?'

'And there are lovely walks all around,' adds Bio-mater.'

'Just as well I packed some casual clothes and foot-wear, then.'

If I have to endure a long journey passively inhaling marijuana, I decide I must try to fill my head with nice thoughts, happy memories. I recall summer vacations spent in our lakeside log cabin in Vermont. All our food was cooked outside over the fire my father built. And the sky in the moonlight, bereft of light pollution, was a magical canopy of twinkling stars. We'd sing and laugh with our neighbours in nearby cabins and become intoxicated on the fabulous smells of the forest and my father's home-made wine.

To my young mind this was heaven, and I began to wonder why people made such a thing about dying.

I am lying on my bed – it doubles as the seating area at the front of the caravan during the daytime. I am staring at a rather large spider weaving its web directly above my face. Mercifully I am not an arachnophobe and am glad of the diversion. Perhaps it will have woven some curtains by morning. What luxury!

There is a good deal of activity going on in the double bed – it serves as the dining table during the daytime. Bio-mater and Sid are screened from my view by two adjacent wardrobe doors that are opened at night to separate our quarters. What made me think a middle-aged couple would contrive to moderate their sexual behaviour in my presence?

Eventually I fall asleep. The nightmare comes when I awake needing the toilet and remember there isn't one. I paddle my feet around in the darkness to locate my shoes, trying not to disturb Bio-mater and Sid. The door is located on my side of the makeshift partition. I grope around, locate the handle and push it open. I forget about the building blocks forming two steep steps and tumble out of the caravan and into a hedge.

Outside, I stumble around in the mean light of my mobile phone trying to remember where the toilet block is situated. It is raining hard and my flimsy negligee offers scant protection. Reason tells me I should pee in a hedge, but I can't, my senses have become too sanitised for such primitive conduct, my lodgings are primitive enough.

My hand eventually makes contact with the roughcast wall of the toilet block. By this time I am so desperate to relieve myself that I lurch into the first cubicle, banishing thoughts of its condition from my mind.

I start to shiver and suddenly the prospect of slipping back into my warm bed becomes very inviting. I step out of the toilet block, uttering a string of expletives, and shamble in what I think is the direction of the caravan.

I am covered in scratches and my bones ache, however, I decide to go for a walk. A long walk, a very long walk. I have my passport, cash and cards in my bag. I will walk until I find an establishment that looks capable of producing a decent cup of coffee. Wales appears quite small on the map, a village or town surely can't be too far away!

It is still early and the little cafe in Brecon, a delightful place, I decide, is just opening its doors to the public. 'I need coffee,' I gasp.

'You'd better come in, then,' replies a chubby lady wearing a wrap-around apron and a bright, warm smile. 'I'll bring you a pot, will I?'

'That would be great!'

'Something to eat, my dear?'

'Um, yes, I am rather hungry, no, I'm absolutely starving.'

'A *Full English,* then?'

'A *Full English* in Wales?'

'We do a much better job of it than they do, I promise.'

'In that case, bring it on.'

'Toast, marmalade, fruit juice?

'Absolutely, thank you very much. I will be needing a cab, do you have a number?'

'Oh, yes, I'll book it for you when you are ready, Tom, the driver, only lives next door. Where do you want to go?'

'Heathrow airport.'

'London?'

'Yes.'

'Well, there's a thing!'

An elderly man comes into the café and sits at the table next to mine. I am wiping my mouth with a cotton napkin, blissfully replete. 'You look as if you really enjoyed that,' he remarks.

'Oh, boy, I did!'

'Good morning, by the way.'

'Good morning.'

'I saw you when you arrived at the campsite. You had a bit of a mishap during the night, I believe.'

'You heard me, I am so sorry about that.'

'No need to be sorry. I am a light sleeper. I am an amateur photographer and always park my camper van there when I'm in the area.'

'The usual, Mr Vernon,' inquires the café owner from behind the counter.

'Yes, please, Edith.'

'They serve a fantastic breakfast here,' I remark.

'Indeed they do, best in the area. You fell out with a bush, by the look of you.'

'Yes, but I'm fine. When you are visiting your biological mother for the first time, you don't think to pack a torch.'

'The lady with the… The colourful lady is your mother!'

'She is.'

'Would you like to talk to a complete stranger? I am a very good listener.'

'Yes, I think I would.'

I acquaint Mr Vernon, Frank, with my situation while he is eating his *Full English*. He *is* a good listener. 'You had built up a picture of her in your mind and she didn't measure up.'

'I suppose so. I know you shouldn't judge a book by its cover, but seeing her was quite a shock. I mean, she is a bit old to look like a punk, don't you think?'

'Perhaps, but it doesn't make her a bad person.'

'I know.'

'You must have gone to great lengths to find her.'

'I did.'

'And she *did* agree to meet you.'

'Yes.'

'You know, Stephanie, appearances can be devilishly deceptive, give her a chance, I say. I think you might have cause to regret it later if you don't.'

I hike back to the caravan buoyed up by a spirit of goodwill. I have flowers in one hand and a box of cream cakes in the other.

Bio-mater is effusive in her gratitude for my offerings; it is slightly embarrassing. 'It's nothing,' I tell her.

'You know that's not true, it's the gesture that counts, especially in our case.' She's astute, Bio-mater. 'Now then, you want to know about me, about why I gave you up?'

'I want to know why you called me Portia Rosaline.'

'Don't you like the name?'

'In context, yes, but it is a bit, a bit theatrical, fitting for a certain type of person.'

'How was I supposed to know what type of person you'd turn out to be?'

'Fair enough.'

'I adore Shakespeare, darlin'. I love the meter, the musicality of his work. It feeds my soul. When you think of how it has inspired great composers and artists…'

'Yes, especially Tchaikovsky and Prokoviev .'

'So, *you* are a lover of the arts?'

'Yes, ballet, opera and theatre. My taste in music is eclectic.'

'Sid and I are performers of acoustic music. We go all over the place doing gigs, that's how we earn our bread and why we're here at present.'

'I see. Where is your next gig?'

'A pub in Brecon, tonight, as it happens. You coming?'

'Of course.'

I can hardly take in what I'm hearing. Bio-mater's voice is full and sweet and velvety, her delivery, effortless. I close my eyes and hear an angel singing.

She holds her audience in thrall as her fingers, so fleet and deft, fall like gentle raindrops upon the strings of an ancient Spanish guitar. Sid flicks a small Irish drum with a wooden tool held between his fingers. The sound is so soft, barely more than a whisper, yet essential, the music's heartbeat. I have rarely heard anything quite so beautiful, evocative or perfect.

'That instrument is called a Bodhran,' the woman in the seat directly behind mine informs. 'And the little stick is called either a tipper or a beater. Sid and Eve are great, aren't they?'

'Yes, they are, they most certainly are.'

'Is this your first gig, dear?'

'Yes.'

'We've been following them for years, ever since they started, really. Sid plays guitar and keyboard and Eve, the flute and accordion as well as guitar. They are so talented, the pair of them. Mind you, Sid sounds like a frog when he sings, but he only sings when he's stoned, so that's okay. You on holiday, dear?'

'Yes.'

I want this woman to stop talking to me because I am feeling so emotional at the moment, close to tears, actually. It is the music, I know it is the music, but it is more than that, so much more.

'Eve had a tough time of it, you know. She had a baby when she was just sixteen and still at college. She knew she wouldn't be able to look after it properly so gave it up for adoption. She told me she never wanted another baby after that, said it wouldn't feel right, that she didn't deserve it. My hubbie and I have kept a scrapbook of all Sid and Eve's gigs, would you like to see it?'

'Yes, I would.' If will shut you up, I think,

The scrapbook is passed to me, but Eve and Sid are about to perform their next number, a traditional folk song, so I hold it on my lap. 'I will look at it in the break,' I tell the woman. She smiles but remains silent.

My eyes are fixed on one photograph. A very youthful Eve is standing on a raised area which obviously serves as a small stage. Behind her, with his hands on her shoulders and his face so close to hers their cheeks are touching, stands a familiar figure.

I become aware that Eve is watching me, our eyes meet. She moves towards the back door of the pub and I know she wants me to follow her. Outside in the garden, she perches herself on a rustic bench and I sit beside her.

'You're smart, darlin', I'm sure you've worked it out,' she says.

'Yes.' I take her hand and hold it tightly in my own.

My gate number comes up on the screen. This is the moment I thought I would be longing for, but instead my heart is full. I walk towards the gate feeling sad, yet peaceful and settled in my mind. I am caught in an emotional embrace; it is comforting.

Eve, a young girl, made a huge sacrifice for me, for my future and wellbeing. It will take me a while to come to terms with that fact.

We are about to land, I will be so pleased to see Jack, the children and my parents again. I will never tell my dad that I know he is my real father because Eve would never have betrayed that truth. It will remain our secret, the bond that binds us.

WHEN THE
BOUGH BROKE

'I am going to tell you your story, Amad, as you snuggle against me, warm and sleepy in my arms, while you are too little to understand my words. One day they will make you cry, and perhaps angry, too. There will be questions, I know, very difficult questions, but I promise to answer them honestly. I love you, my dearest child, that is all you need to know for now.

'I had to get away, Amad, after the funeral. I could not bear the pitying glances, the sickeningly solicitous words of condolence. I could not bear the word *widow*. I booked myself a month long cruise around the Mediterranean. I can't pretend that I had ruled out suicide: to slip into the black waters when others slept or would be to occupied with whatever pleasures took their fancy, or drunk, to notice. I felt so alone, so lost. The cornerstone of my life had fallen and lay in rubble about my feet. He was gone, my darling William was gone, and I could see no life beyond such a monumental loss, such overwhelming grief. There was not a grain of hope in my soul.

'I spotted your boat through my binoculars, whilst standing on the deck of the ship. Your flimsy vessel was laden with people: unmistakably refugees fleeing from their homeland, Syria, apparently. I saw a man stand up, grab you by one arm, spin you around over his head, and hurl you into the water. You landed many metres from the boat. A woman then stood up so hastily the small boat started to rock. I saw her mouth form into a circle of horror as she gazed at the place where you had disappeared; I could her howls of grief and despair, but only in my mind. She raised her arms and face to heaven in supplication, and my own eyes were temporarily blinded by tears. When I looked again, I saw the same man hit her so hard that she toppled into the sea. The woman lay spread-eagled on the surface of the water until it eventually swallowed her up. I know she was your mother, Amad; she made no attempt to save herself because she wanted to be with you for all eternity. Oh, Amad, I understood how she felt, exactly how she felt.

'Shortly afterwards the boat capsized and its passengers became a squirming, thrashing mass, like a great shoal of hungry fish. I later saw the body of your mother lying on the deck of the cruise ship among several others, one being the man who cast you both overboard. He committed you to the horrors of the deep and paid the ultimate price for his cruelty. But you, Amad, were miraculously saved. The lifeboat crew brought you and one hundred or so more on board our ship.

'I paid a greedy steward what he asked to give me care of the toddler in the bright yellow sweater. It was an amount sufficient to pay for his silence regarding your presence in my cabin, and to assist me on disembarkation in England. Money speaks in an obscenely loud voice, Amad. You will learn this as you grow.

'I called in a number of favours from influential friends, and within two months you were officially mine. The precise nature of your installation in my home is unknown to them all, but I doubt they suspect I am capable of smuggling, or human trafficking, or whatever the law calls the importation of an illegal immigrant, even a tiny one as sweet and helpless as you. How little they know about me, about the constant ache that inhabited my heart.

'You see, Amad, all hope of a family died when William died. We had waited until the time felt right to begin the business of having a family; we waited too long, I see that now. We forget that life is not infinite, that our days are numbered and it is not in our power to determine how fate will use us. If only we could learn to embrace and treasure each moment, the world would be a much better, much richer place.

'The name I gave you, in the absence of another, is short for Amadeus: *gift from God.* That is what you truly are, my beloved boy. Amad sounds well, I feel, for a child of your heritage, a heritage I vow I will never undermine or overlook.

'One day you may despise me for my actions, you may say I was selfish, that I brought you here to satisfy my own needs and not yours. But, for now, let there be hope and warmth and peace and harmony. In our cosy little world, where we are everything to each other, let there be love.'

Acknowledgements

Thank you to my neighbour Andrew Bryant for working out my many computer problems. Also thank you to Richard and Sue Fairhead for helping me to publish this book. And to all who have given me help and encouragement.

Printed in Poland
by Amazon Fulfillment
Poland Sp. z o.o., Wrocław

67480484R00226